OTHER BOOM BOOKS BY
JENNIFER L. ARMENTROUT

FRIGID SERIES
Frigid
Scorched

COVENANT SERIES
Half-Blood (includes the novella "Daimon")
Pure
Deity (includes the novella "Elixir")
Apollyon
Sentinel

JENNIFER L. ARMENTROUT

Bloom *books*

Published by Bloom Books, an imprint of Sourcebooks
P.O. Box 4410, Naperville, Illinois 60567-4410
(630) 961-3900
sourcebooks.com

Originally self-published in 2013 by Jennifer L. Armentrout.

Cataloging-in-Publication data is on file with the Library of Congress.

Printed and bound in the United States of America.
LSC 10 9 8 7 6 5 4 3 2 1

To every book lover, big and small—these books are for you.

Chapter 1

SYDNEY

I was in love with my best friend.

And it could've been worse, I guessed. I could have been in love with a male stripper or a drug addict. Kyler Quinn was neither of those things. Although he could easily be passed off as a stripper with those jaw-dropping good looks and messy brown hair.

I saw him before he even knew I was here. There was no way anyone could miss Kyler, not even in the packed Dry Docks, where everyone from the university was out celebrating the start of winter break. People flocked to him, especially the girls.

Always the girls.

I didn't want to say that Kyler looked like a god, because sculptures of Greek and Roman gods typically didn't fall on the attractive side of things. And they were all really small *down there.* I doubted he was hurting in that department, since there was an endless train of women who came back for seconds and thirds. But he was beautiful in a purely masculine way. A nose with a slight hook in it offset broad cheekbones, defined jaw, and wide expressive lips. He'd broken his nose in a fight freshman year.

I still felt bad for that nose.

And when he smiled? Aw, man, the boy had the deepest dimples ever.

His eyes were a warm brown, the color of a rich coffee bean that darkened whenever he was feeling froggy, and I bet he was feeling all kinds of froggy right now.

Right in the middle of the bar, I stopped and leaned my head back. Exhaling loudly, I really wanted to punch myself in the face. Not only was Kyler completely off-limits due to the fact we'd been inseparable since the day he pushed me off the merry-go-round and told me I had cooties for trying to hold his hand, but I'd retaliated by holding him down and forcing him to eat a mud pie the following day. People had a hard time understanding how we were so close. Even I couldn't figure it out. We went together like a lion and a gazelle. Actually, we went together like a lion and an exhausted gazelle who had no chance of outrunning the predator.

I was the gimpy gazelle.

As I made it closer to the table he and our friend Tanner occupied, a blond with legs longer than I was tall plopped down in Kyler's lap. His arms went around the girl's impossibly narrow waist, and a stupid, totally inexcusable sharp pain sliced through my stomach.

Yeah, Kyler might not be a stripper or an addict but he *was* a player.

Veering back toward the bar at the last minute, I almost plowed straight into someone's back. I rolled my eyes. Giving myself a concussion would be perfect. Multicolored

Christmas lights dangled from the edge of the bar, and I thought that was kind of hazardous with all the drunks spilling their drinks. I found an empty stool at the bar and waited for the bartender to notice me. And it was easy to notice me. I looked like I was sixteen, so they usually checked my ID right away. The bartender appeared, asked for the standard, and I ordered the standard—a Diet Coke with rum.

Over the hum of conversation and music, a giggle teased my ears. It was like some kind of damned beacon. No good would come from looking, and there was no reason to ruin the night already. I crossed my ankles. Placed my hands on the bar. Tapped my fingers to the song I was barely paying attention to. Stared at the rack of liquor bottles my other best friend was intimately familiar with.

But I looked, because I was a girl and diving headfirst into girl stupid.

Blondie was straddling Kyler. Her short denim skirt had ridden all the way up her thighs. One would think it wasn't winter outside based on how she was dressed, but then again, I'd wear a skirt like that all the time if I had her legs.

His back was to me, but he must've said something interesting in her ear, because she laughed again. Her hot-pink nails dug into his shoulders, bunching the material of his black sweater. Then she reached up, running her hands through the hair at his forehead, tugging it back.

I couldn't look away now. Like a glutton for punishment, I was fixated on them.

He tilted his head to the side and tipped it back. I could see half his face now, and he was grinning. Not the big smiles that revealed those totally lickable dimples, but I knew he was rocking that half grin of his—the infuriating and incredibly sexy half grin. His hands settled on her hips.

"Here you go." The bartender placed my drink down.

Turning away from what was about to go down over there, I glanced up at the bartender as I knocked a strand of long black hair out of my face. "Thank you."

He winked. "No problem."

The bartender ambled off to help someone else, while I was left to wonder why he'd winked. Thinking I probably shouldn't have let Kyler talk me into coming out tonight, I picked up my glass and took a larger-than-normal gulp. I forced myself to swallow the bit of alcohol, even as it burned my throat.

Just as I placed my drink down, I was hugged from behind. The vanilla-scented perfume and high-pitched squeal gave away the culprit.

"You're here! I saw you from the other side of the bar and tried to get your attention," Andrea said, spinning me around the barstool. Her red curls were twisted in every which direction. My roommate looked like Little Orphan Annie all grown up...if Little Orphan Annie had a potential drinking problem. As evidenced by the beers she was double fisting.

"How much have you had to drink?" I asked.

She rolled her eyes. "This beer's for Tanner, you bitch."

"Since when do you get beers for Tanner?"

Andrea shrugged. "He's being nice tonight. So I'm being nice tonight."

Tanner and Andrea were weird. They'd met last year, and it had been hate at first sight. Somehow they'd kept ending up in the same places, and I guessed they'd tripped and fallen on each other's lips or something. They'd made out a few times, fought a lot more, and now she was serving him drinks. I could never figure them out.

"How long have you guys been here?" I asked.

"About an hour." She wiggled her way between me and some girl on the other stool. "Kyler's Official Girl Parade has been in full force."

I winced. "I can see."

"Yeah, I noticed that you saw. That's why you weren't paying a bit of attention to me." She took a swig of beer. "You coming to the table?"

To the table where Blondie was practically dry humping Kyler? *Sign me up.* "I'll be over in a little bit."

She pouted. "You need to hurry your little ass up and come to the table. Kyler will run the girl off if you're over there, and then I don't have to worry about catching herpes."

"Herpes isn't airborne," I told her.

"Yeah, you say that now, but then it mixes with chlamydia and genital warts, and then you have a superstrain of herpes." Her nose wrinkled. "You breathe it in, and then bam! You'll need antiviral therapy for life."

Andrea was planning on going to med school after college, and I thought she needed to take a few of her classes over again if she believed that was possible. But I knew what the real problem was, and it wasn't the gift that kept giving.

Where there was one girl after Kyler, there were at least two or three more girls hanging on the outskirts. I looked over my shoulder. Yep. Two girls. Andrea didn't want me over there to make sure Kyler behaved. She was just as good at hiding her feelings as I was.

She didn't want one of those other girls to fall into Tanner's lap, which looked close to happening. One of the girls was chatting it up with the tattooed, buzz-cut police officer's son. Tanner appeared only half-interested, saying something to Kyler. Blondie wasn't happy with the lack of attention. She twisted around, scooped up a piece of ice from a drink on the table, and popped it in her mouth. With her other hand, she tugged Kyler's head toward hers as she bent her head down.

"Oh, look at that." Andrea sighed. "I think I saw that once in an eighties movie. Do you think that girl has any sense of shame?"

My stomach dipped like I was poised atop a roller coaster. It wasn't about not having shame. It was all about going for what you wanted. Part of me envied Blondie—a really huge Kyler-sized part of me. "I seriously hope their mouths aren't touching because now all I'm thinking about is herpes."

Andrea pushed off the bar. "Uh…" Their lips were touching. Damn it.

A second later Kyler leaned back, his jaw working as he chewed what I assumed was the piece of ice Blondie had so openly shared.

"Ugh," I murmured, turning back around. Andrea winced, because she knew…she was the only person who knew. "I'll be over in a little while. Going to finish my drink first."

"Okay." She smiled, but sadness crept into her eyes. "Sydney…"

Now I felt like a lame turd. "It's all right, really. I'll be right over."

"After you finish your drink?" When I nodded, she sighed. "You never finish a drink, but I'll be waiting. Don't take forever." She started to turn and then whipped back to me, nearly losing a bottle of beer. "Actually, take your time."

"Huh?"

Her smile spread. "Look who just came in."

I craned my neck to follow her gaze. "Oh."

"'Oh' is right." Andrea bent down and kissed my cheek. "Forget about Kyler the slut. You're better than that. But him?" She nodded at the door. "That's a keeper who's more than willing to end your celibacy."

Heat swamped my cheeks. Before I could argue the use of the word "celibacy," Andrea had skipped off, and I was left staring at Paul Robertson.

Paul was new to our group; I'd met him in my cognitive-processes lab. He...he was good-looking. He was nice and funny. He was perfect, really, but...

He stopped just at the edge of the dance floor, tugging off his skullcap. Scanning the bar, he smoothed a hand over his blond hair. His eyes met mine, and a quick grin spread across his face. Giving me a little wave, he easily navigated the group of people huddled around round tables.

Paul would be perfect for me right now, and for that very reason alone, I needed to stop thinking about the unattainable and start thinking about what was right in front of my face.

Taking a deep breath, I mustered up what I hoped was a sexy smile. There was no better time than tonight.

KYLER

I was already starting to get a headache. By the way the chick was squirming in my lap like she was ready to get it on right now, this was going to be a long night. I crunched down on the piece of ice, half tempted to spit it out.

But that would be sort of rude.

I should have been in the mood to celebrate, except I

wasn't. One more semester of college left, and then what? Join the family business and shit? God, that was the last thing I wanted. Well, not necessarily the *last* thing. Trying to explain to my mom why I didn't foresee a career in bar restoration in my future was probably the last thing I wanted to do. It was never something I wanted to do, but almost four years of college later, I was about to walk out with a degree in business bullshit.

Reaching around the girl, I grabbed the neck of the beer bottle. Across from me, Tanner raised his brows. I smirked as he turned back to whatever the brunette chick was saying to him. Something about getting a wax yesterday and she was outside the mandatory twenty-four-hour waiting period. Seriously? That was pretty much the last thing either of us wanted to hear.

Knowing there was an all-clear on getting down did have its bennies, but Tanner didn't look too into it.

"Kyler," the blond crooned in my ear as she wiggled her ass. "You don't seem happy to see me. I'm happy to see you again."

And apparently I wasn't too into it either. Taking a long drink, I knew I had to proceed with wise caution. Supposedly I knew this girl—like *knew her*, knew her—but I couldn't place her face or her ass, which was all kinds of messed up. How could I not know her when I'd most definitely slept with her at some point?

Fuck.

Sometimes I was sick of myself.

She leaned in, pressing her breasts right up under my chin.

Okay. I wasn't *that* sick of myself. "Honey," I said, fingering the bottle. "I'm going to need to breathe at some point."

Giggling, she leaned back far enough that I could sneak another drink. She ran her hands through my hair, tugging it off my forehead. I fought the urge to knock her hands away. "You gonna play your guitar for me later?"

My brows rose. "I played the guitar for you?" Tanner choked on a laugh.

The girl—and damn, I hoped her friend said her name real soon—frowned. "Yes!" She smacked my chest playfully. "You played it with those awesome, talented fingers of yours, and then you played something else."

Oh.

Tanner leaned back in his chair. "Look at you and your *awesome* fingers."

"My awesome, talented fingers," I corrected him.

Shaking his head, he looked away as the brunette leaned over, tracing the edge of the tattoo that popped out from under his rolled-up sleeves.

"You don't remember?" She stuck out a glossy lower lip. "My feelings are hurt."

I snorted and took another drink, my eyes scanning the now-packed bar. Sometimes I had no idea how I ended up in situations like this. Okay. That was a bald-faced lie. What was between my legs was how I ended up in situations like this.

But it was more than that.

It had always been more than that. "Kyler," the girl whined.

I took a deep breath and turned back to her, giving the girl my most charming smile. "Yeah?"

"You gonna share?"

Before I could respond, she took the bottle from my hand and downed damn near close to the whole thing. My brows shot up. Damn. That was sort of impressive…and annoying.

Her friend giggled. "Jesus, Mindy, take it slow tonight. I am *so* not carrying your drunk ass back to the dorm."

Aha! Her name was Mindy! I felt a little better about this.

Mindy just shrugged as she turned back to me. She leaned in, and when she spoke, all I could smell was beer. "You're so incredibly sexy. Have you ever been told that?"

"A time or two," I replied, wishing for another beer.

Andrea appeared at the table, two beers in hand. One was for her and the other for Tanner, so that sucked. She looked at me and huffed. "Like Kyler needs his ego stroked."

"Kyler needs something else stroked," Mindy murmured, pushing down with her hips.

A look of disgust crossed Andrea's face as she sat on the other side of Tanner. The look didn't bother me. Now, if it were someone else? "Have you seen Syd?" I asked.

Andrea eyed me over the rim of her bottle, her eyes narrowed. She didn't say anything.

I sat back in the chair, sighing. "I invited her."

Tanner arched a brow. "You know damn well Syd's in her dorm, packing for our trip. Actually, she's probably *re*packing for our trip."

A smile pulled at my lips. She probably was obsessively going over what to bring.

"Who cares about her?" Mindy folded her arms, which made her breasts even bigger. Impossible. She looked at her friend. "I need another drink."

"So do I," I said, bouncing my knees so she'd get off. She didn't take the hint. I sighed. "Since you drank mine, why don't you go get us a refill?"

Another pout graced Mindy's lips. "Have you seen how packed the bar is? It will take forever."

"*You* could always get up," Andrea suggested.

I looked over my shoulder at the bar. The damned thing was packed. Shit. Half the university appeared to be here.

Mindy's beer-soaked breath brushed my cheek. "You should go get us a drink, babe. I love Jell-O shooters."

"I'm not your babe." My gaze traveled over the people at the bar. Was that Paul? He didn't come here regularly, only if Syd actually showed up. *Wait a sec...* I leaned to the side to get a look around some huge dude. Was that Syd at the bar? With Paul?

A hand ended up in my hair again. "You were my babe a couple of weeks ago."

"Interesting," I murmured. The dude moved away, beers in hand, and holy shit, it *was* Syd. Her long black hair was down, and her feet were crossed at the ankles. She looked so damned tiny sitting there, I was surprised she'd even gotten served.

I was also surprised that she was at the bar, without me and *with* Paul.

What the fuck was wrong with this picture?

Turning back around, I pinned Andrea with a look. "When did she get here?"

She shrugged. "Dunno."

My irritation spiked. "She shouldn't be at the bar by herself."

Mindy said something, but I wasn't listening. I had this wonderful selective-hearing thing going on right now.

Andrea shared a look with Tanner, a look I ignored. Therefore, the look never happened. "She's not by herself," she said sweetly.

"That's the point." I gripped Mindy's hips. An excited look crossed her pretty face. Too bad I was about to burst her horny bubble. Lifting her out of my lap, I deposited her on her feet. "I'll be back."

Mindy's jaw unhinged. "Kyler!"

I ignored her. I also ignored Andrea's smirk and the eye roll Tanner gave me as I stood and pivoted around.

Syd really shouldn't be at the bar by herself. Being with Paul didn't count. She needed someone to look out for her, to keep an eye on things, because Syd…well, she had this naivete about her that drew dickheads in by the masses.

Dickheads like Paul and other guys like me who pretty much did nothing but get a girl on her back. But I was different, way different when it came to Sydney Bell. And it had been my job since I could remember to keep her out of trouble. Right now was no different than any other time.

Yep, that was exactly the reason I was about to break up this little conversation.

Chapter 2

SYDNEY

"Hey," Paul said, sliding into the spot Andrea had occupied. "I didn't know you were coming out. You didn't say anything in class today."

"Last-minute decision." I took a sip of my rum and Coke. It was already watered down. "How was the final?"

"I think it went well. You?"

I shrugged. "I think I passed."

"You probably aced the damned thing." He stopped, ordering a Sam Adams when the bartender came around. "Are you all packed for the trip tomorrow?"

We were leaving on our annual ski trip to Snowshoe Mountain tomorrow. This was Paul's first time, but Kyler and I had been going up to his mom's ski house since we were kids. This was Andrea's and Tanner's second year, and some of Kyler's other friends would be there, too. We usually had a big group going.

"I was packed last weekend." I giggled. "I'm anal like that."

His easy grin spread. "I still need to pack. By the way, thanks for inviting me. I've never been up to Snowshoe." Surprising, since he'd grown up in the neighboring town, and I figured everyone who lived in Maryland had been to Snowshoe at some point.

"No problem. You said you liked skiing and stuff, so it made sense. Kyler will be out on the slopes all day and night, so you'll definitely have someone to ski with."

Paul's blue eyes drifted toward the table my friends sat at. "I don't know about that."

I frowned and totally refused to see what was happening at the table of sin and sex. They were probably making babies. "What do you mean?"

"I don't get the impression that Kyler's a big fan of mine." That surprised me. Paul was so nice. His gaze settled on me once more, and he shrugged. "Anyway, you're heading back home after you leave Snowshoe?"

I nodded. "Yep, doing Christmas with the family and staying there until spring semester starts back up. You?"

"I'll be in Bethesda part of the time and then Winchester with my mom." He scratched at the label on his bottle, his brows knitted. "Parents divorced a few years back, so I go between houses."

I hadn't known that. "Sorry to hear that."

He smiled. "It's no big deal. I still get to do the whole two-Christmases thing, so I'm not complaining."

After taking another quick sip, I placed my glass down. "Double the presents."

"Double the fun." His gaze fell to his beer. Half the label was gone. "Look. I thought we could do—"

Strong arms wrapped around my waist from behind. I was pulled off the stool, and my surprised shriek was cut

14

off when my back hit an immovable wall of muscle. I was enveloped in a bear hug that smelled of the outdoors and light cologne.

Only one person in this world gave me hugs like this or felt that hard…that good.

Kyler's deep voice rumbled through my body. "When did you get here?"

My feet still weren't touching the floor. "A little bit ago," I said, out of breath, gripping his forearms through his sweater.

"What the hell? Have you been hiding from me?"

Paul leaned back against the bar and grinned, but it was strained. Not that I could blame him. Kyler always kind of burst in and took over every situation.

"I haven't been hiding," I told him, flushing with embarrassment when my eyes met Paul's. "And can you put me down?"

"What if I don't?" he teased. "You're so little, I could put you in my pocket."

"What?" I laughed. "Put me down, you idiot. I'm having a conversation."

"Sorry, Paul, I'm stealing her." Kyler wasn't sorry at all, but Paul gave a resigned nod. Kyler backed away, giving me no choice, because there was no way I was breaking his hold. He turned, dropping into a chair nowhere near the table he'd been at and pulling me into his lap so I was sitting sideways. I was torn between guilt at abandoning Paul so abruptly and the thrill of Kyler's attention.

He looped his arms around my waist. "I'm not happy with you, Syd."

I arched a brow as my heart rate picked up. He was the only person who called me "Syd"—well, the only person I let call me that without kicking them in the shin. "Really? Over what?"

"You're talking to that douche."

"What douche?"

He leaned in, resting his forehead against mine, and my breath stalled in my chest. *Why must he always get so damned close?* And he really, truly, always did. "Paul."

So Paul had been right.

"What about him?" I put my hands on his shoulders to push back, but his arms tightened, holding me in place. "He's nice. Are you drunk?"

"Am I drunk? Aw, now you've gone and hurt my feelings, Syd."

I smirked. "You don't have any feelings."

"Now, now. That wasn't very nice." His impossibly long lashes lowered, shielding his eyes as he lifted his head, rubbing his cheek along mine. My fingers dug into his shoulders as desire twisted tightly in my center. "I have all these feelings, Syd."

It took me a moment to respond. "You're so full of it."

He rubbed his cheek against me again, like a cat seeking a belly rub, and I fought the urge to purr. "I'm full of something."

"Piss and vinegar?" I suggested as I desperately tried to ignore the way my pulse pounded in all the right places.

He chuckled deep in his throat as he leaned back against the seat he'd taken hostage. "Back to the serious nature of our conversation."

"Which is: Why are you playing Santa right now?"

Kyler's lashes lifted, and his eyes drilled into mine. "Hmm, now that sounds interesting. Have you been naughty or nice this year, Syd?"

I opened my mouth, but nothing came out. My cheeks burned as his gaze turned knowing.

"I know what you've been." He kissed my forehead. "You've been nice."

My shoulders slumped. I didn't want to be nice. I wanted to be naughty like Blondie. When she'd been in his lap minutes before, I doubted Kyler had been teasing her. Maybe I should've scooped some ice up and seen what he did, except that would've required me doing so out of a random glass, and that was just gross, especially after all that herpes talk.

I needed to change the subject. "Is it still okay for me to leave my car at your place tomorrow, and you take me home when we leave Snowshoe?"

"Of course. Why wouldn't it be?"

I gave a lopsided shrug. "Just checking."

And just like that, Kyler was all serious, proving he wasn't drunk at all. "You don't ever have to double-check on something like that, Syd. You need a ride at two in the morning, you call me first."

I ducked my chin. "I know."

"Though I'd be curious as to what you were doing at that time in the morning," he added, like the probability of me being out that late was unthinkable. "Anyway, if you knew that, then you wouldn't have to double-check on something like that. I got you."

Tucking my hair back, I nodded. "Thank you."

"You don't need to thank me." He paused and his arms tightened. "He's a douche."

"Huh?" I blinked.

Kyler was staring over my shoulder, his eyes narrowed. "Paul. He's fucking eyeballing us right now. I don't like the way he looks at you."

I *almost* turned around. "He's not eyeballing us, you ass. He and I were having a conversation before you came along, so he's probably waiting for me to come back. And he's not a douche."

"But I don't want you to go back."

I sighed. Was it any wonder why I hadn't been out on a date in forever, when Kyler was my friend? Well, there were other reasons, but still. Kyler acted like a dad and older brother rolled into one. "You're being ridiculous."

He shot me a look that said he knew better. "I don't like him. I can list all the ways that I don't."

"I'll pass."

"You're missing a stimulating list of reasons why."

I rolled my eyes. "Well, I don't like Blondie. I have a thrilling list, too."

One eyebrow arched. "Blondie? Oh. My new friend?"

"Friend?" I laughed. "I don't think 'friend' is the right term for her."

He sighed as he leaned forward, propping his chin on my shoulder. "You're right. That is the wrong term."

"Okay. You must be drunk if you're admitting that I'm right."

"You're such a smart-ass tonight." He slid his hand up my back, and I shivered. "Cold?"

Since there was no way in holy hell I was admitting the truth, I lied. "A little."

"Hmm…you know what?"

The little pressure he was placing on my upper back forced me forward. I placed my cheek on his shoulder and closed my eyes. For a moment, it was easy to pretend we weren't in a bar that was playing crappy music, and even better, that we were together.

Together in the way I wanted to be with him.

"What?" I asked, snuggling closer, soaking up the moment.

"That chick isn't my friend." His breath was warm against my ear, and I loved the feel of that. "You've been my closest friend since I can remember. It's an insult to you to even call her that."

I didn't say anything. Neither did Kyler after that. And we sat there for a little while. Part of me wanted to stand on a chair and shout to the entire bar that Kyler thought more of me than Blondie. But the other part wanted to go home and throw myself in a corner because it wouldn't change how tonight would end. I'd go back to my dorm alone, and he'd take Blondie back to his apartment.

It was the same thing every weekend, and God knew how many times during the week.

No one could replace me in his life. I knew that. I *was* the friend who knew everything about him and whom he trusted above everyone else.

I was Kyler's best friend.

And because of that, he would never love me the way I loved him.

Chapter 3

SYDNEY

The stupid wheels on the bottom of my suitcase snagged on the cheap brown carpet outside Kyler's apartment, throwing me off-balance. Hair flew into my eyes as I teetered to the side. I threw my hand out, trying to steady myself, and at the last second, the items I'd precariously held in my grip started to slip.

I had to make a terrible choice—quickly. Drop the e-reader or the cappuccino.

Both things were necessary for survival, but the e-reader was like a precious wittle baby, so fragile and important to me.

Tightening my hold on the e-reader, I let the coffee hit the floor and go splat, spreading dark liquid across the carpet like a gruesome crime scene.

I sighed.

Well, the yoga classes I'd been taking two nights a week after my psychology and law classes apparently hadn't done crap for my reflexes. I picked up the cardboard cup and tossed it in the trash can by the elevator.

Taking a deep breath, I rapped my knuckles on the door and shifted my weight impatiently. Several seconds passed, and I didn't hear a thing, not even the soft patter of footsteps. I knocked again, and when there was no answer the second time, I turned around and leaned my back against the door.

Kyler was a heavy sleeper. I didn't even bother trying to call his cell. Nothing short of a nuclear bomb would wake him up.

My gaze flicked to the e-reader. Damn it, I'd lost my page. And it was just getting good. Hades had shown up in a convenience store. Sigh. Tapping the screen, I went back several—

The door behind me suddenly opened, and I fell into empty space. I twisted around, my hand colliding with warm, bare flesh. Warm, *hard,* bare flesh. A strong arm went around my waist, catching me before I face-planted.

Oh, dear God in Heaven...

I jerked back, breaking the hold. Air rushed out of my lungs, and my eyes went wide. I was face-to-face with perfect pecs—the kind of pecs anyone would want to touch. My eyes did this wandering thing without my consent, and there was so much golden flesh on display that it was like a scene from *Magic Mike* coming alive. Messed-up thing was that I'd seen Kyler half naked more times than I cared to admit, but doing so never failed to amaze me.

Kyler was an avid runner and skier when the seasons were right, which was reflected in his body. Smooth skin stretched over ridiculously defined abs. He even had those indents on the insides of his narrow hips. There was a little brown mole just left of his belly button. For some reason, I was always fascinated by that tiny dot.

He was wearing boxers—boxers with red Santa hats and

multicolored presents on them. Now that was a Christmas package a lot of people wouldn't mind finding tucked under their Christmas tree.

A lot of people included me.

Heat swamped my cheeks. My brain was *so* going to get a stern talking-to, but Kyler…yeah, he put that "oo" in swoon. Full lips curved into a half smirk, like he knew what I was thinking, and his brown hair was in serious need of a brush. It looked like he'd spent the night with someone running their fingers through it.

My stomach dropped. I'd gone back to the dorm last night before he'd left the bar. He wouldn't have brought Blondie home. Wait. What was I thinking? He *so* would've brought Blondie home.

"You smell like…French vanilla cappuccino."

I blinked. His voice was deep and raspy from sleep. "Huh? Oh, I dropped my coffee. Sorry."

A half smile appeared. "You're early."

"No, I'm not."

"You're early as usual," he continued, stepping aside. He glanced over his shoulder at the sound of water being turned on in the bathroom. He sighed. "You're not going to be happy."

I felt the blood rush out of my face, which was stupid. I totally did not care with a capital *D*. "I'm fine. I can wait in the hallway."

Kyler looked back at me with a frown. "You're not waiting in the hallway, Syd."

He brushed past me and went out in the hall, completely uncaring that anyone and baby Jesus could see him half naked. I got a full view of the lean muscles of his back. He had a tattoo—an intricate lettering that was mostly slashes—curling down his spine. It was some kind of abstract tattoo he'd gotten when he was eighteen. I had no idea what it meant. No one did.

But that wasn't his only tattoo. My lips split into a grin.

He'd lost a bet with Tanner over a football game and ended up with a red heart tattooed on his right ass cheek.

Kyler was a man of his word.

Grabbing my suitcase, he grunted. "What did you pack in here? A legion of fat and angry babies?"

I would've rolled my eyes, but they were glued to the way the muscles in his arm popped. Geez. I needed a lobotomy. "It's not that heavy."

"You've overpacked." He set the suitcase just inside the apartment and then closed the door. "It's only five days, Syd, not a month."

"Whatever," I muttered, daring a glance down the narrow hallway. The water had turned off. "So…"

"Make yourself comfy." As he swaggered by, he tweaked my nose. I smacked at him, but he easily dodged my hand and laughed. "Whatcha reading?"

"None of your business." I followed him into the neat living room. For a twenty-one-year-old guy, he liked to keep things tidy, which was surprising because at home he'd had a maid picking up after him. But it hadn't always been like that for him.

"Nice title."

I stopped behind the olive-green sofa. "Nice boxer shorts. Did your mom get them for you?"

"No. *Your* mom did."

"Hardy har har."

Glancing over his shoulder, he winked as he hooked his

thumbs into the band of his boxers, sliding them down so the very top of his ass peeked out.

"Oh my God." I leaned over the couch, picked up a throw pillow, and threw it at him.

He caught it with startling reflexes and tossed it back. The pillow bounced off my chest and hit the floor. "You liked it." Although I supposed he did have a nice ass crack, I started to tell him that it wasn't something I honestly looked forward to seeing, but the bathroom door with a YIELD sign on it opened.

I held my breath.

Who could it be? When I'd left the bar last night, he'd had a legion of girls surrounding him. The leggy blond whose middle name should've been "Jell-O shots"? Or the sexy brunette who had the deep, throaty laugh I was sort of envious of? I sounded like a hyena when I was trying to be sexy. Was it the redhead who couldn't make up her mind between Kyler and Tanner? It was anyone's guess at this point.

Long, tan legs were what I saw first, then the hem of a denim skirt that was slightly askew. I recognized the legs immediately, but the skintight black turtleneck sealed the deal.

It was Blondie—the ice cube queen.

It had been like fifteen degrees outside last night, with a thin layer of snow covering the streets of College Park, but this chick had dressed like she was in Miami.

And I felt seriously drab in my oversize sweater and worn jeans. Not to mention I felt like I was rocking a training bra compared to this chick's boobs.

She took one look at me and frowned. Black mascara was smudged under her eyes. "Who is this, babe?"

"You met her last night at Dry Docks." Kyler made his way back over to me and picked up the pillow. "Don't you remember?"

Confusion poured into her face, and I figured this was going to take a while.

Kyler's lips curved up on one corner. "You spilled a drink in her lap."

"Oh!" Blondie giggled. "Sorry about that."

"Yeah." I drew out the word. I *had* forgotten about *that*. "No biggie. Smelling like a Popsicle really draws out the guys."

Kyler frowned as he looked at me sideways.

"Has she been here all night?" Blondie asked, her head tilted to the side.

I arched a brow and started to open my mouth, because was this scenario so common that the chick wouldn't have remembered another girl joining in on their party? If so, I really needed to get out more.

"No. She just got here. We're heading out to Snowshoe," he cut in smoothly, rubbing a palm along his jaw. "So…"

Blondie swayed her slim hips right up to him and placed a hand on his chest in a familiar, intimate way. An irrational pang of envy hit me. Touching him was so easy for her. I'd known Kyler forever, and I'd choke on my tongue if I started feeling him up.

"You two are going to Snowshoe all alone? Sounds romantic," she said, a bit of a bite in her words.

"No." Kyler slid out of her grasp. "We're meeting a bunch of friends up there. Soon. So I need to get going."

Blondie wasn't taking the hint, and it was about to get awkward. That was the thing about Kyler. He could charm the panties right off a nun, but he didn't do the morning-after thing. And while he was typically nice, he had the patience of a cornered rattlesnake.

"Man-whore," I muttered as I brushed past him.

Kyler ignored that. "I'll see you later, Cindy."

Blondie hadn't moved. "Mindy—my name is *Mindy*."

I shot Kyler a look, but he was completely unrepentant. Shaking my head, I headed into the kitchen. There were a few cups in the sink, but like all the other rooms in the apartment, things were neater than most I'd seen. Not mine, though. I was so obsessive about it that it drove Andrea nuts. Hopping up on the counter, I crossed my legs and turned on my e-reader. As engrossed as I'd been in the story earlier—so much so that I was sneaking peeks at it at red lights on the way over—I was way too distracted by the muted conversation in the living room.

I eyed the bottle of Jack on his counter. A little early to get started, but the longer he took, the more I wanted a shot.

Who was I kidding? I'd nursed my rum and Coke last night until it'd been completely watered-down Coke and Coke. All our friends had gotten pretty tipsy, celebrating the beginning of winter break. Andrea had puked in the alley behind Dry Docks—she was going to be a joy at the lodge later tonight—and Tanner had been so out of it that he'd been holding up her jacket instead of her hair. Kyler could hold his liquor like a mother, but he'd let loose.

Me? I didn't like the idea of letting loose and losing control. Wasn't like I was uptight or anything, but…okay, maybe I was a little.

Every winter since freshman year of high school, I'd asked myself why I'd agreed on going to Snowshoe. We still had two weeks until Christmas. I could've gone straight home. I couldn't ski, unless skiing consisted of sliding down a snowy

26

hill on my ass. On the other hand, Kyler was a natural on the slopes and a pro at letting go. It was tradition, though, and there was no way I could skip out on it.

"You are really, really early, Syd."

I jumped at the sound of his voice. "I like to be on time."

"Obsessively." He leaned against the counter across from me.

I may have been a little early, but I hated being late. Walking into a class after it had started was worse than a zombie apocalypse to me.

Once more, my gaze dropped to his lower stomach. Had his boxers slipped down? "Can't you put a shirt on? And maybe some pants."

Kyler arched a brow. "I'm pretty sure you've seen me naked, Syd."

An ungodly amount of heat swamped me, which was so inappropriate considering the circumstances of how I had seen him naked. "You were, like, five and had chicken pox. You kept stripping off your clothes. That is *so* not the same thing."

"What's different now?"

Did I really need to explain this?

Laughing under his breath, he pushed off the counter and prowled up to me. Sitting on the counter, I was finally his height. He was ridiculously tall, coming in at six-foot-two, and I was insanely short, barely over five feet. Most of the time, I felt like I belonged in the Lollipop Guild when I was around him.

Kyler reached up and tugged on the hair that hadn't come undone in the hallway. "Pigtails. Sexy."

I shrugged.

He took the end of my right braid and smacked me in the cheek with it. "Do I have time for a run?"

I snatched my hair away from him. "If you don't, then you'll be whiny all day."

Kyler gave me his most charming smile. A dimple appeared in his left cheek, and my heart skipped a beat. "Want to join me?"

Waving the e-reader, I made a face. "Do I look like I want to go running with you?"

He leaned in, placing his hands on either side of my legs, which made him way, way too close. Even if I weren't nursing an undying lust for him, I wouldn't be immune to his proximity. Kyler oozed sex appeal, a dangerous mix of looks and intelligence wrapped in an air of unpredictability.

I inhaled—oh, wow, did he smell good. Not like he'd drunk a trough full of alcohol last night and then had wild-monkey sex for hours. Oh no, he smelled like man and a fine cologne I couldn't place.

Man, I couldn't believe I was smelling him like some kind of creeper extraordinaire.

Leaning back, I looked away.

"You'll have fun. I promise. Come on." He tugged on my braid again.

I shook my head. "There's snow and ice everywhere. I'll break my neck. Actually, *you* might break your neck. One day of not running isn't going to kill you."

"Yes, it will."

Keeping my gaze focused on the photo stuck to the front of the fridge, I clasped my hands together. It was a picture of us together, in elementary school, dressed in our Halloween costumes. He'd been a werewolf, and I'd been Little Red Riding Hood. It had been my mom's idea. "I can't believe you even *want* to go running after all you drank last night."

He laughed, and his breath was warm against my

cheek. "I can handle it. Don't forget, you're drinking with the big kids."

I rolled my eyes at that.

Closing the space between us, he kissed my cheek. "Go sit someplace more comfortable. I won't be that long."

When I didn't move, he made a disgruntled sound deep in his throat and then placed his hands on my hips. Without any effort, he lifted me off the counter and set me on my feet. He gave me a little smack on the ass, which sent me scurrying out of the kitchen.

I plopped down on the couch, glaring at him. "Happy?"

Kyler cocked his head to the side and looked like he was about to say something, but then he just grinned. "I'm going to teach you to snowboard this week. You know that, right?"

Laughing, I leaned back against the overstuffed cushion. "Good luck with that."

"You have such little faith in me. I have skills."

"I'm sure you do," I said dryly, staring at the narrow Christmas tree in front of his window.

A laugh burst out of Kyler, a nice deep laugh, and my muscles tightened. "Wouldn't you love to know the full extent of my talents?"

"If I did, it would be easy to find out. I could ask about ninety percent of the girls living on my dorm floor."

Grinning shamelessly, he backed out of the room, heading toward his bedroom. "Actually, it would be more like eighty-nine percent. I didn't sleep with the girl at the end of the hall. She just gave me—"

"I don't want to know."

"Sound jealous, don't you?"

"Not likely," I replied, turning my e-reader back on.

"Uh-huh. Keep telling yourself that, sweetheart. One of these days, you're going to admit that you're madly, deeply in love with me. It's my boyish charm—hard to resist."

"If you'd gone with your body being irresistible, it would've been more believable."

He laughed again as he turned. I watched him disappear from the room with a sinking, weird feeling in my stomach. It was the painfully embarrassing truth that Kyler never knew. He might joke with me and tease me, but he was clueless when it came to how I felt about him, and it had to stay that way.

I tipped my head back and closed my eyes, groaning softly.

Girls were like flavors to him, and I wasn't one he wanted to taste. He'd been like that since high school, and I'd accepted it as the way it was. It had to stay that way because I knew that if Kyler discovered how I truly felt, our friendship would be over in a heartbeat.

Chapter 4

KYLER

Shit. Shit. Shit.

My feet pounded the cleared parts of the sidewalk, which weren't much, and my breath puffed into little white clouds. I really could've skipped the run this morning, but I needed to get out and get moving.

I needed to run.

The burn in my muscles and the cold air worked as one hell of a brain cleaner, but the sour shit was still in my stomach, and that had nothing to do with the alcohol I had drunk last night.

I should've fucking known better.

Sydney was always obsessively early. Today would've been no different. It all stemmed from fourth grade when she'd gotten to school late and had to walk into the classroom by herself. Everyone was staring at her when she tripped and dropped her rainbow-colored notebook. The class bully—Kris Henry—laughed at her, which got half the class laughing.

I punched him for it. Got called to the principal's office for that, but it had been so worth it to knock that dough-boy on his ass. God, just thinking about it made me want to punch Kris Henry again.

And I wanted to punch myself in the nuts, while I was at it, for this morning.

The last thing I wanted Sydney to do was witness the walk of shame. Wasn't the first time, but every time it happened, I swore it would be the last time. Except there never was a last time.

Rounding the city block, I crossed over to the small park and moved onto the grass. My mind went in a really weird direction. When I'd first met Syd, my life was nothing like it was now. My mom and dad could barely make ends meet running the bar they'd bought. Food stamps were what put food on the table and my clothes were bought at the local Goodwill. As twisted as it was, it had been only after my father passed away, when I was in middle school, that the bar took off.

A fucking car accident had stolen his life, and he'd never gotten to see their dreams fulfilled.

Mom had invested his life insurance in the restoration business. Now she had money and an insanely successful business, and I'd been prepped to take it over, but you could put my ass in brand-new sneakers, designer jeans, and a new car, and I still was the same white-trash boy from the trailer park who couldn't believe the pretty little girl in class wanted to be friends.

My head went in an even weirder direction. I thought about the time I'd climbed a tree to get into Syd's bedroom. She'd been sick with mono, and our parents had been keeping us apart for obvious reasons, but I'd been worried about her. Syd had always been small, and I felt like I needed to take care of her.

I fell out of the damned tree that day and nearly broke my leg.

Our parents didn't try to keep us separated after that, and it didn't matter because, a week later, I ended up with mono anyway. But she had been so happy when I'd finally gotten my dumb ass in her bedroom. Even as sick as she'd been, when she'd seen me, her smile had lit up her face, and her blue eyes had sparkled and shit.

I'd always been a sucker for her eyes.

And it had always been like that. Year after year, when she saw me, she always smiled and her eyes would get so bright and so blue, I couldn't help but find them beautiful. So seeing her look disappointed when some random girl stumbled out of my apartment was killer.

Man, I'd fucked up this morning. One fuck-up among hundreds, if not thousands, and each time I was scared shitless that it would be the last time. That she would get fed up with me—with the girls, the partying, the whatever—discover that she was a thousand times better off without me, and walk out of my life.

And it was going to happen eventually. I knew it.

Circling the park, I picked up speed as I avoided the patches of ice. Sydney was perfect—the actual embodiment of the perfect woman. She was practically pristine and fresh. She was untouchable.

She was everything to me.

I'd spent the better part of my life trying not to fuck up for Syd and yet somehow failing miserably. I'd seen the look in Syd's eyes when Mindy came out of the bathroom this morning, and I knew she thought I'd slept with the chick last night. Which didn't take a huge leap in logic, but it wasn't like I didn't have standards or a moral code, for fuck's sake.

I was pretty sure I hadn't invited Mindy back, but she'd ended up at my place anyway. I'd deposited her drunk ass on my couch and locked my bedroom door, and that had been that. I didn't blame Syd for thinking the worst, and there was really no point in correcting her assumption.

It didn't change anything.

Sydney Bell had always been, and would always be, a few pedestals too high for me.

SYDNEY

About an hour later, Kyler was freshly showered and wearing clothes. A shame to cover up that body, but he still managed to look good in worn jeans and an old U of M hoodie, with his damp hair falling across his forehead.

He slung a black guitar case over his shoulder, and I couldn't help but get excited—the boy could play. And those fingers? The way he strummed them over the strings had my imagination skipping through the gutter gleefully every time he played.

There was nothing sexier than a guy playing the guitar. Okay. Maybe a guy on a motorcycle. That was pretty hot, too. I sighed as I followed him outside, tugging my gloves on.

I needed to get laid because my mind was really becoming disturbingly fixated on sex. Pretty hilarious, considering I really didn't count the first—and only—time I'd had sex. And honestly, I didn't get what the big deal was. I knew there had to be something because it was all anyone ever talked about, and considering Kyler's endless supply of girls there had to be more to it than pushing, pain, and awkward noises. Shoving those thoughts out of my mind as we headed outside, I focused on something less embarrassing.

"Do you think that huge storm is going to miss us?" I had watched the news while he'd been out running, and they'd given an update on the nor'easter. Earlier in the week, they'd said it was going to miss West Virginia, but it looked like the storm was moving farther south than expected.

Carrying his luggage and mine, he stopped behind his Durango. "We're going to a ski resort, Syd, where there's snow. A little more isn't going to hurt."

I went to pick up my suitcase, but he nudged me out of the way. Glancing up at the gray sky, I started nibbling on my fingernail. "But they're saying this could be the storm of the century or something like that."

He chuckled as he reached out and pulled my hand away from my mouth. "Like snowmageddon?"

I grinned. "Yeah, like that. Should we call Andrea and see if they want to wait and find out if the storm is going to miss that area of West Virginia? I know she's coming up with Tanner and the rest. Paul is driving up by himself."

The smile slipped off his face as he shut the back window and headed to my side of the car. He held the door open. "Who invited that douchebag, anyway?"

I hauled myself into the passenger seat, suddenly worried that I'd really screwed up. "Paul is not a douchebag."

"He's a dickhead." Kyler shut the door. I watched him lope around the front of the SUV and climb in behind the wheel, where he picked up the conversation. "Who invited him? Andrea?"

I'd figured Kyler's dislike of Paul had been a one-night, too-many-drinks kind of thing. "What's up with the name-calling? Paul's pretty cool, and he's been nothing but nice to you. What's your deal?"

Kyler eased the SUV out into traffic. The set of his jaw was so hard, I thought his teeth would crack. "I just don't like him."

I frowned, shaking my head. "Okay. Anyway, *I* invited him, so I hope you aren't a jerk to him."

"*You* invited him?" He cut me a quick look before stiffly returning his gaze to the road. "You invited him to my mom's place without asking?"

Staring at him, I had no friggin' clue where this attitude was coming from. Kyler could be moody sometimes, though. Apparently this was one of those moments. "I totally said I was inviting him *weeks* ago, and you didn't have a problem with it then."

"I must've been drunk when you asked me," he muttered, taking the road leading to the beltway. "Paul? Do you like him or something?"

"What?" I gawked at him. "He's a nice guy."

His long fingers drummed on the steering wheel. "That's not what I asked."

It took me a couple of moments to answer. Paul *was* really nice and funny, and I probably wouldn't kick him out of my bed for eating crackers. "No," I said finally. "I don't *like him*, like him."

Kyler didn't say anything to that, and he didn't say anything until we hit the beltway. "I think he likes you."

I arched a brow, remembering how he'd accused Paul of eyeballing us last night. "You think he likes me?"

He nodded curtly.

Andrea had said the same thing countless times before, but I'd always thought it was her way of trying to get me to obsess over someone other than Kyler. "How would you even know that, since you obviously aren't BFFs with him?"

"Why?" Easily hitting the express lane, he glanced at me. "Does knowing he's got the hots for you change the way you think of him?"

"What?" I threw my hands up, frustrated. "This is a stupid conversation."

Kyler flashed a quick grin, but his eyes were so dark, they almost seemed black. "And I'm a guy. I know when another guy wants a chick. It's in the way the guy looks at a girl. Says it all."

I chewed on my thumbnail. Maybe there could be something there, because pining away after Kyler was stupid, and if Paul was willing... "You're full of it."

"He stares at you every time we go out." He paused and reached over, tugging on my sleeve until I dropped my hand. "And if you want to know how he stares at you, it's like he's pretty much fucking you with his eyes."

"Oh. Wow. That's romantic." A secret little rush of pleasure zinged through me because it was nice to know someone thought I was desirable, even if it wasn't the person I wanted.

He snickered. "It's the truth. Though I don't know what the guy is thinking."

I turned to him slowly. "What does that mean, exactly?"

"Trying to get with you," he finished, his eyes narrowing as he peered at the green EXIT signs. "He's out of his mind. You're not..."

A slow burn filled my stomach, traveling through my veins like acid. I knew I wasn't the kind of girl who had guys dropping their undies for her every day, but I wasn't so bad off that a guy would have to be out his mind to want to hook up with me.

Anger bubbled up like water boiling over, but a deep hurt festered underneath it, fueling my words. "I'm not what? A girl who randomly hooks up with guys she meets in bars? Someone who obviously has taste and a sense of self-worth?"

His brows flew up. "Whoa. That's—"

"That's the kind of girl you go for," I cut in, clenching my hands into tiny fists. "And just because I'm not like that, then no other guy could possibly want to be with me? Maybe Paul just has taste and doesn't have a thing for girls named *Mindy*."

"Okay," he said slowly. A muscle popped in his jaw as he stared straight ahead. "First off, the last time I checked, I have superb taste. Secondly, I'm an adult. So are the girls I hang out with. Thirdly"—*How many points is he going to make?*—"it's okay to have fun, Sydney. Fun. As in something that exists outside of reading books and going to class."

My mouth dropped open. "I know how to have fun, you ass."

Kyler smirked. "That's bullshit. You're the most uptight person I know. You're—"

"If you say 'frigid,' I will kick your ass and crash this car." My heart thumped painfully. "Seriously."

He looked at me then, almost like he was startled. "I wasn't going to say that, Syd. I would *never* say that."

"Whatever," I muttered.

"Anyway, you've distracted me from my final point."

"Oh, do tell."

The infuriating half smile was back. "There isn't a damned thing wrong with the *friends* I bring home."

"But there's something wrong with me?" The moment those words left my mouth, I wanted to punch myself. I didn't think I could possibly sound more pathetic.

"Other than the fact you should wear a sign that says 'interact with at your own risk'? No. Nothing at all wrong with you, sweetheart."

"Oh, shut the hell up."

Kyler drew in a deep breath and let it out slowly, a sure sign he was close to losing his patience. "Sometimes I don't even know how we're friends," he said, running one hand over his head. "Honestly, I don't."

Tears sprang to my eyes, and I quickly turned my attention to the side window. Pressure clamped down on my chest, a powerful ache that made it hard to breathe. We really were the lion and the gimpy gazelle.

"Me neither," I whispered.

The drive was painfully awkward, on a level that jumping out of a moving vehicle seemed like a viable option. We hit a traffic snarl halfway there that added another hour and a half to our trip, and then we hit a snow squall. After our little argument, Kyler had turned up the radio, leaving it on the hard-rock station the whole way. Yep. He wasn't in a better mood.

Sometimes I don't even know how we're friends.

Ouch.

This wasn't the first time Kyler and I had bitched each other out, but usually we weren't stuck in a car together immediately afterward. I couldn't even lick my wounds in private.

About an hour out from Snowshoe, we stopped at a gas

station to fill up. As he headed into the store to grab munchies, I called to check in with Andrea.

"Where you guys at?" I asked, staring at my uneven thumbnail.

Andrea's voice was muffled. "We're stuck outside Frederick. We hit this huge-ass snowstorm. It's totally snowing us down. Ha. Did you get that—hey! Shut up, Tanner. It was funny. Tell him it was funny, Sydney."

"It was funny," I replied. "Back to the snow—is it a part of the nor'easter? Has it changed paths?"

"Looks like it." She paused. "We might have to pull over soon and wait it out, so we're going to be late."

Late? More time alone with Kyler. Great. I wanted to bang my head against the dashboard.

"What's going on with you?" Andrea asked. "It's the start of winter break, our senior year, and you sound like someone ran over your cat and then laid it on your bed."

Ew. I made a face. I had such weird friends. "I don't know. Kyler and I kind of got into an argument earlier, so it hasn't been a fun ride."

Andrea laughed. "You guys argue all the time."

"This was different."

There was a pause, and then her voice was really low. "Was that girl with him when you went over to his place this morning?"

I cringed, knowing Tanner and whoever else was in the car could most definitely hear the conversation.

"I knew it!" she exclaimed. "He's such a sleazeball sometimes. You—"

"It's all right, Andrea." I peeked out the window. "Hey, he's heading back. Call me when you guys know your ETA. Be careful."

"You, too."

Kyler hopped in, shaking the fine dusting of snow out of his hair. Then he reached into his plastic bag and pulled out a ginger ale—my favorite—and handed it over.

"Thank you," I said.

He grumbled something incoherent.

I took a deep breath and dared a glance at him. He was ripping open a bag of beef jerky as he pulled around the gas pumps. "I just talked to Andrea. They're stuck just outside Frederick due to the snow. They're going to be late. Maybe we—"

"We'll be fine."

And those were pretty much the last words we exchanged. The rest of the ride was silent. Even though I still wanted to unbuckle my seat belt and hit him a few times in his stomach, I didn't want to start winter break like this. We still had to drive back home to our families.

It seemed like forever before we saw the sign for Snowshoe just beyond Marlinton. The steady flurries had died off by then, sparking hope that we were just going to be clipped by the monster storm and nothing else.

Snowshoe Mountain really was beautiful. Like a winter wonderland with fresh snow and the main lodge rising several floors, majestically placed between the tall, snowcapped elms and slopes. Down on the narrow streets between the condos and businesses, the lampposts lining the streets and the many chalets nestled together always reminded me of the North Pole. With the heavy clouds and the approaching dusk, the shimmering white lights circling the posts and draped over the smaller fir trees were already glowing.

We passed the Starbucks just as their Christmas lights

blinked on and a group of people spilled out of their doors, laughing and carrying steaming cups of coffee.

Man, I missed my cappuccino.

As we crested the hill, I spotted the ski lifts off in the distance. Those things scared the crap out of me. Feet dangling into thin air, and you're just supposed to jump? While it's still moving? Yeah, not my idea of a fun time. Curling up by a fire and reading a good book? More up my alley.

I dared a quick peek at Kyler. The tension had eased out of his jaw, and his eyes were lighter, already filling with a gleam of excitement. He loved Shay's Revenge, the nastiest slope Snowshoe had to offer. Just looking at the fifteen-hundred-foot vertical drop made me want to vomit.

Quinn Lodge was right next to the slopes, and it was one of the larger privately owned homes. Two stories high, with multiple bedrooms and a pimped-out basement with a big screen, pool table, and various other boy toys. It would be ours for the week.

Kyler hit the brakes and hopped out, keying in the security code to the garage door. With a loud rattle, it slid up. Out of habit, I unbuckled my seat belt and wiggled into the driver's seat. Kyler disappeared into the garage, and a second later, light flooded the space.

I barely reached the pedals, but I eased the massive SUV into its spot between the three snowmobiles, the headlights shining on a stack of ski equipment. After killing the engine, I opened the door and started to hop down, but Kyler appeared in the space.

Before I could utter a word, his hands were on my hips. My breath hissed between my teeth at the intimate contact. It was the second time today he'd gotten all grabby hands with my hips. Not that I was complaining, but heat simmered in my veins, curling my toes inside my boots, and my poor body could only take so much.

"Here," he said, his voice light. "You're about the size of a teacup chihuahua. You'll hurt yourself."

Kyler lifted me from the Durango, and I gripped his upper arms. Hard muscles flexed under my hands, and a smart-ass retort died on the tip of my tongue. He was touching me, which probably meant he wasn't pissed at me anymore, and since his fingers were wrapped around my hips, I hadn't the foggiest idea why I'd been mad at him.

"There you go, safe and sound."

I mumbled something—no clue what it was. Knowing that if I looked at him, as close as our mouths were, I was likely to plant my lips on his and really embarrass myself, I kept my eyes fixed on his scuffed black boots. A kiss? I shouldn't even be thinking that, for a multitude of reasons. He only saw me as his friend, and God only knew where his mouth had been in the past twenty-four hours. Thinking that should have dampened my arousal, but it didn't. My imagination pictured his hands slipping around my hips to cup my ass. My skin tingled all over at the thought of that. Warmth flooded my cheeks, and I sucked in a sharp breath.

"What are you thinking?"

My head jerked up at the deepness in his voice, and he let go of my hips. I immediately missed his touch. "Uh, nothing—nothing at all."

He arched his brow but said nothing. "Want to head in and turn on the lights while I get the luggage?"

Happy to get away, I nodded and practically ran toward the door. What the hell was wrong with me? My hands were shaky as I opened the door into the small hallway that led

43

into the basement. As I smacked my hand along the wall, I told myself to get a grip. I could not spend the entire week lusting after the unattainable.

Finding the light switch, I flicked it on and hurried around the covered pool tables. The air smelled of cinnamon and pine. By climbing the stairs, I entered the first level. The house's interior was as beautiful as the outside. A wide, square foyer led to the large living room, with a spacious kitchen and formal dining area beyond.

Kyler's mom must've been here recently. A Christmas tree stood in front of the windows in the foyer. There were two presents under it.

Curious, I walked over to the tree, my boots silent on the hardwood floors. I knelt and picked up the red-and-green wrapped one, reading the little note attached to the sparkly bow.

Sydney—open this once you're home and it's Christmas morning. No cheating!

Love, Mary

I smiled as I placed the present back under the tree. There was one for Kyler, too, and hanging from the windowsill behind the tree were several stockings, each one for our friends. Kyler's mom was awesome. Besides the fact she'd made a billion bucks starting her own company, she was one of the sweetest women I knew.

"What have you got over there?" Kyler asked, placing the guitar case down outside the living room.

Standing, I turned around, thrilled to find that I hadn't immediately started drooling or caved to the silly notion of brushing the strand of hair that had fallen across his forehead.

"Your mom left us presents, but we're not allowed to open them until we're home and it's Christmas."

He laughed as he rounded the stairs leading to the second floor. "I bet it's a cheesy Christmas sweater."

I followed him upstairs. "Your mom would never give a cheesy gift."

"No. That's usually *your* mom."

"So true," I replied, sliding my hand along the polished banister. Mom was such a cornball when it came to Christmas. "You know, I can carry my own stuff."

"A girl shouldn't carry luggage." He glanced over his shoulder. "Especially someone who weighs ninety pounds."

I rolled my eyes at that. "I don't know what girl you're talking about because I'm pretty sure my ass alone weighs ninety pounds."

"Uh-huh." He stopped at the top landing. There were five bedrooms, each with their own bathroom. "Which room do you want? Andrea is staying with Tanner, right?"

Depended on whether they were ready to kill each other by the time they got here, but I nodded. "Any room works, really."

"How about this one?" He strolled down the hall, stopping between the last two. The room he normally stayed in was directly across. I couldn't help but think he'd hear anyone who came in and out of this room. Not that I'd have any traffic.

Him, on the other hand? I sighed. His room would be like a bus stop.

When I nodded again, he nudged the door open and headed in, placing my suitcase on the deep-brown bedspread. "I was thinking about heading down to the main lodge to get dinner. You want to come with?"

It would probably be a good idea for me to stay back and give him space, but I was hungry, and I...well, I wanted to spend time with him. "Sure. When do you want to head down?"

"In about an hour or so." Kyler headed for the door and stopped, glancing back at me. He looked like he was about to say something, but then his lips tilted up in a half smile as his hand tightened around the strap on his oversize duffel bag. "See you then."

I waited until he'd shut the door behind him before I dropped onto the bed and stared up at the wooden beams. I really needed to cut this shit out. I'd made it this long without letting my attraction get in the way. This week couldn't be any different—I couldn't risk destroying our friendship. Lusting after Kyler was only going to end one way: A broken heart.

And a whole lot of sexual frustration.

Chapter 5

SYDNEY

After dragging my stupid butt off the bed, I opened my suitcase and dug out my toiletries. In the bathroom that was the size of my dorm room, I freshened up the best I could. I wanted to take a shower, but my hair was way too long and heavy to go through the annoying drying process again.

While I untied the braids, I noted there would be no need for blush. My cheeks were still flushed and my eyes a bit too big as I threaded my fingers through the links. Freeing one braid completely, I leaned forward as I moved on to the other side, staring at my face. Was that a zit popping up on my chin?

I sighed. Why not? Perfect.

A smattering of freckles covered the bridge of my nose, and my lips were grossly bare. They needed some color. My best feature—or at least what my mom always told me—was my eyes. They were a bright shade of blue that stood out against my dark lashes and hair.

Finishing with the braids, I shook my head, happy to

discover my hair fell in tousled waves down my back instead of looking like I'd taken a crimper to it. I rummaged in the makeup bag, pulling out a tube of mascara and lipstick. After a few swipes of each, I went back to the bedroom and started toeing off my boots. If I couldn't shower, then I could at least put something fresh on.

After yanking out all the clothes I'd brought with me, which were way too much for a week, I realized I didn't have anything remotely sexy with me. A bunch of jeans and sweaters. There was a cami I could wear under a cardigan, but I'd freeze my ass off in that. Then again, I really didn't own anything sexy. And seriously, who was I trying to impress?

Kyler, whispered an evil, bitchy voice. That evil voice wasn't helping.

After pulling off my jeans, I left them on the floor and tugged the bulky sweater off, letting it join the messy heap. Standing on the tips of my toes, I held up a pair of dark skinny jeans. *These could be cute with a turtleneck.* Not that the evil, bitchy voice in my head was right or anything. There could be a hot ski instructor at the lodge for all I knew, and maybe my bedroom would turn into a train station instead of a bus stop, and I—

The bedroom door suddenly opened. "Tanner just called. He said…"

My heart stopped, and the jeans fell from my suddenly boneless fingers. Oh my God…I couldn't even think. I just stared at Kyler. There I was, standing in my bra and panties. Couldn't forget the knee-high snowman socks because they provided oh-so-much coverage.

Both of us were frozen, struck absolutely immobile by my nakedness. Time stopped, and Kyler…he kept staring at me. I couldn't remember the last time he'd seen me naked or at least half naked. Not since I'd developed breasts, probably, and they weren't much to stare at. Someone had once said more than a mouthful was a waste, but I sincerely believed that saying had been made up by girls with small breasts like me just to make ourselves feel—oh dear God, my brain needed to shut up.

Heat infused my cheeks and traveled down my neck and then even farther south, to the edges of the white lace bra, because Jesus H. Christ, I couldn't have been wearing something sexier than a white bra and striped boy shorts?

Fuck. Me.

And those were the worst two words to even think because now I was thinking about that, and Kyler was still staring at me like he'd never seen a chick in bra and panties before, which I knew was *so* not the case. But he *was* staring at me in a way I had to be completely imagining after years of hopeless wishing, because there was a heat in his eyes, an intensity that felt like a caress against my flushed skin. My lips parted as my pulse sped up, pounding through every point in my body.

He stared the way he'd said Paul stared at me. Kyler had never looked at me like that.

The muscles in my stomach tightened, and there was a sharp sensation snaking down my spine. My knees felt wobbly.

"Jesus."

His voice was a hard explosion that jarred common sense into me. I dove toward the bed, yanking an oversize sweater off it and holding it to my front. "Don't you know how to knock?"

He thrust his fingers through his hair. "Shit."

I stared at him, my entire body burning for two different reasons. Shit? That was all he had to say? Not "baby, I want to lick your body" or "ew, cover that shit up"? At least with that last one, the word "shit" became a viable part of a sentence.

And then Kyler laughed—laughed so hard, I thought he was going to physically hurt himself. "I'm sorry," he gasped. "But you should see the look on your face."

My mouth dropped open. "Get out."

His laughter went up a notch, deep laughs that sent shivers skating over my skin. I grabbed the first thing off the bed and threw it at him.

Kyler's hand shot out, and he snatched my projectile out of the air. His brows went up, and my stomach hit my toes. Something red and lacy and *bulky* hung from his fingertips.

Oh, sweet baby Jesus on a merry-go-round.

It was my bra—my Victoria's Secret push-up bra. The kind that had so much padding in the cups that it added five pounds once I put it on.

I clamped my mouth shut to stop the scream building in my throat.

Kyler's gaze flicked from the bra to me, then back to the bra. "Do you *wear* this thing?"

Unable to answer, because I was pretty sure my response would be all stabby-stabby, I said nothing.

He walked it over to the bed and laid it down like it was some kind of wild animal about to wrap itself around his face. His lashes swept up, his gaze meeting mine. Humor danced in his eyes. "No wonder your suitcase was so heavy."

"Get out!" I yelled.

Laughing under his breath, he backed away slowly. "Don't you want to know what Tanner called about?"

I shifted my weight from one foot to the next. "And if I say no?"

"I'm still going to tell you." He flashed a grin. "They've met up with the rest of the group, but they're staying the night in Frederick. It's snowing really bad down there."

At this point, I expected anything and everything to go wrong. "Crap. Do you think it's going to get bad here?"

"Don't know. Guess I'll go check the news while you put some clothes on." Kyler started toward the door and added, "Floozy."

"Shut up, you non–door-knocking peeper."

"Nice undies by the way," he said, dipping his head back in the room. "I like the color scheme. Do they have the day of the week on them?"

I screamed.

KYLER

Closing my bedroom door behind me, I tipped my head back against it and stared at the exposed beams in the ceiling.

Mom was into the whole rustic look. I thought it made the house look unfinished.

I focused on the deep oak beams, desperately trying to get the image of an almost-naked Syd out of my mind. Wasn't working. The beams morphed into hips and breasts.

Jesus. H. Christ.

Holy mother of God, that was *not* what I'd expected when I'd opened that door. I also hadn't expected Syd to be so...*curvy* under her clothes. She was a tiny thing, barely reaching my chest, and I'd assumed she was all straight lines and little else, since the last time I'd seen her so damned close to naked was in junior high school. Since then, I hadn't even seen her in a bathing suit.

Boy, was my assumption so far off, it was ridiculous.

The girl had hips on her, sweetly flaring out from a narrow waist. For someone so short, her legs looked a mile long when there was nothing covering them. And those breasts?

I scrubbed my palm across my jaw and closed my eyes.

They were small, but the size fit her perfectly, and I bet they were perky as hell under that chaste white bra, and the tips would be a sweet, dusky pink—whoa. What in the hell? I needed to stop thinking about her breasts. Totally off-limits. But because I was a dude and once that image took hold, I pictured them in my hands and her back arching into my touch—

"Shit," I growled. Lust stirred with a vengeance—that heated, almost-crazed kind of lust that never amounted to anything good.

And the way she'd been looking at me? No. No way. I had to be imagining that shit because this was Syd, for chrissakes. She was *my* Syd, but never in *that* way. And there was no way she could be looking at me with those damned baby-blue eyes of hers filled with want. Like she had wanted me to do something about the fact she'd been standing there with barely anything on.

Like she had wanted me to *see* her. Aw, hell, I *had* seen her.

And there was a good chance I was losing my damned mind, because Syd had never looked at me like that. She simply didn't think of me that way or—as far as I knew—any guy that way. Not since that asshole Nate had screwed

52

her over. Ever since then, she just didn't date. And I was okay with that because I hadn't met one guy who was good enough for her, especially not me, not after what she'd said in the car on the way up here.

I pushed off the door and crossed the bedroom. After yanking my hoodie over my head, I tossed that and the shirt underneath onto the bed.

I headed into the shower, not because I really needed one, but because I had to get my head on straight before I did something stupid.

And there was a lot of stupid in me—a whole lot.

I was still rocking the hard-on of my life, which I told myself had nothing to do with Syd, when I stepped into the hot spray of water. Probably had more to do with the fact I hadn't gotten laid last night. Yeah, that sounded good. There was only one way to fix this without a cold shower. Resting my head against the slick tile, I reached down and closed my eyes.

It was fast. It was hard. And I thought about the wrong person the whole time.

SYDNEY

I stared at the back of the bar, eyeing the bottles of liquor like they were the only things that could cure my humiliation. And they could, because if I drank enough, I probably wouldn't care that Kyler had seen me in my undies and laughed.

He had *laughed*.

The bar was packed, everyone talking about the

snowstorm that was now apparently going to make West Virginia its own personal snow bitch. It was too late to leave. All we could do was hope it wasn't as bad as they were predicting.

Spying an opening, I squeezed myself between a girl with a lot of blond hair and some dude in a flannel jacket. I glanced over my shoulder and sighed. Kyler was where I'd left him, his attention riveted on the statuesque brunette he apparently knew from waaay back. Her name was Sasha. She looked like a Sasha.

Ah, listen to me. I was being such a bitter bitch.

I watched her place a hand on his shoulder and lean in so that her breasts—much bigger than mine—pressed against his arm. She said something and he smiled. Not the full smile that showed off those dimples, but more like the cat that was about to eat an entire cage of canaries.

Kyler looked up at that moment, his gaze finding me across the crowded tables. I turned away and found myself staring at the bartender's slim black tie. Fancy.

He smiled. "What can I get you, honey?"

Since "a brain" wasn't provided in a bottle, I went with the next best thing. "A shot of Jose."

The bartender's brows rose a little. "ID?"

I dug out my license and handed it over.

He checked it out and then handed it back. "Barely twenty-one." Surprise colored his voice. "I would've pegged you for eighteen."

"Story of my life." I leaned against the bar, handing over my credit card to open a tab.

The bartender laughed as he turned, grabbing a bottle off the racks. I never knew what to do at bars. It was like an awkward experience in trying not to stand out and look like

I didn't belong. It didn't help that I apparently looked like a teenager.

"Tequila?" said a voice from behind me. "A girl after my own heart."

I turned and looked up, and up. An honest-to-goodness guy stood behind me, one *not* wearing a lumberjack flannel jacket.

Dark brown hair curled along his forehead and temples. He looked nothing like Kyler—stockier and broader.

Perfect.

"You're a fan of tequila?" I asked, finally finding my voice.

An easy smile appeared. "Nothing warms you quite as fast as tequila. You need that around here."

"You're a local?"

He nodded. "I work here during the winters."

"Ski instructor?"

"How'd you guess?"

Thinking about my desire to hook up with a ski instructor earlier, I almost laughed. The shot of tequila landed on the bar top, and I took it. I might not have been very into drinking like everyone else, but I knew how to take a shot. Tipping my head back, I put the small glass to my lips. What I hadn't expected was for my throat to catch fire.

The tequila coursed down like gasoline and spilled into my insides. Eyes watering, I turned back to the bar, dragging in deep gulps of air, desperately trying to stop my gag reflex. "Holy shit…"

Mr. Ski Instructor laughed as he patted my back. "You okay? The first shot is usually brutal."

"Yeah," I gasped, blinking the tears out of my eyes. Once

I was sure I wasn't going to hurl it back up on him, I turned around. "Wow."

He grinned. "It's not that bad."

"Oh no, not at all. I think I was already flammable."

"I haven't introduced myself," he said, sticking out a free hand. A bottle of beer occupied the other. "My name is Zach."

"Sydney." I shook his hand. His palm was slightly calloused.

He held on to my hand for a little longer than necessary. When he finally did let go, he propped a hip against the bar. "So you're obviously not a local."

"No." I tucked my hair back and smiled.

"You with him?" He gestured over his shoulder toward Kyler with a jerk of his chin. When I nodded, he cocked his head to the side. "Friends, or...?"

"Friends," I answered automatically, and the burn of tequila seemed to lessen the sting of saying that.

Zach's brows rose. "I don't think I've known Kyler to be just friends with a pretty girl before."

His compliment was lost in the reality of his statement. "Well, I've known Kyler all my life." I took a breath and let it out slowly. "So you know Kyler?"

He nodded. "I don't know him very well, just from the times he comes up here. So...is it just you two?"

"We're up here for a couple of days with some friends. Well, most of them haven't made it yet. I'm from Hagerstown."

"Oh. Pretty cool town." He took a sip of his beer. "Where are your friends at?"

"Outside Frederick," I told him as I glanced over my shoulder. I couldn't see Kyler through the mess of people. Not that I was looking for him. "They hit the storm, so they're going to try to come up tomorrow."

Zach shook his head. "Ah, I don't know if they're going to make it. The snow is supposed to move in here overnight, and they're saying it's going to be a huge storm."

I was *so* not trying to think about that.

His easy smile spread, and I realized he was really good-looking. "Think it's time for a second shot? It's on me." My gaze flicked past Zach, to where Kyler was, still with Sexy Sasha. He wasn't paying any attention to her now, though. Instead, he was staring at me like he was seconds away from getting up and storming across the bar to tell me I was up past my bedtime.

He wouldn't dare.

Kyler's eyes narrowed. He would.

A couple of months ago, while out celebrating my birthday, during one of the very rare times I did drink, he'd made me go home before I'd even gotten to the second Sex on the Beach, citing something along the lines that the crowd at the club was getting too rowdy.

Anger and frustration swirled, mixing with the shot of tequila. Kyler had said I didn't know how to have fun. I was apparently as interesting as a statistics formula on a Monday. Maybe that was kind of true. At that moment, part of me wanted to go back to the house and pick up the book I was reading. Maybe eat some buttery popcorn, too. Oh, and I'd brought that pair of fuzzy socks that were so toasty and—

"Sydney?"

Out of all the crazy moments to think about Nathan Balers, he popped into my head right then. I hadn't really thought about him in over a year. He'd been my only real boyfriend, the guy I'd dated for two years in high school and most of my freshman year in college.

Looking back, I couldn't say if I'd been in love with

him or not. At the time, it seemed like it. The only guy I'd been interested in other than Nate had been off-limits—still was—and Nate had been it for me. Patient. Funny. Smart. Cute. While we did other things—namely me doing other things so I didn't feel like the crappiest girlfriend in the world—we waited until our freshman year in college to have actual sex. It wasn't something for me to write home about. And apparently it wasn't for him either. The sex had hurt, and when it had stopped hurting and had started to *almost* feel good, it was over. Nate broke up with me a week later.

In a text message.

A few days after the text, Kyler overheard Nate running his mouth at a frat party. He'd supposedly been telling the guys that I was so frigid, he could barely keep it hard.

And that was the fight that had ended with Kyler having a broken nose and Nate with a broken jaw and a severe limp that had lasted several weeks.

Nathan Balers could go screw himself.

I knew how to have fun. I knew how to lose control. And I wasn't frigid.

Smiling, I turned back to Zach and said, "Another shot would be great."

Chapter 6

SYDNEY

Another shot turned into several more, and I honestly lost track of them. At some point, I learned that Zach was the most hilarious person on the face of this Earth, or at least it seemed that way, because I couldn't stop laughing. Then again, I'm pretty sure I would've laughed at a massive car pileup on the interstate.

When someone kicked on the jukebox and "Country Roads" started playing, I had no idea what the lyrics were, but I sang along anyway. And when Zachie Boy caught my hand and started to pull me toward a little dance floor near the hall leading to the restrooms, I didn't protest.

Though the bartender did. "You might want to sit this one out, honey."

"I'm fine." A big old smile was plastered on my face.

Zach tugged on my hand. "You heard her. She's fine."

The bartender's gaze moved from me to him. "She's not a local, Zach."

"He knows that," I pointed out.

"Keep that in mind, Zach." The words sounded like a warning to me, but that didn't make sense, and Zach was pulling me over to the square patch of floor anyway.

We started dancing, and our legs brushed. When I turned around, his hands landed on my hips. I didn't mind. I didn't think I cared about anything. Music thrummed through my veins. Or maybe it was the tequila. Either way, it didn't matter. Within minutes, sweat dotted my brow, and I lifted my hair off my neck. The movement tugged my shirt up, exposing a slice of skin.

Fingers whispered along my stomach, startling me. "You're so incredibly hot," Zach said, his palm flattening against my belly, his fingers climbing farther up my stomach. "Seriously."

My brows rose at that statement. Then again, besides Sasha, there weren't a lot of prime pickings, and I did feel hot as I swayed my hips to the beat of the music.

Zach lowered his head, rubbing his chin along the side of my face. The slight stubble made me shiver. "We should get—"

My butt vibrated, distracting me. "Hold on a sec," I said, stepping away as I pulled my cell from my back pocket. It was a text from Andrea. I glanced up. "I'll be right back. It's my friend."

Zach's smile slipped a little, but he nodded. "I'll be waiting."

I slipped back into the hallway, and it was a little cooler and quieter.

Her message read:

Bored. U?

Me: At a bar. Dancing with ski instructor.

I sent that with a big, goofy smile.

Rly? Where is Kyler?

That knocked the smile off my face.

Me: With some chick named Sasha.

We exchanged a couple of texts while I used the girls' room, and I was happy that I only stumbled a little bit. By the time I was back in the hallway, Andrea wanted to know what else I was planning to do with Zach.

Me: IDK. Dance more?

Show him your Tiya.

"Show him your Tiya?" I said out loud. I couldn't be that drunk. Shaking my head, I sent her a quick text back.

Me: Tiya?

A second later:

Tits! Damn u autocorrect!

"Oh. Tits. That makes sense," I mumbled, sliding my phone into my back pocket. Andrea gave such great advice.
"You're standing by yourself talking about tits?" Kyler asked from behind me.

I gave a little shriek and spun around. "God…"

His sexy half grin appeared. "I need to keep a better eye on you, if that's what you talk about when you're alone."

Could I just crawl under a barstool and die? "It's Andrea."

He cocked his head to the side. "You're talking about Andrea's tits?"

"No. My tits."

Interest flared in his eyes, darkening the hue. "Well, this keeps getting better."

I clamped my mouth shut, wanting to physically remove myself. "No—never mind. I have to go."

"Go where?" He caught my arm as I brushed past him, bringing me to an unexpected stop. In the cramped hallway, our thighs brushed. He lowered his head, his eyes narrowing. I swayed a little, and a slow grin split his lips. "You're drunk."

"I am only a little tipsy." I tried to pull my arm free, but he held on. "I have to get back to Zach. We were dancing. And he said I was incredibly hot, so I would like to dance with him more."

"Come again?" he said, his eyes widening.

"He said I was hot." I stared up at him. "What? Does that sound so hard to believe?"

With his free hand, Kyler reached over and tugged my sweater down past my waistline. I squirmed farther away. "I'm not saying that. Sasha knows him. Said he's a creep, and I have to agree."

"Oh." I started laughing. "Does Sasha know him? How?"

Kyler frowned. "Because Sasha is from here, and yes, they used to date or something, Syd. I told you I knew her."

"I bet you *know her*, know her."

His lips pursed, and he didn't respond for a few seconds. "Not like that, Syd. Sasha and I aren't like that."

He hadn't had sex with Sasha? *Wow, we must be the last two women on the face of the Earth.* "Well, you should get back to Sasha. I will get back to the creep."

He sighed and tipped his head back. With his hair falling back from his face like that, he looked like an angel staring up at the heavens.

All right. I was quite possibly very drunk.

"Why don't you come over and sit with me?" He tugged me closer, and for a moment, I stopped trying to get away. My thighs bounced off his legs, and I was staring at his chest again. Unfortunately, he was wearing his hoodie.

I leaned in, pressing my cheek against his chest. He smelled *amazing.* I closed my eyes and breathed him in.

Kyler chuckled softly. "How much did you drink, baby?"

"I don't know," I mumbled. "A couple."

He let go of my arm and dropped his over my shoulders. "What were you taking shots of?"

"Tequila." I sighed.

He let out a surprised laugh. "Ta-kill-ya? Oh shit."

I giggled. "It's not that bad. Kind of burned, but ya know, now I don't feel anything at all."

Kyler laughed again. "I bet you don't."

"Mmm…"

He got a hand between his chest and my face, placing his fingers on the tip of my chin. He lifted my head. "Are you going to come back and sit with Sasha and me?"

I jerked away and stumbled back a step. He had me right up until the whole "Sasha and me" bit. Disappointment seeped in, threatening to kill my buzz. I knew I shouldn't feel bad—or feel anything at all—but I did.

"I'm going to dance some more. See ya."

Kyler's atrocity of curse words was lost in the pounding

of my heart. As soon as I exited the hallway, Zach was there, grabbing my hand. "I thought you'd gotten lost."

"Nah," I said, letting him pull me toward the dance floor. "I was—"

An arm snaked around my waist, pulling me to a stop. For the first time in my life, I was literally stuck between two boys. Huh. And here I'd thought it would be more fun than this.

"Hey now." Kyler's breath stirred the hair around my temple. "Where do you think you're going?"

Good question.

Zach turned around, frowning when he saw Kyler. "And I was having such a good night. What do you think you're doing?"

"It's not really any of your business." Kyler's arm tightened around my waist.

Oh dear…

Zach's grip was firm. "Well, nice to see you again, but we're about to go dancing."

"I think she needs to sit down." Kyler stepped around so that he partially blocked me. "All right?"

Indignation rose. "I don't need to sit down."

"Well, you heard your *friend*," Zach replied, tugging me forward. "She doesn't want to sit down, so I think you should just let her do what she wants."

Kyler laughed—a cold, nasty laugh that warned of trouble as he caught my other arm, holding me in place. "Yeah, I don't give a fuck what you think, and I'm sure you already know that, but I can tell you right now, what's on your mind is *not* going to happen."

Whoa. This was weird. For two people who barely knew each other, there was a lot of hostility here.

"Excuse me?" Zach said, his eyes narrowing.

"Yeah, you heard me just right."

I don't know what happened next. Zach's grip on my hand tightened, and I yelped out of surprise. The next thing I knew, Kyler let go of my arm, and his hands slammed into Zack's chest, knocking him back several steps.

"You don't touch her," Kyler growled. "You get that? Not now. Not ever."

I was pretty positive Kyler was overreacting.

"You don't know who the fuck you're dealing with," Zach warned, taking a step forward.

"He's a ski instructor," I felt the need to explain. Yep. Fountain of helpful knowledge right here.

Kyler got right up in Zach's face. Well, he was much taller, so he pretty much looked down his nose at the dude. "I know exactly who I'm fucking with, *buddy*."

"Is that so?" Zach started forward, but Kyler was too fast. He caught the ski instructor by the shoulder and pushed him back into the paneled wall. The checkered dartboard rattled around the nail it hung from.

"Better think again," Kyler said. "I have no problem wiping the floor with your face."

I tugged on the back of his sweater. "Kyler, come on. Let's go."

Kyler ignored me.

"You think you little rich fucks can come up here and push people around? Yeah, not happening." Zach's eyes flicked over Kyler's shoulder. "That goes for little cockteases, too. Seems like your taste in females is the same."

"What?" Now pissed off for a whole different reason, I tried to get around Kyler. "I am not a cocktease, you asshat."

"Whatever." Zach shrugged off Kyler's hand and edged

65

around him, about to tuck tail and run, but not before he threw out a "you two have a great time up here."

Kyler looked like he was about to follow him across the bar, but the unfriendly faces that had started paying attention—probably locals—had him thinking otherwise. "God, where do you find these creeps, Syd?"

"Hey!" I smacked his back. "He wasn't a creep until you got involved."

"Whatever. You don't know him." He reached down and took my hand. The weight felt different and about a thousand other things I couldn't figure out. "Come on. Let's go back to the house."

His tone carried no room for argument. Stopping by the table, he said his goodbyes to a pouty Sexy Sasha, and then we headed to the door. A whole group of big dudes was doing the evil-glare thing from the corner, Zach among them, but Kyler didn't notice. And the evil-glare thing from a group of big dudes born and raised in West "by golly" Virginia could be a pretty frightful thing. Brought up images of dark backwoods and graves in hastily covered ditches.

Shuddering, I realized I was freaking myself out.

As soon as we stepped outside, harsh wind smacked me in the face. I gasped. "Holy crap, it's cold as balls out here!"

"Balls are not cold, Syd. Trust me," said Kyler. "Didn't I say you should wear a coat?"

"Bah!" I pulled free and started stomping through the fresh snow that had fallen since we'd gone in. It was only a couple of inches, but I was kicking it up everywhere. "We should have driven down here."

"*You* wanted to walk." He pulled his hoodie over his head and off. "Here—put this on." I shook my head and started down the hill, but Kyler sighed as he stepped in front of me, his jaw set in a determined line. "Lift your arms."

"What if I say no?"

His lips twitched as he held his hoodie out. "I'll hold you down and dress you."

That kind of sounded like it would be fun. Actually, Kyler holding me down and *undressing* me sounded even better. I sighed, completely lost in the fantasy. We could be like snow bunnies getting it on.

Kyler stepped closer, tipping his chin down. "What are you thinking about?"

"Snow bunnies," I replied.

He let out a deep laugh. "Come on, lift your arms and tell me why you drank so much. Please?"

"Since you said 'please'..." I lifted my arms and felt him step forward. He slipped the opening over my head and then moved on to the arms. "I just wanted to have fun."

"Nothing wrong with that." He got my left arm into the sleeve, and then he started working on the right arm, his brows furrowed in concentration. "But you've had fun before without drinking so much."

"So?" I balled my fist, and he sighed, trying to work the sleeve around it. I giggled as I straightened my hand. "What's the big deal?"

"There isn't one." He tugged the hoodie down, and it swamped me, ending just above my knees. "There you go."

When I looked up, he'd stepped back, and he had this strange look on his face—like approval. "Aren't you cold?" I asked.

He shrugged, stretching the material of the black thermal he'd had on under the hoodie. "I'll be fine."

I opened my mouth to say "okay," but something totally different came out. "I don't want to be boring anymore."

"What? Shit." Kyler thrust his fingers through his hair. "Baby, you're not boring."

"Yes. I am."

His eyes pinched at the corners. "Sydney, you are so far from that. I shouldn't have said that shit in the car. You're perfect—"

"Just the way I am?" I finished for him. "Isn't that from *Bridget Jones*?"

"Maybe." One side of his lips tipped up.

"You are such a vagina."

Kyler nudged me. "But seriously, Syd—"

"I don't want to talk." I was suddenly about a million times more uncomfortable. Walking again, I heard him keep pace with me a few steps behind. "Talk. Talk. Talk," I muttered.

Snow kept falling in a steady, light shower that coated my head and shoulders. I had an urge to tip my head back and catch snowflakes on my tongue, but I ended up throwing my arms out, tipping my head back, and belting out, "If you want a woman with a tight little kitty, then find one with itty-bitty titties!"

Kyler got an arm around my waist, laughing. "God, you are so trashed."

"You haven't heard of the song." I leaned into him, wrapping my arms around his waist, but my grip ended up around his thighs. Odd. "It's by Haven Palen Pole."

He held me up. "That would be David Allen Coe, baby."

I frowned. "That's what I said."

"Whatever you say."

We walked—or shuffled along—about a yard, and then I walked straight into a mailbox. I grunted. "Son of a bitch jumped right out in front of me!"

Kyler stopped, shaking his head. "You are a hazard to yourself right now."

"I'm fine." I waved him off, edging around the tricky inanimate object as I shot it a dark look. "I'm watching you."

"Let me help you," he offered. "Okay? I'll get us both home in one piece and keep us far away from ninja mailboxes."

Sounded like a good plan, but when Kyler wrapped his arms around my waist and lifted me, practically tossing me over his shoulder, I was *so* not expecting it. I let out a squeal and immediately started squirming.

"Behave." He smacked my ass. "Hey!"

He smacked it again, and I got in a good punch to his kidneys. My butt was too cold to really burn, but his grunt brought a smile to my face. This whole position wasn't really good for the alcohol sloshing around in my stomach, though. Kyler took three steps, and I decided I *needed* to get down. I reared back suddenly, and he stumbled to the side. He stepped into a snowdrift. I wiggled down his front, causing our legs to tangle.

"What are you doing?" he asked, trying to get a grip on me.

"Down." I swung back and ended up taking our legs right out from underneath us. Kyler twisted at the last moment, taking the brunt of the fall in the drift, and I landed on top of him.

Neither of us moved for a second, and then his hands clamped down on my hips. Under me, his chest started to move slowly and then faster. Loud laughter barreled out of his throat, bringing a happy smile to my face.

I planted my hands on his chest and lifted my head.

He stared up at me, smiling.

My breath caught and I felt dizzy. "You're beautiful."

Kyler reached up, brushing my hair from my face and tucking it back behind my ear. "I think that's my line."

"You think I'm beautiful?"

His gaze roamed over my face like he was committing every freckle to memory. Giddiness swept through me, like I was caught in a bubble. "I've always thought you were beautiful, Syd."

The world was bright and shiny and new. "Really?"

"Yeah," he replied, his hand falling away from my hair, back to my hip. "Yeah, I have."

There was nothing else for me to do. I only had one option. Kyler had said I was beautiful, and I'd waited forever to hear him say that.

So I kissed him.

Chapter 7

SYDNEY

Or at least I tried to.

My aim was completely off. My lips collided with his cool cheek.

"Syd," he said, and the way he spoke my name, like it was caught between a curse and a prayer, hollowed my stomach.

His hands slid up to my waist, under the hoodie and my sweater. His fingers brushed my bare skin, and I felt the contact in the sharpest, most delicious way. My back arched, and it all seemed like the go-ahead to me. I rolled my lower body down onto his, and I sucked in a sharp breath as I felt him pressing against the softest part of me. Kyler made a deep sound in his throat, his fingers digging into my sides and setting fire to my nerves.

Kyler moved so fast. The world turned upside down, and I was suddenly on my back, and he was above me, his hair falling over his forehead in a messy sweep. Hey now! I liked where this was heading.

Tiny snowflakes covered his head, glimmering in the

dim streetlamp. Cold snow crept under my clothing, but I barely felt it. I was on fire. I was burning up from the inside, my senses were all over the place, and it was the best feeling I'd ever had. I reached up, letting my fingers thread through his soft hair. His reaction seemed to be instinctive He closed his eyes and tilted his cheek into the palm of my hand. Warmth blossomed in my chest.

"You have no idea what you're doing," Kyler said, catching one of my hands and holding it down in the snow, next to my head. His fingers circled my wrist in a firm grip.

I wiggled under him. "Yes, I do."

His eyes closed again, and when they reopened, they were like black pools. "You're so drunk, Syd."

"Nuh-uh." I managed to get a leg out from underneath his, but then he sat up, pulling me along with him. A second later, I was on my feet, and the sky did a little jig. "Whoa."

"Yeah, 'whoa,' exactly," he said, his voice deeper than I'd ever heard it. "Let's go home."

"But—"

"Sydney," he snapped, and I flinched. "You are drunk. The only thing I'm going to let happen is me getting you home."

There was that tone again—the one that said, "Shut up and do as I say." Usually I balked at that, but I was shocked into listening. He took my hand again and started walking back to the house. I stumbled alongside him, confusion eating away at me along with the tequila. I didn't understand. He was attracted to me. He'd said I was beautiful and that he'd always thought I was beautiful, and I'd felt him. Like, I'd felt how attracted he was *against* me. There'd been no hiding that, but he'd rejected me.

Kyler had rejected me.

And he didn't reject *any* woman.

I wanted to cry—to sit in the snow and cry. Humiliated, confused, and still more than a little horny, I forced myself to stay quiet and to keep walking. Both were equally hard. Diarrhea of the mouth was building in my throat. No good could come from that.

It took forever to get to the house, and by then I couldn't feel my hands or legs, and I didn't think the snow had anything to do with that.

Kyler let go of my hand as he turned on the lights. The harsh glare hit me hard, causing the room to make like a Tilt-A-Whirl. He was right there—perfect timing, too, because I was sure my legs had stopped working.

Lifting me, he cradled me close to his chest as he started toward the stairs. "You shouldn't have drunk so much, Syd. There was no reason for that."

I burrowed my face into his shoulder. Being admonished for drinking too much by Kyler Quinn was the height of irony and embarrassment, but he was right. I was so drunk, I could admit I was drunk.

Kyler said nothing as he carried me upstairs and to the room I was staying in. He said something when he placed me on the bed, but the moment my head hit the pillow, I was blissfully and luckily out cold.

KYLER

What in the fuck had just happened?

Seriously. I was waiting for some divine intervention to offer an explanation.

73

I stared down at Syd, totally convinced that when I entered Snowshoe, I must've walked into some kind of warped reality where seeing Syd half naked, watching her get drunk off her ass, and then having her try to kiss me was run-of-the-mill.

I was absolutely struck stupid and kind of pissed, too. If I hadn't been with her tonight, she would've hooked up with some random ski instructor. And fucking Zach at that? Acid burned in my stomach. Holy shit, that didn't sit well with me at all.

And I was also sort of turned on, but then again, she had just been wiggling in my lap like any number of the girls back at school did. And she'd felt really damned good wiggling in my lap—too damned good and real hard to turn down.

Man, I had no business even thinking about this. Of course, I was attracted to her, but I couldn't go there because if I really started to acknowledge that, then I'd have to get real about other things.

I scrubbed my hand over my face. Syd was drunk, really drunk.

The girl needed to stay away from Jose.

She shifted, her brows pinching as she whimpered softly. I was by her side before I even realized I'd moved. "Syd?"

No response from her, but I could tell she wasn't comfortable. Straightening, I bit back a curse. I couldn't leave her like this. And what if she got sick? After grabbing a pillow from the head of the bed, I slipped a hand under her neck and placed the pillow underneath. She didn't wake but flopped onto her back.

I grinned and wondered if she even knew she had lain down the wrong way on the bed. I was going to go with a no. Moving to the head of the bed, I sat down and gently tugged off her boots. They were some kind of fake sheepskin or something and came up to her knees. The wedge soles were damp from the snow.

Placing them near the chair in the room, I turned in time to see her trying to sit up. "Syd?"

She mumbled something, and the only thing I made out was the word "hot," and then she started tugging at the hoodie I'd made her put on. Within seconds, she got it stuck around her head.

I laughed as her arms dropped to her sides.

Her voice was muffled, but it did not sound friendly. Then she bent over, trying to pull the hoodie off that way. Good God, she was going to suffocate herself.

"Hold on," I said, sitting beside her. "Let me get this off."

She smacked at my hands, but I got her head free, and she went for her sweater underneath.

Sighing, I grabbed her wrists. "Syd, let me get this for you."

Her eyes were completely glazed over, and I doubted she had any idea what was going on, but she settled down enough that I was able to get her sweater off, leaving her in her tank and jeans.

"I need…" she mumbled, leaning forward and resting her forehead against my shoulder. "I need to get undressed."

I chuckled as I wrapped an arm around her back, holding her up. "Baby, you just took off two sweaters."

"Pants." She wiggled up into my lap, so her legs were on either side of mine, and sighed. "I'm going to sleep."

Turning so she didn't slip out of my lap and hit the floor, I smiled against the top of her bent head. "You're going to sleep just like this?"

75

"Uh-huh."

I laughed again. "You can't sleep in my lap."

She burrowed closer, curling up in a little ball. Goosebumps spread across her arms. "Why not?" she grumbled pitifully.

"It's not going to be very comfortable." I brushed her hair off her cheek as I leaned back, searching her face. Eleven freckles. That was how many were sprinkled across her nose and cheeks. Thick lashes fanned her cheeks. Was she asleep? "Syd?"

"Mmm…pants."

My brows rose. "You want your jeans off?"

She pressed her cheek against my chest and tapped my leg once. I guessed that was drunk Morse code for yes. Swearing under my breath, I knew what I was going to have to do. Something I never thought I'd do with her.

Laying Syd on her back, I watched her lashes flutter up. The color of her eyes was like the clearest blue skies of summer. She murmured, "You're so…pretty."

"Come again?" I said, choking on my laugh. "Did you just call me 'pretty'?"

She started to roll onto her side again, but I stopped her. "Pants," she repeated, reaching down, her fingers fumbling on the button of her jeans. "Off."

I froze for a second, not sure if I should laugh at her one-syllable responses or dive-bomb out the nearest window. Undressing Syd was never on my bingo card, especially when she was drunk. But I didn't want her to wake up and, in a drunken stupor, crack her head open trying to get undressed. With Syd, anything was possible.

Shit.

I could do this. I could do this and it wouldn't be weird and I wouldn't be turned on by it, because it was Syd and she was drunk and it wasn't a big deal. We'd grown up together. I was pretty sure I'd pissed in front of her on more than one occasion. Hell, I thought I'd done that about a month ago after a night of drinking moonshine. I could take off her pants and not feel like a total fucking pervert.

I should've drunk more tonight.

Taking a deep breath, I quickly unbuttoned her jeans and undid her zipper. The striped panties peeked out as the material parted. Double shit. I closed my eyes as I tugged them down her hips. She wasn't helping. Not a single bit. She was out cold. I got a hand under her back and lifted her far enough to get the jeans past her ass. I kept my eyes shut as I pulled them down her thighs. My knuckles brushed her legs, and I didn't think about how soft her skin was because that was really inappropriate and then some.

Triple shit.

It felt like freaking forever before I got those damned jeans off, and only then did I realize she was lying the wrong way again. Cursing under my breath, I went over to the chair and grabbed the blanket off the back. I spread it over her, tucking it along her sides, and then I got the pillow back under her head.

Picking up her jeans, I felt her cell phone. The whole backside of her jeans was wet. I pulled the cell out and tapped on the screen. Nothing. Hell.

I headed downstairs, trying to get her cell to turn on as I checked the front door and made sure it was locked, turned up the heat, and made my way to the kitchen. The phone still wouldn't turn on. Recalling something Tanner had said about rice, I pulled out a bag and buried the phone in it.

Needing to check on Syd, I returned to the bedroom

she was in. The moment I saw her, I was rooted to the floor. All I could do was stare at her. My heart was beating pretty fast, and for no apparent reason.

Finally, I sat beside her and pulled the blanket up her bare shoulder. I didn't want her getting cold. I started to get up, but what if she got sick or needed something in the middle of the night? Syd never drank like this. God only knew what was going to happen.

There was a good chance I was overreacting, but I stretched out beside her. Maybe a second passed, and in her sleep, she rolled onto her side, wiggled her way over toward me so that her head was nestled against my chest, and folded her hands under her chin. Damn. I could've gotten up and gone into my own room. I could've set the alarm and checked on her in a few hours. I could've put a trash can by the bed.

But I didn't. I stayed.

SYDNEY

My head was pounding like my brain was holding its own personal rock concert somewhere near my temples. My mouth and throat felt like sandpaper. And I was freezing. I didn't want to open my eyes, but there was this strange noise—a soft humming. It took me a couple of seconds to recognize the song.

Dave Matthews's "Tripping Billies."

Kyler.

Forcing my eyes open, I found myself staring at the ceiling...from the foot of the bed. Odd. And the room was dark, like it was still night outside. Even more strange was the fact I was in my tank top and panties. Nothing else.

Oh God...

I didn't even remember getting in bed or taking off my clothes. Entire sections of last night were nothing more than a blur. What I did remember I prayed to God was just a weird dream.

"Look who decided to grace the world with her presence."

At the sound of his voice, I turned my head. Kyler was sitting beside me, facing the large windows. He was wearing a long-sleeved sweater, and he looked a hell of a lot better than I felt.

"Hey," I croaked.

Turning toward the head of the bed, he grabbed something off the nightstand. He handed me a glass of water and two aspirins. "Take these and drink up. You're going to need them."

Shoving the blanket down, I took them and shivered. "Why is it so cold in here?"

Kyler leaned onto his elbow, watching me. "I have bad news, badder news, and baddest news."

"'Badder' and 'baddest' aren't words." I finished off the water, handed it back, and then tugged the blankets up to my shoulders as I pulled my legs to my chest, trying to suck in some of the warmth.

"Good to see the tequila didn't damage your brain cells."

I winced. "I don't know about that."

A fond smile appeared. "Well, here's the bad news. Last night, when you decided to knock us down into the snow"—*Aw, hell, that hadn't been a dream*—"and rolled around? You got your cell phone soaked."

I closed my eyes. "Shit."

"I put it in some rice last night. Hopefully it will turn on after that." He poked my blanket-covered arm. "I have high hopes that it will."

"Thank you," I mumbled, opening my eyes. "What's the badder news?"

"Well, this is a two-part thing, which includes the badder and the baddest news. Remember that pesky snowstorm? They gave it a new name—Saint Snowmas."

"What?" I made a face. "That's a stupid name."

"I agree." He sat up. "But the Saint Snowmas storm turned into a nor'easter on steroids. If you look outside right now, you'll see that it's snowing pretty steady—nothing too bad, but they're saying it's supposed to get real bad and real quick. Here's the badder part: the gang turned back this morning. No one can make it up here."

I sighed. "Well, at least that's the safe and smart decision. Are we leaving soon then?"

He brushed his hair back from his forehead. "And here's the baddest part. Even though it's not the apocalypse outside right now, we have no chance of making it home if we leave. We've got to head east, and the storm is coming in from the north and the east. We're stuck for several days before we can even try to leave."

My heart thumped. "Here?"

"Here," he repeated, nodding. "The storm is moving really slowly. They're saying it will dump most of the snow tomorrow and through Wednesday."

"Holy crap." My stomach tumbled over. "How much snow are they calling for?"

"Somewhere between 'a lot' and 'holy fuck.'"

I flopped onto my back and stared up at the ceiling.

"We could be stuck here all week in the middle of a blizzard?"

"Could be. I think we'll be out sooner than that, but depends on how fast they work everything." He nudged my leg. "I cranked up the heat, so it should get warmer. Hopefully when the brunt of the storm gets here, we won't lose power."

My eyes widened.

"We have a backup generator that will run the essentials if we do, but let's not think about that right now."

"Sure."

Being stuck here alone with Kyler hadn't really set in. Normally that wouldn't be such a big deal, and truthfully I usually would've looked forward to something like that, but there was this nagging dread in the pit of my stomach.

I frowned, trying to pull together the memories into something that made sense. I remembered the tequila shots and Mr. Ski Instructor. "Did you get into a fight last night with the guy I was dancing with?"

Kyler's lips thinned. "You mean the creep you were dancing with? We didn't get into a fight, per se, but we didn't part on friendly terms."

Wiggling an arm free, I rubbed my brow. My skin felt gross. That couldn't be why I felt so uncomfortable. There was more. There had to be. I remembered going outside and Kyler making me wear his hoodie. Speaking of which... "Please tell me I undressed myself last night."

A half smile formed. "Is that what you want to hear?"

I smacked my hand over my heated face. "Oh my God..."

He chuckled softly. "You helped undress yourself, and I didn't peek. And I already saw your unmentionables earlier, so..."

I groaned. "Thanks for reminding me."

"You're welcome." He paused, and then he took a heavy breath. My muscles tightened in warning. "How are you feeling?"

That innocent question didn't match his tone. There was something about last night. *Last night.* What the hell had happened?

…And then it all came back in a horrifying rush. I'd practically molested him in a drunken stupor.

My body jackknifed into a sitting position, and I almost knocked Kyler off the bed, but that was the least of my worries. The movement rattled my poor brain, and horror swamped me. "Oh my God. Oh my God, I tried…you…" I was so embarrassed, I couldn't even speak the words.

Kyler sat back, a muscle flexing in his jaw. "I was sort of hoping you wouldn't remember."

He was hoping I didn't remember? I smacked both hands over my face and moaned. Had I been that bad? Had it been that bad for *him*?

"Hey." His voice softened, and his fingers wrapped around my wrists, gently pulling my hands away. "It's okay, Syd."

"No, it's not," I moaned, ducking my chin. "I molested you."

Kyler laughed. "You didn't molest me. Okay. Maybe just a little, but you wouldn't be the first girl to get all—"

"It's not funny!" I cried.

Two fingers landed under my chin, and he tipped my head up. "It's no big deal, Syd. People do a lot of things they normally wouldn't when they're sober, and you were really drunk."

The problem was that I had wanted to do that while I

was sober, and apparently it was just a big joke to him. I cast my eyes to the blanket. "I'm sorry."

"You don't need to apologize, baby. It's not like it was a horrific experience," he added dryly.

My gaze swung to his, and that was when I remembered the better moment of last night—him telling me I was beautiful, that he'd always thought I was beautiful. Some of the unease slid away. "It wasn't?"

His lips quirked in that adorable way of his. "I'm never going to complain about a girl crawling all over me."

Okay. That wasn't a declaration of mutual lust, but it was something I could work with. "Then why...then why did you stop me?"

He blinked once and then twice, as if he couldn't believe I was asking the question. "I'd been drinking last night, Syd, but I wasn't that drunk."

A slice of pain hit my stomach, and I froze, staring at him. "You...you weren't that drunk?"

"No." He looked confused.

I swallowed, but the lump rising in my throat got stuck. In all the years I'd known Kyler and he'd been sexually active, I'd seen him take girls home when he was sober, tipsy, drunk off his ass, and everything in between. He was equal opportunity when it came to having sex. Short. Tall. Skinny. Round. White. Black. Tan. Pale. Oompa Loompa color.

"That hasn't stopped you before." And I couldn't stop myself from talking.

Kyler thrust his fingers through his hair and then clasped the back of his neck. The shorter strands flopped back onto his forehead. He didn't answer at first, and the longer the silence dragged out, the more I wished I'd kept my mouth shut. "You're different, Syd."

So I was different, and apparently he had to be really drunk to get with me. Tears rushed into my eyes, and I had to get away from him. We were too close. I needed space before I completely lost it and humiliated myself more. I started scooting across the bed, grabbing the quilt to cover myself. I needed to get away.

"Hey." Kyler jumped to his feet. "Sydney, what are you doing?"

"I need to go to the bathroom." I slid my legs out from the covers. The breath I took was shaky and short as I wrapped the patchwork quilt around me. My feet hit the cold floor, and I took a wobbly step, smacking my toe into the edge of the suitcase. I hissed, and a tear sneaked out, rolling down my cheek.

He started walking around the bed. "Let me help."

"I'm fine." That damned lump was at the top of my throat. I reached the bathroom door as my stomach lurched. Maybe I was going to hurl instead of cry. I didn't know which was better.

"You don't look fine."

Pushing open the door, I slid inside and quickly shut it behind me, locking it. I couldn't even look in the mirror. I squeezed my eyes shut, but it was hopeless. Tears eked out, streaming down my cheeks.

"Syd?" He was right outside the door. "What's going on?"

"Go away, Kyler." Sitting on the rim of the bathtub, I pulled the quilt up to my chin. My stomach was churning. I lifted the lid on the toilet.

The doorknob rattled, and I sank to my knees. I couldn't even see the toilet, but I hoped I hit it. "Sydney!"

The quilt slipped from my fingers, and I grasped the sides of the toilet. "Go away!"

A moment of silence stretched into minutes. Then all those stupid shots came back up, leaving my insides feeling wrecked, and my heart—well, it was cracked for a whole different reason.

Chapter 8

KYLER

Wincing at the sounds coming from inside the bathroom, I moved away from the door and then went back, trying the doorknob again. She'd locked me out. God knew I could help her, hold her hair and shit, but she'd actually locked me out.

Damn it all to hell and back again; I wanted to kick the door in.

I didn't, though. I'd seen the look on her face, like I'd crushed her. But I didn't get why.

I stared at the door, taking a deep breath. *Why did you stop me?* Had she really asked that question? Was she still drunk? It seemed obvious to me. Syd had been way too drunk to even be considering masturbation, let alone sex.

Backing away from the door, I turned and headed downstairs. I checked her phone—still didn't work—and then I checked the news. Still calling for the storm of the century, and outside, the snow was starting to really come down.

I did just about everything to stop myself from checking on Syd and from really thinking about what she had asked me. I even called my mom.

She answered on the second ring, sounding breathless. "Hey, honey, please tell me you're not on your way home. I don't want you trying to drive through a blizzard or putting Sydney in a car."

My lips split into a grin. "We're going to wait it out, Mom."

"Good." Relief was evident in her voice. "Tony and I were so worried you were going to try to get out of there and hit the storm on the way."

I meandered through the various rooms, stopping in the sunroom. "What's it doing there?"

"Snowing like crazy, honey," she replied. "Did anyone else make it up there?"

"No." I moved a plotted plant to a different stand. "They hit the snow coming up."

"So, it's just you and Sydney?"

"Yep."

There was a pause. "Interesting."

I frowned. "What's that supposed to mean?"

"Nothing," she said, but she said it way too innocently. "Are you taking care of Sydney?"

I thought of last night. "Yeah, I always do."

"That is true." Another pause had my brows slamming down. I did not trust her weird silences. "You know, she treats you real good, honey."

My mouth opened, but nothing came out.

"That's a good girl with a good head on her shoulders. You'd be—"

"Okay," I cut in. I was *not* having this conversation with

her. There was only one other conversation I dreaded more than talking about girls with my mom.

Mom laughed, and then she said, "Oh. Before I forget—Tony wants to take you to the club in Bethesda we're looking into remodeling. He wants to see what you think of it."

I came to a complete standstill. Aaand there was the other conversation. "Why?"

"Because we probably won't make a move on it until late spring," she explained, and I could hear the TV in the background. She must've been in her home office. "The owner is holding out and thinks they have enough money to get them an additional four months, but we'll see. Anyway, it works out perfectly. It can be your first restoration."

"Huh?"

"You're graduating in the spring, or did you forget that?" Excitement hummed in her voice, and my stomach sank. "This works out perfectly. You get to show us your goods with the club in Bethesda. Tony wants to take you down there while you're home over break."

My eyes widened as I turned from the windows. "I don't know, Mom. I might not have time for that."

"Oh, pooh on that. You'll have time."

I said nothing.

Mom went back to talking about the weather, but I was barely listening. Ever since the restoration business had taken off, it was just assumed I would be a part of it. At first, I really didn't have anything against it. Good money—great money, even—my own hours, and I could travel, but it didn't appeal to me now.

It wasn't what I wanted, what I cared about.

But Mom had sent me to college for this. Telling her that

there was something else I wanted to do with my life was tantamount to throwing all that money back in her face—money that had started with my father's life insurance.

I got off the phone pretty quickly after that and found myself in the basement, holding my guitar in my hands and staring into nothing. Back to Syd—always back to Syd.

A huge part of me was just confused. Completely, utterly confused by her question, but the other part? I was pissed. Did she think I normally slept with girls who were so fucked up, they couldn't walk straight? There was a huge, vast difference between that and being drunk. Was that how she really thought of me?

Disgust rolled through me, and my hand tightened around the neck of the guitar.

I had never slept with a girl who didn't know what she was doing. If I even thought for one second that a girl was too drunk, nothing happened. Just like with Mindy. Then again, perception was all that mattered. All Syd saw was me going home with girls after drinking. I'd slept with a lot of women, so it didn't take a huge leap of logic for her to think that I slept with every one of them and that she wouldn't be any different.

"Fuck," I muttered as I sat on the couch across from the covered pool table.

The muscles in my stomach tightened. How could Syd think I'd treat her like a drunken one-night stand? The whole idea sickened me. I wasn't perfect, but fuck, this was Sydney.

She would always deserve far better than that, and far better than me, no matter how deep she lived inside me.

SYDNEY

I stayed hidden in my room until I was seconds away from chewing my arm off. By then it was late afternoon. I'd stopped hurling and crying hours ago, and from what I could see out the bedroom window, the snow was coming down in waves and the wind was picking up.

Heading downstairs, I stopped at the bottom of the steps and strained to hear where Kyler might be. There was the distant hum of the TV from the basement, so the coast was clear. I hurried through the foyer and into the kitchen.

The room was cooler due to the floor-to-ceiling windows in the front. I wrapped my arms around myself and walked over to the glass. Staring out the window, I watched the wind pick up the flakes, spinning them into little funnels as it tossed them across the snow-covered driveway. There had to be several inches of the new fluff since last night. And it was supposed to get worse?

Man, we'd picked the worst time to come here.

Turning away from the window, I went to the fridge and opened it. Kyler's mom had done us good, though. Food and drinks stacked the fridge and freezer. I bypassed the more complex stuff and went with bologna and cheese. But when I went to put the items back in the fridge, I sighed and made one for Kyler—ham, cheese, and extra mayo. I didn't know if he'd already eaten or not. I didn't even know why I did it—maybe out of habit—or maybe it was just because even though Kyler had stared at me like I was nuts for asking why he hadn't hooked up with me, I still loved him.

God, I was lame.

After wrapping his sandwich in a paper towel, I ate mine quickly and downed an entire can of soda in minutes. The food settled weirdly in my stomach, and I guessed it was a product of drinking half my weight in tequila. I couldn't believe I'd drunk that much and hadn't died, considering I had no tolerance for alcohol.

When I was done, I really didn't know what to do. I didn't want to go back upstairs, and I wasn't ready to face Kyler just yet. Would I ever be ready after I'd tried to kiss him and was then rejected? The guy had pretty much had his dick in just about everything. He'd had his dick in some chick two nights ago.

God, that should've grossed me out, but it really just made me feel all the more lame.

As I roamed the upstairs, I could hear a strumming riff or two coming from downstairs. I quietly made my way to the edge of the stairs that led to the basement.

Kyler was playing the guitar.

Leaning against the wall, I closed my eyes. Kyler had a talent when it came to playing music. Even as a kid, he could pick up almost any instrument and learn how to play it in record time. I, on the other hand, made musical instruments run in the other direction.

He was playing a Dave Matthews song, not missing a note at all. A smile pulled at my lips as I listened. Each note was perfect, rising in tempo as the song continued. I don't know how long I stood there and listened, but when he stopped, I was bereft.

With nothing else to do, I slipped on my boots, jacket, and hat. Slipping out the front door, I pulled my gloves out of my pockets and put them on. Snow always made me feel better. I liked shoveling. It was weird, but it helped me think.

It was brutal outside, though. The wind whipped down the valley. There weren't any other houses near this one, and other than the forest full of pines, the land was empty.

I made my way carefully down the stairs and hit the ground. Last night the snow had been packed down, but now it came up to my calves, and it was wet and heavy. I waded around the stairs and made my way to the front of the garage. Looking around, I saw the shovel propped against the wall under the stairs.

Sigh.

Shuffling back up the slight incline, I grabbed the shovel and turned, taking a sheet of snow to the face. It stung like a bitch.

"Jesus," I muttered, shaking my head.

After dragging the shovel out to the driveway, I started clearing a path. There wasn't any point to it. Wind was blowing snow back onto the tiny section I'd cleared, and when Saint Snow Dumbass or whatever they were calling it finally got here, it would be a total whiteout, but I liked the burn in my arms and how everything seemed different outside, freezing my ass off and sweating at the same time.

Maybe trying to kiss Kyler and getting rejected hadn't been such a bad thing. I could learn from this experience. Get some perspective or something, because it was probably well beyond the time I should let go of this stupid unrequited-love stuff.

He didn't want me. I wanted him.

The only way to fix this was to find someone else. And there was Paul. Nothing was wrong with him, and before Kyler had hijacked me at the bar, there was a good chance he had been going to ask me out. At least that was how it'd sounded, and according to both Kyler and Andrea, Paul was attracted to me. He didn't need to be swimming in beer to want me, so he got bonus points right there.

Too bad Paul wasn't snowed in here.

Oh, who was I fooling? Even if Paul were here, it wasn't like I'd be spending the entire time in his bed or something, but he could've been the perfect distraction.

I stopped, brushing snow off my face. Using Paul as a distraction was really shitty, but if I could just let go of Kyler, I could fall for Paul. Couldn't I? He was nice and handsome and fun. As far as I knew, he didn't sleep around. We had career goals in common.

My heart didn't like the idea, though. It felt like I was betraying Kyler or something, and that was just stupid. But I felt…icky even considering it.

Everything in my life was where it needed to be. I would graduate in the spring, then enter grad school, and for the most part, I had my shit together, but relationships? I'd missed the boat on that one. It was the one thing I couldn't fix or figure out. I was twenty-one, but it was like I was stuck at sixteen when it came to my love life.

In reality, I was stuck on one word: *frigid*.

It seemed stupid to be so affected by some guy saying that, especially with my psychology background, but that one word summed up years of a relationship and my own actual, real sexual act.

I couldn't get past that, just like I couldn't get past Kyler. Half tempted to throw myself face-first into the snow, I began shoveling with vigor. I had half the snow moved off a decent section of the driveway when I heard something rumbling in the distance. Turning around, I held the ends of my hair back from my face and tried to see through the snow. What the hell was that noise? There was nothing around here. We were too far from the street to hear anything, and I doubted anyone was up on the slopes today. Dropping the shovel as the noise—the hum of an engine—grew louder, I still couldn't see anything. Thinking I might have some tequila still left in my veins, I twisted around, and then I saw it.

Two small headlights belonging to a snowmobile were a couple of yards away from me, flying over the snow and kicking up loose flakes.

My brain absolutely refused to comprehend what was happening at first, but instinct kicked in. Air expelled from my lungs in a painful rush. It was coming fast—too fast. I froze for maybe a second, and then I started backpedaling, panic making my movements clumsy.

"Hey!" I yelled, waving my arms, but the wind carried my voice away.

The snowmobile was heading straight for me! Didn't they see me? My heart turned over.

Twisting away, I turned and tripped over the handle of the shovel. My knees sank through the snow, and I quickly pushed myself up, fear coating my insides in ice as I looked over my shoulder. It was right on me, so close that I could see the white helmet with the red and yellow stripes down the center and the dark shield covering the face. I couldn't get out of the way. It was going to run me over.

A tiny part of my brain, one that wasn't completely overcome with panic, couldn't believe this was how I would die. Being run over by a rogue snowmobile during a blizzard? Life was so cruel.

Something hit me in the waist, and I was flying ass over teakettle. I hit the part of the driveway I'd just cleared for no freaking reason. Black starbursts filled my vision, and the last thing I remembered was hearing my name, and then there was nothing.

Chapter 9

SYDNEY

I must've been out for only a few seconds—long enough to leave me feeling disorientated when I blinked open my eyes.

Kyler's hands were on my cheeks, his brown eyes nearly black. "Sydney! Say something, baby. Talk to me."

My tongue felt like a wool brush. "Ouch."

He stared at me for a moment, and then he laughed. A second later, he pulled me into a sitting position and to his chest. He was so warm, I wanted to crawl into him. "Jesus, you scared the shit out of me."

What did I do other than almost get run over? I buried my head in the front of his sweater as I clutched his sides. "I think I saw my life flash before my eyes. It was pretty lame."

His embrace tightened, squeezing me until I thought he'd crack a rib. "I didn't think I'd get to you in time, that..." He trailed off, pressing his lips against my chilled forehead. "I knew I should've come outside when I saw you go for the shovel, but I know how you like doing that shit." There was a pause, and then he cursed again. "Syd..."

"I'm okay." And I was, other than a little shaken up and having a soaked and frozen butt. "They didn't see me. Close call."

"Didn't see you?" Kyler pulled back, fury etched into the striking lines of his face. "There's no way that asshole didn't see you."

"What?"

Kyler stood, bringing me along with him. I was a little wobbly, so he held on as the wind whipped at us, throwing sheets of icy snow around us. "The asshole had to have seen you. I could see you from the porch!"

My heart tripped up. "But…"

"He saw you." Anger hardened his voice, giving it a scary edge. "Come on. Let's go inside and get you warmed up."

Before I could process what he was saying, he swooped me up and started toward the porch steps. "I can walk," I protested.

"This makes me feel better, so don't even argue with me."

I did start to argue, but when I opened my mouth, I ended up taking in a mouthful of snow, which caused me to hack up a lung. Attractive. Once inside, Kyler didn't put me down until we were in the living room and in front of the fireplace.

"What do you mean the person on the snowmobile saw me?" I asked as he worked the logs in the fireplace. "That means they were doing it on purpose."

"That's what I said," he all but growled. There was a bright spark as he stoked the flames to life, easing some of the bone-chilling cold. "He saw you. I don't know why someone would do that, but they did."

I opened my mouth again, but nothing came out. I

didn't know what to say. I couldn't believe anyone would've purposely tried to run me over. It wasn't like Kyler to be so paranoid, but I didn't know anyone here, so it wasn't like I'd had a chance to piss someone off badly enough for them to want to run my ass over.

"I don't want you going outside by yourself," he said, his back still to me as he messed with the fire.

"Okay," I said, only because I didn't want to start an argument.

He stood, shaking the wet flakes out of his hair. "You should get out of those clothes before you get sick."

Feeling a little bit like a misbehaving child and not sure why, I left to do what he asked. Since it was late and I doubted we'd be going anywhere, I changed into a pair of flannel pajama bottoms and a long-sleeved shirt. When I went back down, Kyler had changed into dry sweats, and the fire was going strong.

He handed over a blanket, and I wrapped it around myself, grateful. I felt like the snow had gotten inside me. I sat beside the fireplace, watching the flames lick at the bricks. Outside, the wind was really starting to pick up, rattling the house. It seemed like it was finding every little crack and making its way inside.

I clenched the blanket tighter as I scooted closer to the fire, shivering. Kyler watched me for a moment, and then he stood from where he was sitting on the couch. Grabbing another blanket, he walked over to where I was and sat behind me. I stiffened.

"It's okay," he said. "I have an idea." He spread his legs out on either side of me and then got an arm around me. Tugging me back, he wrapped the blanket around us. "See? We're like a burrito."

I stayed put, not leaning against him, but I could already feel the warmth coming over me. Being this close to him was nerve-wracking in a way it never had been before, so it took me a few moments to find my voice. "It's a pretty cool burrito."

"I think so." A couple of moments passed. "What do you think the gang is doing back home?"

I focused on the flames. "Probably hanging out with family. I think Andrea was going to go to Tanner's parents' house."

"Are they together?" Confusion marked his question. "I never know what's going on between those two."

I laughed and began to relax, loosening my white-knuckle grip on the blanket. "I really don't know either. It's anyone's guess."

"Those two are crazy. I don't even think they've gone out on a date."

"They haven't. I don't think they've done anything, but I still bet they'll end up married with tons of babies."

Kyler chuckled as he leaned back against the foot of the recliner behind him. "You know what I was thinking?"

I glanced over my shoulder at him. His head was tipped back, exposing the expanse of his neck. He had a sexy throat. Hell, the boy had a sexy everything. A smile tugged at my lips as my chest warmed. "What?"

"I was thinking about changing majors."

"Huh?" I laughed. "You're graduating in the spring, Kyler."

He grinned as he lowered his chin. His eyes were a warm brown. "Is it too late for that?"

"Probably." I wiggled around so I was half facing him. He spread out one leg, giving me more room. "You don't

98

want to do business management? Like your mom and stepfather?"

Those full lips of his pursed thoughtfully. "Honestly?"

"Yeah." Business management might have sounded lame to some people, but there were a lot of stable careers in that and money to be made. Especially for someone like Kyler, who had the connections needed to start his own business, which according to the last time I'd talked to his mom, was following in her footsteps. I really tried not to think about that because it meant that once we graduated, I'd stay in Maryland to get my doctorate, and Kyler would start traveling, like his mom. After spending more than half my life with him within arm's length, I wasn't sure how I'd handle the separation.

It sort of struck me then, my sudden inability to ignore my wild-monkey lust for him and my feelings that were stronger than friendship. We'd be separated sooner rather than later. Knots filled my stomach.

His eyes met mine, his expression suddenly serious. "I don't know."

Truth was, Kyler had the luxury of changing his mind this late in the game. His family had enough money that he could hold off graduating. He could go back and get another degree. He could do nothing. My parents were nowhere near as wealthy as his. My dad ran his own insurance office, and Mom taught at the local private school, so there'd been a college fund for me, but if I decided to change my mind now or take a few years off before grad school, my parents would kick my ass from here to home and back again.

"What do you want to do?" I asked, but I already had a suspicion. "Travel the world as a millionaire playboy?"

"Ha. Funny." He flashed a quick grin. "Seriously?"

I nodded.

"Restoring old bars and shit? I don't know about that. Don't get me wrong. It's not a bad job."

"No, it's not. But?"

The light in the ceiling flickered as the wind gusted. He smiled, and I released a breath. "You know how my minor is in biology, right? And I've been adding a lot of math classes in?"

"Yeah," I said, relaxing into him. He seemed to be okay with that because he shifted so my head was against his chest and his arms were clasped around me. "I just figured something was wrong with your brain for taking those classes."

He laughed. "Nah, my brain functions normally, most of the time." There was a pause, and then he said, "I was thinking about going to vet school after graduating."

My eyes fell shut as my heart did this stupid squeeze-floating thing. Kyler's biggest soft spot had always been animals. Once, in the third grade, he'd found a pigeon outside on the playground. Its wing had been broken, and left alone, it would have surely died.

He'd kicked a fit—and I mean, refusing to sit at his desk and everything—until the teacher had dug up a small box.

Kyler had marched out onto the playground and scooped up the little bird. He'd also made his mom take it to the vet.

A pigeon—a creature no one else would've given a crap about. He'd become my hero in that moment.

"Syd?" There was uncertainty in his voice, like he worried I might think giving up a career where he could make millions for one where the main payback would be helping animals was insane. I inhaled a shaky breath as I snuggled closer. I couldn't have Kyler the way I wanted him. I knew that, accepted that. The drunken version of me didn't, obviously, but still, I was proud to call him a friend.

"I think it's a great idea."

"You do?" He sounded surprised.

I smiled. "I think it's wonderful. It's something you feel passionate about. You should do it."

Kyler didn't respond, but I felt some tension seep out of him. Something I hadn't really noticed until then. Maybe that was what he needed. Affirmation.

As we sat there in silence, watching the flames create dancing shadows along the wood walls, I realized something else in that moment. Even though I knew all we'd ever have between us was friendship, I loved him.

Oh man...

I would *always* love Kyler Quinn. I was so screwed.

Chapter 10

SYDNEY

We were going to lose power. The wind was going crazy outside, beating at the house and the power lines. Why no one had thought about running those suckers underground was beyond me.

Lights flickered on and off for the entire evening. Around nine, the snow started coming down so fast and thick, I couldn't see anything outside the windows. The white stuff blanketed the limbs on the pines, weighing them down. I'd gone to bed hours ago but couldn't sleep. My mind was obsessing over everything—me molesting Kyler, the killer snowmobile, and how long we were going to be stuck here. The wind wasn't helping. It sounded like the house was going to cave in on me.

Frustrated, I turned away from the window and tightened the quilt I had wrapped around my shoulders. I crept out into the hallway, not wanting to wake Kyler.

I made it halfway down the hall before I heard a door creak open. "Syd?"

Sighing, I turned around and nearly started drooling. Kyler stood in the bedroom doorway, shirtless in pajama pants. His stomach...why did his stomach have to look like that? All rippled and hard and stuff...

"Syd?" He stepped out, closing the door behind him. "Are you okay?"

"Aren't you cold?" I sort of wanted to smack myself after saying that.

He grinned. "I wasn't until I got out of bed."

"Good point." I shifted my weight, feeling like a turd. "Sorry. I didn't mean to wake you."

"It's okay." He sauntered over to me, all 100-percent man, and I kind of hated him for that. "You can't sleep?"

I shook my head as I stifled a yawn. "The wind, it sounds like it's ripping the entire—"

A loud crack interrupted and caused me to jump. From the window at the end of the hall, the sky lit up with a shower of sparks, and then the entire house rumbled for several seconds. Overhead, the hallway light flickered twice and then went out, plunging us into complete darkness.

"Shit," Kyler said, and I felt his hand on my back. "I think the power just got knocked out. The backup generator should kick on."

I blinked, trying to get my eyes to adjust, but I could only make out his silhouette. The lights hadn't come back on, but I could hear something gearing up, like a low-level hum. Air was blowing out of the vents in the hall, nowhere near the power from before, and didn't curb the cold sneaking into the house.

He cursed again. "Stay here."

"I'm *so* not moving."

I heard him walk back toward the window. "Well, triple

103

shit. One of the pines just came down, hitting the power lines." He turned, aggravated. "The backup will only run in emergency mode—heat at a minimal, enough to keep the fridge cold and the pipes from freezing, stuff like that." He was back in front of me again, his breath warm against my forehead. "Go back into the bedroom while I check downstairs and make sure everything's okay."

"Okay." Nervous, I tightened my hold on the blanket. My heart was pounding fast. "Do…do you have to go?"

His hand was on my back again. "I'll just be a few minutes."

"Sorry, but all I can think about are those people who were stranded in the snow and had to eat one another."

Kyler laughed deeply. "Baby, that was like in the eighteen hundreds or something. We'll be fine. I'll be right back."

"You're not going to be saying that when I start chewing on your leg like a zombie." But I put my hand on the wall, using it as a guide to my room while he moved through the darkness like a damned cat.

Once inside the bedroom, I scurried over to the window. Snow fell in gusts, but with it covering everything, the entire ground glowed in the dim moonlight to my dark-adjusted eyes. A giant pine had snapped in half, a black silhouette against the snow. I shivered. Being stranded sucked badly enough, but having only backup power with the snowstorm of the century now just gearing up? *I think God just smote us.*

I headed back to the bed and climbed under the covers, tucking them under my chin. I lay on my side, watching the door. When I heard footsteps a few minutes later, I tensed.

Kyler carried a candle, and its soft glow cast shadows over his cheekbones. Placing it on the nightstand, he sat beside me. "I'm sorry about this."

"Why are you sorry?"

"Coming up here every year is my idea. You could be home, but now you're stuck up here, worrying that we're going to start eating each other."

I laughed softly. "I don't really think we'll start eating each other."

"Well, I hope if you do, you don't start with my face. I'm told it's my most valuable asset." I could hear the grin in his voice, and it made me smile. "But it's going to get cold, Syd."

"I know, but it's not your fault. I like coming up here."

He was silent for a moment. "You know, I never understood why. You don't even like to ski or do anything like that."

I chewed on my lower lip. "I like to spend time with you—with everyone." My cheeks heated. "I just like doing this with everyone."

Kyler reached over, and in the dim light, he found the strand of hair against my cheek and tucked it back. "I'm glad you came."

I got all kinds of warm at hearing that. "Only because you'd be all alone right now."

He laughed deeply and then cut a look toward the window as the wind screamed. "Nah, that's not the only reason."

Now my heart was doing jumping jacks.

Kyler picked up the edge of the blanket. "Scoot over."

My eyes popped wide. "What?"

"It's going to get cold in here, and I know you're not sleeping because of the wind. I'll stay with you until you fall asleep." He paused. "And besides, I am freezing my ass off right now."

"Okay." I stuttered that word like an idiot as I scooted over. Then I rolled over onto my other side because I was sure I couldn't face him in bed.

He slid under the covers, and even though a few inches separated our bodies, I could feel him. Totally weird, but my entire back warmed, and the urge to wiggle back and *really* feel him was hard to ignore.

"You're okay with this?" His voice sounded like it was right in my ear. "I guess I should've asked that before I told you to move over, huh?"

"Yes," I whispered. "I'm okay with this."

"Good." He settled onto his side, and I knew he was facing me. We were spooning! But we weren't touching, so I guessed that didn't count. "Because I think this bed is way more comfortable than mine, and I kind of don't want to leave."

I really didn't want him to leave either. This was like heaven to me. I closed my eyes, soaking up his nearness like he was my own personal sun.

"Do you remember doing this when we were kids?" he asked.

"Yeah, I do." But it was *way* different now. Back then, it had been so chaste, and we'd just been two kids having fun during a sleepover. Before I'd wanted to jump his bones and do all kinds of naughty things to him.

And now I was thinking about those naughty things, like rolling over and pressing against him, placing my lips against his. Touching him. Him touching me. Getting naked.

I really needed to stop thinking about those kinds of things.

"Syd?"

"Yeah?"

There was a pause. "I promise I won't hog the covers this time around."

I smiled even as my chest squeezed. "I'll hold you to that."

———

I didn't know how I'd fallen asleep with the object of my lust sleeping beside me, but I must've because I could tell hours had passed before the roaring wind woke me. I started to sit up, but I couldn't move. When what held me down sunk in, my eyes flew open, and the air rushed out of my lungs.

Kyler's arm was curled around my waist, but more than that, his entire body was snug against mine. Every deep, steady breath he took moved through me. His warm breath danced along the back of my neck, sending shivers down my spine. There was no way I could sleep next to him when he was spooning me—*really* spooning me this time. I doubted even a nun could have that kind of willpower. I wiggled away, getting a couple of inches between us, before the arm around my waist clamped down.

I held my breath.

Kyler dragged me to him, fitting my back to his front and—holy snow bunnies—he was aroused. I could feel him through our pajamas, long and thick, pressing against my rear.

My body immediately responded, going from sleepy to "well, hello there" in a matter of seconds. Didn't matter that I told my body not to or that I really had no idea what to do with all that. Warmth flooded my veins and an ache hit my core nonetheless.

This was *nothing* like the sleepovers we'd had as kids. "Kyler?"

He murmured something and managed to move closer, his chin finding its way to the sensitive area between my neck and shoulder. Shivers raced across my skin. I might have stopped breathing. The arm around my waist shifted, and his hand slid down my lower stomach. The movement had bunched up my shirt, exposing a decent bit of skin. Heart pounding against my ribs, I bit down on my lip until I tasted blood.

Kyler's fingers brushed against my bare skin, causing me to jerk back. A deep, sexy sound came out of him, and he rolled his hips forward, pressing into me as his fingers splayed, slipping under the loose band of my jammies. Never a big fan of wearing undies to bed, I was bare under the bottoms, and his fingers were so, so close. I had to be dreaming because this couldn't be happening, and I never wanted to wake up.

His warm lips brushed the side of my neck. I thought it was by accident at first, and then his mouth was against my pulse, placing a hot kiss there. Those tiny kisses kept coming, traveling down my throat. I moved unconsciously, exposing more of my neck as I arched into him, and then his hips moved in a slow, sensuous thrust that left me spinning. If this was what he was capable of half asleep, I couldn't imagine what he could do fully awake.

I'd probably be a changed woman.

And then his hand slipped farther down, brushing my center and the knot of nerves there. Sharp, exquisite sensations pulsed, robbing me of the ability to form coherent thoughts or recognize what was really happening. My body went on autopilot, kicking my brain out of the equation. I leaned back, parting my legs as his fingers grazed my most sensitive area. It seemed so easy for him, to know what to do. A finger split the wetness between my legs, moving slow and deep. In. Out. *Oh God*. Every part of me throbbed. My eyes were wide, but I wasn't seeing anything. I tried to keep quiet, but a throaty moan escaped.

The wonderful hand stilled, and the chest against my back rose sharply. "Syd?"

"Yeah?" I didn't move.

Kyler jerked back, and the bed dipped as he shot to his feet.

Holy crap, I'd never seen anyone move so fast. I rolled onto my side and started to rise, but the look on his face stopped me.

"Shit. I'm so sorry." His voice was gruff—deep and thick. "I was asleep. I thought I was dreaming—*shit*."

Disappointment swelled so quickly, it squelched the desire. He *had* been asleep—completely asleep. Not half asleep, like that was any better, but at least then he would've been half-aware of what he'd been doing.

What had I been thinking? That he'd woken up in the middle of the night and decided he could no longer resist me and all my hotness? He'd probably been dreaming of Sexy Sasha from the main lodge.

"Say something, Sydney, *please*."

At the anxiety in his voice, I realized how stupid I'd been—how stupid I was continuing to be. I squeezed my eyes shut. "It's okay. No big deal. It's all right."

There was no answer, and after several moments, I opened my eyes, scanning the room for Kyler. It was empty. I was alone with just the violent wind.

KYLER

Holy shitstorm, there were no words for what I'd just done.

I couldn't believe it.

My heart was throwing itself against my ribs as I closed the door to my bedroom and backed away. I sat on the bed, but it was more like falling because my legs were weak. That *wasn't* okay. It was a big deal. And it wasn't all right.

I was hard and throbbing, and at the same time, I felt sick. How could I've done that in my sleep? There was an easy answer, but still. I'd been dreaming about her—about Sydney. After seeing her in her bra and panties yesterday, and after last night, no wonder she was starring in my porno dreams. Shit. It hadn't been the first time I'd had that kind of dream about her, but to act on it?

I'd had my hands on her and my fingers *in* her—in *Syd*. "Oh shit."

What if I hadn't woken up? How far would it have gone? She was untouchable to the likes of me.

I started to get back up, to go to her and apologize again, but I forced myself to stay put because as the shock wore off, I remembered what had woken me from one the best dreams I'd had in a long time, which had turned out to not be a dream.

Syd had made a sound.

And the sound coming out of her hadn't sounded like fear or disgust. Every cell in my body had recognized that breathy, low moan. She had been enjoying it. Better yet, Syd seemed like she'd been awake for a while. She had to have known what I was doing, and she hadn't stopped me.

Holy shit, she *hadn't* stopped me.

Not only had she not stopped me, she had been *soaked*. And boy, did I know what that meant. But for the first time in my life, I had no idea what to do with *that*. My brain couldn't digest it, even though my body knew exactly what to do.

Flopping onto my back, I groaned, and the sound echoed in the room. I stared at the ceiling, knowing I was more likely to sprout wings and fucking fly than I was to get any more sleep tonight. Especially when damn near every part of me wanted to get back in her bed and pick up exactly where I'd left off.

Chapter 11

SYDNEY

Kyler avoided me the next day like I was some ugly chick he'd drunkenly brought home from a bar and couldn't get rid of. The whole thing was about ten levels of awkward and a basement full of someone-kill-me-now.

As I made us cold-cut sandwiches for the second day in a row, he lingered at the edge of the kitchen, and when I handed him his plate and our fingers brushed, he jerked back, knocking the plate out of my hand. Honey ham and swiss cheese went flying. Mayo splattered along the pretty tile.

"Shit," he said. He'd been saying that a lot lately. He knelt and started scooping up the mess. "Sorry about that."

I stood there, my hands shaking. I wanted to cry. Like an angry baby who wanted to be fed level of crying. Mumbling something I didn't even understand, I went over to the counter and grabbed some paper towels. With every intention of helping—and somehow cleaning up the more important mess—I went back to where he was and bent over.

At that very second, Kyler stood, and the top of his head

smacked into my chin, snapping my head back. Sharp pain burst across my jaw as I stumbled back, dropping the paper towels as Kyler cursed like the F-word was going out of style. Standing up, he reached for me, but the laws of gravity were totally against me. I knocked into the heavy-ass oak kitchen table, shaking it. Perched in the center was a vase that his mom had commissioned over five years ago, which started to wobble from side to side.

I spun around, reaching for the stupid purple-and-pink work of art. It was like one of those really bad movies where a series of accidents led to something priceless being destroyed. I practically dive-bombed the table, catching the vase a second before it committed suicide off the edge.

"Oh my God," I whispered, out of breath.

Kyler appeared at my side, helping me straighten up without any more bodily injury. "Are you okay?"

I couldn't feel my chin. "I'm fine."

He took the vase from me and waited until I backed away from the table before he placed it back down. "I'm sorry. I could've knocked your teeth out."

There was nothing for me to say, so I stood there, trying not to come in contact with anything. "Are *you* okay?"

"I have a hard head." That he did.

And then the awkwardness of the decade was back. We both stared at each other. Heat crept into my cheeks, which was amazing since it was so damned cold in the house.

Kyler went back over to the mess and grabbed the paper towels. I started to make him another sandwich. "Don't," he said, looking over his shoulder. "I'll make myself one."

I didn't know why that stung like a giant mahogany wasp had landed on my nose, but it did. It *hurt*, cut right through me. Appetite slaughtered, I left the kitchen and walked aimlessly, ending up in the sunroom on the other side of the living room.

It was freezing in this room, with the floor-to-ceiling glass windows. Huddling down in my heavy sweater, I sat on one of the wicker chairs and stared out over the snow-covered yard. Wind whipped the snow, creating drifts at least six feet high against the shed out back. Beyond that, the forest crept in. I could see the lifts off in the distance, swaying back and forth as the wind kicked them around. I took a deep breath and let it out slowly. I couldn't help but think about how it was going to be when we finally got out of here. Would our friendship ever be the same? I couldn't see how it would be.

Lowering my chin so that it dipped under the hem of my sweater, I closed my eyes. The moment I did so, I regretted it because in that room, with nothing but the wind to focus on, I thought about what had happened between Kyler and me last night. How was I ever going to forget that?

"Syd?"

I lifted my head at the sound of Kyler's voice. He was standing just inside the doorway of the sunroom. "Hey."

He ran his hand through his hair. Something he must've been doing all day, because his hair was adorably disheveled. "I'm sorry about what happened in the kitchen."

My entire body felt like it had been slipped into a fruit juicer. "You can stop apologizing. It was an accident. I'm okay. So are you. Nothing is broken."

"You left your sandwich in the kitchen."

"I'm not hungry. I'll get it later."

He looked at me for a long moment and then turned his gaze to the windows. "It's crazy out there, isn't it?"

I followed his gaze, feeling close to tears. "Yeah, it is."

A couple of seconds passed, and then he sat beside me. He leaned forward, dropping his hands on his bent knees. "Sydney, about last night—"

"Please don't apologize for that again. Okay?" I didn't think I could bear it if he did.

Kyler tensed. "How can you be okay with that? I felt you up in my sleep. Wait. I didn't just feel you up. I was *touching* you."

The way he said it made me think of those dolls social services showed kids who came into their offices. My gaze traveled over his profile. For the hundredth time, I found myself wishing things were simpler between us.

He glanced at me. "That wasn't what I intended when I got in bed with you last night. I just want you to know that."

I sucked in a sharp breath. Well, if I thought my heart couldn't take any more bitch smacks, I'd been so, so wrong.

I had to know. "Was it so bad?"

"What?"

Looking away, I pushed to my feet and walked over to the window. Maybe I just needed to grow some lady balls and confront this head-on. Obviously, we'd damaged our friendship already. The only way to repair it was if we got past this crap. Psychology 101. Avoidance was the fun and easy way, followed by denial, but neither ever worked. I needed to tell him that I was attracted to him, that I wanted him. Maybe once we cleared the air, I could move on. Honesty was always the best route to take, but I wasn't sure I could grow balls that big.

But if I didn't, then we'd continue this way. Having stilted conversations.

I heard him take a breath. "You're thinking something," he said. "You're thinking something really important. If you're pissed at me because of last night, you can tell me instead of trying to protect my feelings. I'll understand. I wouldn't hold—"

"I'm not mad at you." I faced him, folding my arms. He looked away. "And how could I be, when I tried to kiss you when I was drunk? That would make me a hypocrite."

"They were two totally different situations, Syd. You didn't try to grab my junk."

I would've if I had better reflexes while intoxicated. That was the truth—not something I'd admit, but I had to get it out there. "Why did you stop last night?"

He stared at me like I was insane. "I was sleeping, Syd! Hell, you thought you molested me while you were drunk? I seriously did that to you."

"I didn't mind." My voice came out weak, a barely there whisper.

Kyler jerked back.

I shook my head. "I wasn't asleep, Kyler. I knew what you were doing." Now he really stared at me, and I lost my breath. It was either now or never. All those moments had led up to this. I could tell him I was glad he'd stopped, say something stupid and change the subject. Or I could tell him what I wanted—what I'd been wanting for so very long. If I did, there was no going back.

"Sydney…" His voice carried a warning.

I took a deep breath. "I want what the other girls have had."

"What?" His eyes widened, darkening.

My cheeks burned like I was sunbathing in hell. "I want that—I want *you*. I want to be with you." I watched him stand, and for a second, I thought he was going to leave the room. Knots formed in my stomach, so tight that I thought

I'd hurl, but he just stood there. "I'm not asking for you to be my boyfriend or to marry me. I know you don't do relationships. I know you're not into that kind of thing."

"And you're not either?" Derision dripped from those words. Now my entire body flamed. He said that like I was Miss Relationship USA. It made me go on the defensive, and the need to prove I wasn't a frigid little Goody Two-shoes hit me hard.

"Not with you. I just *want* you. For one night. That's it."

Kyler went very still. I didn't even think he breathed. Then his eyes narrowed on me. "That's what you want?"

My hands twisted in front of me, and I whispered, "Yes."

"And that's it?" He prowled a step forward, and my heart tripped up as I took a step back. "Say it a little louder, Syd."

Throat dry, I swallowed and went with a minimally louder "yes."

Another measured step from him, and I found myself backing up until I hit the glass window. A slow, predatory smile graced his lips, and heat flooded my veins in a maddening rush. "Since when?"

Words were so hard to form. "For…for a while."

"How long?"

"A long time." Oh God, my heart was going to explode.

He shook his head. "That doesn't tell me much."

"Long enough," I said.

"And what is it again that you want?"

I wasn't sure if I could speak, not when he was looking at me like that. "You."

"You're going to have to be a little more detailed than that, baby." He stopped in front of me, and I had to crane my neck to see his expression. "Waiting…"

Was he really going to make me go into a detailed thesis?

I started to look away, but his fingers landed on my chin, holding my gaze to his. His eyebrow arched. "I...I want you."

His gaze dropped, and even though I wore a heavy sweater, I felt bare and vulnerable. I shivered and my nipples tightened. Everything in me tightened.

"You've said that already. You've also said that you want what the other girls have gotten. You know what that is?"

I nodded the best I could.

Kyler lowered his head so that his lips were a scant inch from mine. "I fucked those girls. That's it. No strings. No commitments. Nothing. And that's what you want? You want me to fuck you?"

No. I wanted more, so much more, but he wouldn't go for that. "Yes."

He sucked in a sharp breath as he dropped his hand. Anger flashed across his striking face—real anger, brightening his cheeks.

I knew I'd screwed up then. Disappointment crashed into me with the force of a wrecking ball. This was it. He was turning me down again. The back of my throat burned with the finality of it because this was it—I couldn't clear the air any better than this. I wanted to kick myself in the head. I'd brought this on myself and most likely ruined our friendship, for real this time. *Screw psychology. I should've continued with the whole avoidance thing.*

"Turn around," he ordered.

I blinked. "What?"

"Turn. Around." The authority in his voice sent a rolling shudder through me, but I was frozen there, staring up at him. His eyes were wider now, and they glimmered like polished onyx. I was trapped in his gaze. "I'm not going to tell you again."

Part of me wanted to ask what he thought he was going to do if I didn't listen, but I did turn around because I had seen the heat in his eyes. Maybe I was hallucinating all this. Maybe I'd tried to race from the room and had fallen and hit my head. Always possible. Or maybe I'd gotten a concussion from the snowmobile of death and the earlier knock I'd taken from Kyler's hard-as-hell head.

"This is how I do it." His heavy, deep voice caused me to jump. Chuckling, he brushed the mass of hair off my neck, tossing it over my shoulder, and then his breath was warm and hot along my nape. "Sometimes standing, sometimes against the wall like this, or sometimes on our knees, with me behind them."

Oh. My. God. Totally made me the queen of creepers, but I'd always wondered how he did it. I stared out into the snow, but I didn't really see anything. Heat blossomed low in my stomach, rushing through my veins. I licked my lips and then bit down as a hand skimmed my hip before settling on the curve of my waist.

"I don't do it any other way, not with girls I *just* fuck." Another hand landed on my other side, his fingers gathering the material. "And that's what you want, Syd? You want me to fuck you from behind?"

My breath hitched, and a deep ache started between my thighs. "I..."

"Which way?" he asked, then shifted closer. His lips brushed my cheek, and I could feel him all along the back of me even though he wasn't pressing against me. "Do you want to do it like this? Or we can get down on our knees. I'm fine either way."

OhGodOhGodOhGod...I had no idea what to say. The only time I'd had sex, it was missionary, and I honestly didn't know how this would work with the height difference or—

"You're thinking, Syd. Did you change your mind?"

Was that what he wanted? Or did he just expect that of me because he'd heard what Nate had said? I was frigid, and frigid girls sure as hell didn't do *this*. I squeezed my eyes shut. "Like this."

A muttered curse came out of him, and my eyes flew open. Was that the wrong thing to say? But then his hands fisted my sweater, and before I could say "orgasm," he tugged my sweater right over my head and off me.

And then I was standing there in my jeans and bra. Not the grossly padded bra—thank God—but a bra. Holy crap, we were going to do this—he was going to *do me*. We were going to fuck. A little bit of unease wiggled its way through me. There was nothing romantic about that, nothing sweet and affectionate. Fucking was just that—fucking. And he didn't sound particularly happy about any of this.

This was all wrong.

Kyler's large hands landed on the bare skin of my sides, and I jerked at the contact. "Put your hands on the glass, Syd."

All thoughts fled my mind as the heat expanded deep within me. My body responded shamelessly to his order and the deep timbre of his voice. The windowpane was cool under my palms.

"Good." One hand drifted over my skin, moving to just below my belly button and over the band of my jeans. His hand flattened. "Keep your hands on the window."

He pulled me toward him as he seemed to lean over me, so I was slightly bowed and nestled against him but still touching the window. I could feel him hot and hard, pressing into my back, and sensation trilled through my veins.

"You should've said something earlier—that this was all you wanted." There was a tightness to his words, a hard edge I didn't understand. He was definitely ticked off, but he was doing this.

Confusion and lust swirled inside me, and I didn't know which way I was going.

His other hand started to move, skimming up along my ribs, sending shivers through me. "I would've...helped you out a long time ago," he said.

I couldn't think, not when his hand drifted over my upper stomach and then over the cup of my bra. A moan escaped me as my back arched. "Kyler..."

"Shit." His hand stilled as his hips pushed forward. With his other hand still holding me in place, there was no escaping the slow, torturous pump or what it meant. Not that I wanted to. I pushed back against him, and he groaned deep in his throat.

His hand moved away from my bra, and I whimpered. But then he reached between us and, with incredibly nimble fingers, undid the bra quicker than it'd taken me to fasten it. The material slipped down my arms, and I let go of the window long enough for the bra to hit the floor. Cold air hit my chest, dueling with the heat battering me from the inside.

He wasn't in front of me, but I knew he was looking at me. As tall as he was, it didn't take much. There was a slight reflection of us in the window, and I could feel the intensity in his gaze. The tips of my breasts tightened even more, becoming almost painful.

Then his hands were on me, and my entire body sparked to life. His fingers moved over me, gently exploring the swell of my breasts, teasing the tips. He lowered his lips to

121

the spot below my ear, pressing a hot little kiss there. "Damn it, Sydney."

His fingers caught my nipple, and I cried out, moving my hips back against his in a silent plea. He trailed kisses down my neck, over the slope of my shoulder, and all along, he kept touching me until my breasts felt heavy and swollen. It had not been like that with Nate.

Kyler nipped at the side of my neck. "You…you deserve better than this, baby. Damn it, you deserve better than this." I was pretty sure I was getting exactly what I deserved—and happily, too. One of his hands left my breast and traveled down my stomach. With a flick of his finger, he undid the top button and slipped his hand into my jeans. "Tell me to stop," he said, kissing along my jaw. "Tell me."

"No," I breathed out. "I don't want you to stop."

He muttered something beyond my understanding, and then he kissed where my pulse pounded. His hand slipped under my panties, and then he was cupping me with his long fingers. "You're so ready for me, aren't you?"

I flushed, sort of embarrassed because I was oh-so-ready, but then he moved his thumb against the center of me, and I cried out his name, shaking as sweetly sharp pleasure rose so quickly, I was dizzy.

"God," he groaned, his hips grinding against me as he worked a finger inside slowly. "You keep saying my name like that and this is going to be all over before it gets started."

"Kyler," I begged, because seriously, I was at the point of begging.

His finger hooked, and I was so close already. He started a slow rhythm that was so gentle that it bordered on madness. "You're so tight," he said, and I'd never heard his voice like that. Raw. Primal. "Damn, baby, you haven't done anything since...?"

I shook my head. "No. No one since him."

"That's what I thought, but..." He shuddered, but his hand...his finger didn't break rhythm. The slow, steady thrust built a fire inside me that quickly spread. My hips moved against his hand, and I could hear his soft breaths in my ear, and each time his hips pushed against mine, it brought me one step closer to release. Every muscle tightened, and I was going to explode. I was going to—

A loud crack whipped through the room like thunder, and the window in front of us exploded.

Chapter 12

SYDNEY

Glass and snow flew into the air as I let out a surprised shriek. That was *so* not the kind of explosion I'd been aiming for.

Kyler spun around, using his body to block mine, but not before tiny sparks of pain lit up my chest and stomach. I gasped as cold air roared into the room and wind tore around us. A floor lamp toppled over. Paintings on the wall rattled.

"Holy fuck!" he shouted, bringing us down so that he was almost crouched over me. "Are you okay?"

"Yeah." I carefully put my hands on the cool, wet floor. "You?"

"I'm good." His hands slid down my bare back, and then he placed my sweater over me, wrapping it around my shoulders. "Stay down, okay?"

I nodded as I tugged on the sweater. Scooting on my knees to the wicker sofa, I looked over my shoulder. Kyler stood slowly, his hands balled into fists at his sides.

"What happened?" I asked, shivering.

He moved closer to the shattered part of the glass. A whole section was gone. Jagged edges rose from the wooden pane. "I don't see anything or anyone out there."

"Any*one*?"

"There aren't trees close enough to do any damage to the back of the house."

"But the wind—"

"The wind is strong enough to blow a fallen limb, but there aren't any limbs down below." He turned around, brushing his hair out of his face. When he saw me huddled against the sofa, his jaw hardened. "Are you sure you're okay?"

I pulled the sweater closer, ignoring the raw stinging as it brushed against certain areas. There were more important issues. Like, for example, how a window had just blown up. "I'm okay, really. What do you think happened?"

Kyler shook his head as he knelt in front of me. "I don't know. Maybe the window got so cold that when..." *Is he blushing?* "That when you pushed against it, it shattered? I don't... What the hell?"

My heart skipped a beat. "What?"

He leaned over to the right and picked up something that was lying on the floor. In his open palm, I saw a small, round pellet. "Son of a bitch," he said, standing and whirling around in a graceful move I'd seen him pull off on a snowboard. "I'm not an avid hunter or anything, but this looks like goddamn buckshot."

"What?" My shriek had to have burst his eardrums. "Are you serious?"

He nodded. "Fuck a duck, that's what it looks like."

I couldn't believe it. "But doesn't a buck shell, like, spread out? Wouldn't we've been hit?"

125

"I don't know." He tipped his head back, and the edges of his brown hair grazed the collar of his hoodie. "If someone aimed for the top of the window, it's possible the spray would've missed us."

I shivered again, but this time it had nothing to do with the cold. "You really think someone was aiming for us?"

Kyler said nothing.

"That's crazy," I whispered. Then I added, louder, "Do you think it's a good idea to be standing in front of the window, if that's the case?"

"No one's out there now, and neither of us was paying attention before. Someone could've been standing right in the open for all we know."

"Watching us?" I was hot and cold all at once. Our eyes met, and then I looked away, swallowing against the sudden nausea. I'd been topless, and his hand had been... Someone could've been watching that?

Someone with really bad aim?

"Could it have been someone hunting?" I asked, hopeful.

His brows formed a deep V. "In this kind of weather? It's a blizzard out there."

"It's West Virginia. People hunt here in all kinds of conditions."

Kyler turned back to the broken windowpane. "If that's the case, a bear must've been hanging from our roof."

I would have rather believed that than someone shooting at us, but after the guy on the snowmobile, I wasn't so sure I could consider the two situations to be coincidences. But it didn't make sense. I couldn't imagine anyone being *that* mad at us. Fear trickled in, though, as icy as the wind.

What if that shot really had been on purpose?

KYLER

Pure motherfucking rage boiled my blood, where a few moments ago, a different kind of anger had been lighting me up from the inside. Lust fueled by an indignant disbelief and anger. Syd wanted me to fuck her like a one-night stand? Like that was all I was good for, and that would be good enough for *her*?

What. The. Fuck.

But really, that wasn't the most pressing issue at the moment.

I'd deal with that later.

My gaze traveled over the shattered window, stopping on the upper-left corner. There was a tiny hole, and the glass fissured out from that point, forming a spiderweb that spread up to the edge of the jagged shard.

I'd bet my rosy-red ass cheek that there were more little holes on the outside, closer to the fascia and gutter. Someone had aimed a fucking shotgun at the house. Whether they'd intended to hit either of us was up in the air. There was no way to control buckshot, but most people could get it to go in the general direction they wanted.

Son of a bitch.

Whoever was responsible for this had been out there, watching us for God knew how long. They would've seen everything. Syd had been partially exposed.

My hands curled into fists as heat traveled down my spine. I was going to kill someone.

"Is it okay if I stand?" Syd asked.

I nodded and then glanced over my shoulder as she

127

climbed to her feet. She looked incredibly small standing there, clutching the heavy sweater to her chest with her shoulders hunched over. Anger punched me in the gut, quickly followed by the sharp taste of fear, the kind of fear I'd never experienced before.

Syd could've been hurt or worse. That was twice in a matter of two days. Horror and fury mingled inside me, forming a tangible ball that settled in my stomach. I could've lost her, and I honestly didn't know what life would be like without Syd. I didn't want to even think about that.

"Are you sure you're okay?" I asked again. "You're not hurt or anything, right?"

She shook her head slowly. "I'm really fine. Just a little freaked out."

I thrust my fingers through my hair. "I want you to stay out of this room, Syd. Hell, stay the fuck away from windows altogether."

"No problem." She inched toward the doorway before stopping. Our eyes locked, and a sweet flush spread across her cheeks and down her throat, to the edge of the sweater she still held. I wanted to go to her and take her in my arms and tell her everything was going to be okay, but I didn't move.

She looked away first, biting her lower lip. I turned back to the window stiffly, knowing I should say something— something about what had happened between us. Under the anger and the fear for Syd, lust still simmered, but there was nothing to say at this moment…or nothing I was willing to say, at least.

I felt rather than heard Syd leave the room, and it made me all the more tense. Possibly being shot at was a real libido killer.

I needed to call someone—the state police—and see what we should do. The likelihood of anyone making it out for an investigation was slim, but I needed to report this.

My gaze narrowed on the snowy ground below. I didn't want to think it, but I was a realist. I wasn't sure we were so safe here anymore, and I also knew that everything had changed between Syd and me. And that change was irreversible.

SYDNEY

After hurrying out of the sunroom, I went upstairs. It was much cooler up there in the hall and in my bedroom. Darkness was settling in, even though it was only late afternoon. I went into the bathroom, pushing the door closed behind me. Enough light came in from the window above the shower for me to see what was going on.

Standing in front of the mirror, I slowly unwrapped my sweater and winced when I got a good look at myself.

My poor boobs!

Tiny, angry-red cuts were dangerously close to my nipples—like, this could've been a hell of a lot more painful than it was. There were smudges of blood on my breasts and my upper stomach. I ran my hand over my stomach and winced. Just above my belly button, there was a small piece of glass embedded in my skin. Nothing requiring major surgery or stitches, but blood made me squeamish. Pain was even worse. I had no tolerance, having never broken a bone or experienced anything major in my life.

I hobbled from one foot to the other, freezing my nips off

as my fingers hovered over the shard of glass. I could do this.

All I had to do was pull it out. That was it. Nothing major. But I couldn't even pull out a splinter without asking Andrea or my mom to do it.

I reached for it and then winced, pulling my hand back. I did that over and over for at least five minutes, until I tipped my head back and let out a loud, frustrated groan.

"Syd? You in there?"

Jumping at the sound of Kyler's voice, I banged my hip into the edge of the sink. "Shit!"

The door swung open, narrowly avoiding a head-on collision with me. I yelped, crossing my arms over my chest—not sure what the point was in that, considering he'd been all up on it ten minutes ago—as he stormed into the bathroom, looking like he was ready to take on a rabid grizzly bear.

His dark brown eyes searched every exposed inch of me. Then he was right in front of me, grasping my shoulders. "You're bleeding." He sounded pissed. Kyler's eyes narrowed as a muscle popped in his jaw. "You told me you were okay."

"I am," I said in a tiny voice.

"When someone is bleeding, that usually means they are not, in fact, okay." He shook his head as he let go of my shoulders. "Jesus. Sit down and let me take care of you."

"I can't sit down." I winced.

He lowered his head so that he was almost eye level with me. Up close, I couldn't make out the difference between his pupils and his irises. "Why can't you sit down?"

I shuffled from one foot to the other, feeling incredibly vulnerable since I had no shirt on and all. "There's this piece of glass stuck in my skin, and I think sitting down is going to make it worse."

"What?" he shouted, and I flinched. "Why in the hell didn't you say something downstairs?"

"Because I didn't know it was stuck in my skin, and it really isn't a big deal, but—"

"But you don't even like splinters. Jesus, Syd...where is it?"

I pointed to where the tiny speck of glass was.

Kyler went down on his knees, and my eyes went wide.

All kinds of dirty thoughts exploded in my head, totally inappropriate at that moment, but the button on my jeans was still undone and, well... "I can't see it," he said. "You're going to have to come downstairs where there's more light."

"I'm—"

"You are *not* okay, and you are *not* going to argue with me over this." Jaw set in a determined line, he reached around me and grabbed a towel off the rack. He tucked it over my shoulders, folding it across my hands. "Come on."

Realizing there was a good chance he'd just drag me downstairs, I followed him out of the bedroom and into the hall. He told me to wait there while he disappeared into the hallway bathroom and returned with peroxide and a little first aid kit in his hand.

I sighed. This was going to suck. Could be worse, I knew that.

He could be plucking out buckshot.

We ended up in the kitchen, much to my dismay. There were a lot of windows in there, but we really didn't have much of a choice.

Kyler positioned me so I was just below the window, but close enough that he could see. Getting on his knees once more, he parted the edges of the towel with a frown. "Damn, that's a piece of glass."

"Told you."

His head bent, and several strands of hair fell across his forehead as he dug around in the little box with a red cross. "You can't leave it in your skin, Syd. It will get infected."

"I wasn't suggesting that. I was just sort of hoping my skin would quickly and naturally reject it."

He laughed as he pulled out a pair of tweezers, causing me to swallow hard. Images of me running screaming from my mom as a child whenever she'd wielded those tiny instruments of pain assaulted me. He held them in his elegant fingers as he looked up. "You're going a little green, Syd."

"I don't like tweezers," I whined.

A small grin appeared. "It's not going to hurt."

"That's what everyone says, but I know it's not true. It is going to hurt because you're going to start digging around and—"

"I'm not going to dig around. I'll have it out before you know what I'm doing. Promise."

I wanted to run from the room, but I forced myself to stand there beside the window like an adult. "Okay."

"You sound pitiful," he remarked as he tucked the edges of the towel into the back of my jeans, exposing my stomach. He placed his fingers on either side of the glass splinter and pulled the skin taut.

The tweezers hovered over my skin, and I cringed away.

"You big baby, stop moving."

"Shut up."

He chuckled. "This isn't going to work if you keep squirming away from me every time I get within an inch of the glass. You're making this worse by delaying it."

Sounded logical, but I wasn't a fan of logical thoughts right now. After I managed to move a full foot before Kyler cornered me between him and the counter, he distracted me. "I tried using my phone to see if I could get a hold of the main lodge. You know, to ask if anyone else has been having problems with windows being shot out or psychos on snowmobiles."

"Okay." I obsessively stared at the top of his bowed head as he continued.

"I couldn't get a call out. Looks like the storm is messing with cell service, too. Couldn't even get on the damned internet, but from what I remembered of the weather alert, we have about another day of heavy snow, and then it should taper off."

"How long do you think it will take them to clear—" There was a pinching sensation that caused me to yelp.

Kyler's head shot up. "Sorry, but good news, baby, I got it out." He waved the tweezers around. "See? Wasn't too bad."

"It wasn't." I smiled as he went back to studying the minor cut. His long lashes fanned down. "Thank you."

"My pleasure." He grabbed the bottle of peroxide and wet a cotton ball. "It will probably take a day for them to get the highways cleared and another one to get the roads around here."

There was a little burn as he swiped at the cut. "Three more days?"

"Probably." He stood gracefully and put the bottle on the counter, along with a few more cotton balls. "Let me take a look at the rest of you."

I blanched. "I don't have any more glass stuck in me."

"Forgive me for thinking you might lie to avoid the tweezers." He cocked his head to the side, and I felt my heart trip up. "I want to see the rest of it."

But that would mean I'd have to expose my breasts, and while he'd been all friendly with them earlier, this was different. We'd been caught up in the moment. Things had been hot, and this was about as hot as an ice storm. Not to mention he hadn't said a thing about what had happened between us. Neither had I, but I'd lost my lady balls after the window exploded.

Kyler sighed. "You have to make everything so damned difficult."

"No, I don't."

He shot me a bland look and then grabbed my hips. Giving me no other choice, he lifted me onto the counter. "There you go."

"Bastard," I grumbled.

He ignored that. "Let me see your chest."

I flushed about a thousand shades of red.

"Do I need to point out the fact that I just saw your—"

"No!" I cried out, horrified. "Don't point that out. It doesn't make this any easier."

His lips twitched as if he was fighting a smile. "I promise I'm going to be totally clinical about this."

Well, that didn't really make me feel any better either.

He held up his hands. "How about this? I'll treat you like you're a cat or a dog that needs to be examined."

"What?" I scowled. "Gee. Thanks."

Kyler laughed then. "Come on, Syd, stop being such a girl."

"I *am* a girl!"

"Trust me, I know." Before I could decipher the huskiness of his voice, his hands shot out, gripping the edges of the fluffy towel. "Let the towel go."

"No." I held on tighter.

"Sydney," he growled. "Let. It. Go."

Seeing that he wasn't going to let it go, because he was in full wannabe-caretaker mode, I focused on his broad shoulder as I loosened my grip on the towel. The material gaped down the front.

Instead of pulling the towel off, he investigated the little nicks that were below my breasts and in the slight valley between them. Swearing under his breath, he pulled a clean washcloth out of a drawer and ran it under the water.

Coming back to where I sat, he shook his head. "You could've lost an eye." Or a nipple, but I didn't think adding that would be helpful. "This is going to be a little cold. Don't want to use up the hot water." When I nodded, he gently wiped away the blood before taking the soaked cotton ball to the cuts.

He worked quietly and diligently, tossing the used cotton balls in the trash when he was done. Then he returned to his spot in front of me. His eyes met mine for a brief second before he slid his fingers under the towel, brushing the skin of my shoulders. I shivered and quickly looked away, biting down on my lip.

This…this was about to get interesting.

Kyler didn't say anything or seem to have moved once the towel pooled around my hips. I kept my gaze trained on the mat in front of the kitchen sink while I felt his eyes move away from my face and down my neck, following the fast-traveling flush across my breasts. The urge to cover myself was hard to suppress, but I wanted him to look.

I wanted him to like what he saw.

Although I knew this was supposed to be clinical, the tips of my breasts puckered under his scrutiny, and the unfulfilled ache in my center thrummed to life with a vengeance. I was breathless as he picked up the cloth and leaned in.

"Are you cold?" he asked.

I briefly hated him.

His chuckle was low and deep, irritating me further. "I'll make this quick."

"Yeah, you do that." I squirmed, torn between being extremely turned on, angry, and uncomfortable to the max.

Kyler moved the cloth in small circles between my breasts, every pass coming closer and closer to their aching tips. My breath was increasing, and now I wasn't sure if I wanted him to know I was confused by what had gone down between us. He'd wanted me—obviously—but nothing had been spoken about it since we'd left the sunroom. Had he changed his mind once he'd cooled down?

With the next circle, the sleeve of his shirt brushed my nipple as I sucked in a sharp breath. It happened again, on the other side, and I had no idea if he was doing it on purpose.

I gripped the edge of the counter until my knuckles hurt. My pulse pounded as he shifted so that he was standing between my legs. His hand shook as he gently swept the cloth over my right breast and then the left. I squeezed my eyes shut and tried to think of something gross, but all I could think about was him touching me and how his fingers had felt.

So not good.

I was beyond clean by the time he tossed the washcloth aside, and the peroxide burn came next. Might have made me a complete and utter freak, but the little stings somehow heightened my arousal.

"Perfect," Kyler murmured.

I looked at him, and a fevered anticipation swelled like it was my own personal Christmas morning. "Perfect?"

He was staring at my chest, and then he dragged his eyes up. "Everything's perfect." He set the bottle aside and then pulled the towel around my shoulders, covering me. "You're going to be fine."

The bubble of yearning burst in a shower of epic failure.

Kyler started to back away, his movements jerky. "I'm going to…check the garage for one of those weather radios. I think Mom had one up here. And I need a tarp. Yeah, a tarp for the window."

I stared at him.

He made it to the doorway, stopped, and rubbed his palm along his jaw. "You can get a sweater now. *Please* put a sweater on."

I didn't know what made the next words come out of my mouth. Maybe it was the leftover adrenaline from the window exploding, mixed with raging hormones that had had a taste of what it would be like to be with Kyler. I honestly didn't know, but I was pissed and confused.

And God knew that was a terrible combination, but I had my lady balls back.

"Why do you want me to put my sweater back on when you're the one who took it off?"

Kyler lowered his arm slowly, his hand forming a loose fist. "Syd, I…I really don't know what to say."

Sitting on the countertop like a kid had me at a disadvantage. I hopped down, keeping the towel clenched around myself "What do you mean, you don't know what to say? I think we pretty much covered the bases earlier."

He took a measured step forward, his shoulders tensing. "Look. This isn't the time for this right now. I need to get the tarp. I need to figure out if someone really did shoot out the damn—"

"How are you going to figure that out? Been majoring in CSI without me knowing?"

He arched a brow. "No need to be a smart-ass."

"And there's no reason why we can't talk about this now. I want—"

"I know what you want, Syd." Anger flashed across his striking face once more. "Trust me, I totally understand. You want me to fuck you like a drunken one-night stand."

I flinched back. That was *so* not what I really wanted.

"What? You don't like the way that sounds? Well, I don't like the way it sounds either."

Yeah, he really was pissed. A muscle throbbed in his jaw, and his eyes were a dangerous black. "I shouldn't have let it get as far as it did because that's not going to happen. That's not what we're about. And we're never going to be about that."

Chapter 13

SYDNEY

Lady balls were so freaking overrated. So was snow.

I used to love the snow, but right now I hated it because it had me trapped right here. And this was officially the last place on the planet I wanted to be.

The temps had dropped even more once evening crept in on us. I paced the length of the living room, my arms folded across my chest in spite of the heat from the fire. Three more days with Kyler. I couldn't make it.

I heard his footsteps coming up the stairwell from the basement, and I froze in front of the fireplace. My heart thumped as loudly as the wind outside. He appeared, carrying a bundle of blue tarps. Our eyes met for the briefest second, and then he headed for the door at the opposite end of the room, toward the sunroom.

"Can I help?" I asked, wincing as my voice cracked in the middle.

Surprise flickered across his stony face, and I wasn't sure why. Sure, I was embarrassed and pissed, and "confused" should have been my middle name at this point, but what had Kyler really done? I'd thrown myself at him—more than once. Asked him to fuck me like a cheap date, and he *was* a guy—a guy who was probably used to having sex just about every other day. Of course, he was going to act on it in the heat of the moment. He hadn't done anything wrong. If anything, he was the only one in this situation trying to do the right thing. Apparently he valued our friendship more than I did.

It was all on me.

Kyler looked away, shaking his head. "I got this. Just stay in here and keep warm."

I watched him close the door behind him, my chest squeezing. As soon as I heard it latch, I smacked myself on the forehead. "God. I *suck*."

Turning from the door, I tugged my hands through my hair and winced at the slickness. There was a good chance his head had cleared once he'd realized I hadn't showered this morning. The whole conserving-hot-water thing sucked. He'd taken a cold one this morning, and I figured I could probably take a quick one that would get the grime off.

And it would also serve as the perfect distraction.

Hurrying upstairs, I ignored the chill in the air and stripped off my clothes in the bedroom. Before I went into the bathroom, I laid out a pair of sweats and the cream-colored sweater I'd fallen in love with. I'd wanted to wear it out here, with tight jeans and boots. In the store, I had hoped that when I wore it, it would somehow trigger something in Kyler that flipped the friendship switch to "let's get it on."

What had my mom always said? If wishes were fishes… Sighing, I went into the bathroom, ignoring the way my entire throat burned. I wanted to rewind the past couple of days, start all over. I couldn't change the way I felt about Kyler. That was a lost cause, but I could've stayed away from the liquor at the lodge, and I could've kept my mouth shut afterward.

Too bad there wasn't a rewind button on life. I'd be pressing the hell out of that.

Adjusting the water so that it was lukewarm, I stepped into the shower, wincing at the coolness under my feet. I figured keeping the water temp down would help. Without wasting time, I grabbed my shampoo and lathered up. The little cuts on my chest and stomach stung, serving as a reminder of what had happened.

Had someone really shot out the window? Had someone been aiming for us? I shuddered as I grabbed the conditioner. I slathered it through my hair and immediately started washing it out as I grabbed the bodywash and loofah. Suds were everywhere, sliding down my stomach and thighs, pooling in the basin of the tub.

I wanted to go home.

Tears filled my eyes, and I squeezed them shut. I wanted to go home so badly and forget these days, but I knew how pointless that was. I would never forget those moments with Kyler.

Fuck you like a one-night stand.

That wasn't what I wanted, but I would've accepted it. I wasn't sure what that said about me—that I could love someone so much, I'd accept whatever scraps they tossed my way. It wasn't right. It was the epitome of *weak*. I knew that, but it didn't change the fact that if Kyler climbed into the shower right now, I'd let him do whatever he wanted. My chest hurt in a way I was slowly growing accustomed to.

Icy water sprayed me suddenly, forcing out a surprised

shriek as I jumped a good foot in the air. I scrambled to the back of the tub, my feet slipping out from underneath me.

Oh no…

I lost my balance. Arms flailing, I grabbed the first thing my fingers touched. The shower curtain caught my weight, and for a second, relief washed over me, but then the tiny hooks snapped. The curtain tore, and my legs went out from underneath me. I hit the slippery, soapy tub on my ass. Brittle pain spread across my tailbone as I sucked in a breath. The curtain fluttered around me, creating a weak shield against the frigid water.

The small vent in the bathroom wall stopped rattling, and whatever little heat had been coming out, keeping the pipes unfrozen, disappeared.

The bathroom door swung open, slamming into the wall, and I had a wicked sense of déjà vu as Kyler burst into the room. "Sydney, what…?"

I smacked at the faucets, turning them off as I tried to keep the plastic curtain around me. Of course, it was practically see-through, because why would I expect anything else? I was going strong on humiliation.

The water trickled to a stop as I lifted my head, peering through wet, cold hair at Kyler. He was crouched by the tub, his eyes wide. "Are you okay?"

I clenched the curtain to my chest. "I think…I broke my butt."

His lips mashed together as he looked to the side, grabbing a towel from the stack across from the toilet. "Here," he said. "Let me help you."

Little bumps spread across my skin as I knocked his arm away. "I'm okay."

"What happened?"

I shot him a withering look. "I fell."

"I got that part." He held up the big, dry towel.

"The water went ice-cold, and I wasn't even in the shower that long. Not even a minute," I grumbled, trying to figure out how to get the towel without exposing everything.

Brows knitted, he reached over to the vent and put his hand in front of it. I took that moment to snatch the towel and scoot out from under the curtain. Wrapping it around my chest, I stood on shaky legs. My backside really did hurt.

"Shit," Kyler said, standing. "I think the damned backup generator is out. Fucking great."

I didn't need to ask what that meant. Pipes would freeze. Food might spoil, but with the freezing temps creeping inside, that part was doubtful. At least the stuff in the fridge might stay good. The only heat would come from the fireplace.

Kyler grabbed my arm and helped me out, like he expected me to fall again and break my neck. At that point, anything was possible. What little heat had been running upstairs had completely vanished. An excited chill ran up my spine as we entered the bedroom.

He ran his hand through his hair. "I've got to go outside and check it out. Stay in here, okay?"

"Wait." I started to follow him around the bed. "Is that smart? What if someone really did shoot out that window, Kyler? I don't want you going outside."

"I'll be okay." He headed for the door.

"Kyler—"

"Someone has to check it out, Syd. I'll be okay. Just wait for me downstairs, where it's...sort of warm." He paused, and his expression lost most of the hard edge. "Seriously. I'll be fine."

143

I didn't like this at all, but he was out the door. If someone was going all hillbilly psycho outside, I didn't want him out there.

Aaand I was freezing my unmentionables off.

After quickly changing into the sweats and the sweater, I hurried downstairs and pulled on my snow boots. If Kyler was out there with potential bad stuff going down, I could be out there, too, at least keeping an eye out for him while he put some gas in the generator.

I grabbed my jacket off the back of the kitchen chair. Zipping it up, I opened the front door and took a face full of blowing snow. "Holy snowballs in hell!"

Kyler's footsteps had barely made a dent in the drift of snow covering the steps leading off the porch. Unwilling to fall again, I held on to the banister as I carefully shuffled through the packed snow. Not once did my boots sink through and hit the wooden steps. Jesus. This was some heavy snow.

In the fading light and through the whirling snow, I could see the downed pine tree to my left and the snapped electric lines whipping in the wind. There was a slight path in the snow, where it had to have been disrupted by Kyler.

I followed it around the house, wading more than walking. My hands were shoved deep in my pockets, but I already felt the cold biting into them. I couldn't feel my nose or my cheeks as I rounded the side of the house.

He was crouched beside a pile of snow, a shovel clenched tightly in his hands as he stared at the backup generator.

"Kyler?" The wind carried my voice to him.

His head snapped in my direction, and he rose quickly. "Syd? What in the hell are you doing out here? I told you—"

"I know." I waddled closer to him, my teeth chattering.

"But you shouldn't be out here by yourself." I pulled out my hand, tugging my wet and now-icy hair back from my face. "I can keep watch."

"Jesus, you're going to catch pneumonia!" Red splotches colored his cheeks.

"That's n-not true. You can't get a cold from a w-wet head." Sniffling, I turned my attention to the generator, my eyes narrowing against the stinging wind. "Is it ou-out of gas?"

He stared at me for a moment, his expression stormy as he turned back to the generator. "No. There's gas in it, but someone cut the fucking lines going into the house."

My mind rebelled against what he had said, but I saw a long disruption in the snow, leading away from the generator to the surrounding woods—a trail that looked to have been made by skis. "No. No w-way."

Kyler moved through the drifting snow with more ease than me and reached behind the generator, pulling out sliced wires. "Completely cut."

I stared at those wires, my heart sinking. Fear slushed its way through my system. "This isn't g-good."

"No." He dropped the wires and turned to me. "We need to get back inside. Now."

I wasn't going to argue with that or when he dropped his arm around my bent shoulders, tucking me close as he herded me back inside. I had no idea how he wasn't cold or how his fingers weren't numb. Maybe it had to do with the time he'd spent skiing and snowboarding.

Maybe I was just a wuss when it came to the cold.

Kyler quickly unzipped my jacket and slid it off my shoulders. "You really shouldn't have come outside, Syd. I told you I'd be okay."

"But someone cut the wires. They could've still been outside." Shivering, I let him pull me into the living room. "You could've been attacked or...or been covered in snow."

He tugged me down to the thick carpet in front of the fireplace. I cringed back from the warmth; it was almost too much against my ice cube skin.

"I can handle myself," he said, crouching beside me. "It's you out there that worries me."

"It shouldn't." I fixed my gaze on the bright orange and red flames.

"Why wouldn't it?" He ran a hand through my wet hair, brushing off the snowflakes. My eyes closed when he made another sweep, and I wanted to push into the touch, like a cat seeking more petting. "When I heard you say my name outside, my freaking heart practically stopped."

"Dramatic," I murmured. His hands lingered in my hair, and in those moments, I forgot about the mess that we had become.

"It's true. The idea of you being out there with some fucking asshole running around scares the shit out of me."

"Do you think we're safe here?"

He didn't answer immediately. "It's going to get cold. We're going to have to sleep down here, but there's enough wood in the back of the garage to last us. I know that's not what you meant, but I don't think anyone can get in, and besides, if they do, they aren't getting out." I opened my eyes. Kyler nodded toward the wall near the fireplace. Several rifles were on display.

"They actually work?"

He nodded as he rose and unhooked one of the rifles. He propped it against the wall. "It's also loaded. No safety. So don't play with it."

146

"Wasn't planning on it," I said, my gaze moving to where the curtains parted above the window. Night would be here soon, a very cold night, but he was right. That wasn't my big concern.

"I'm not going to let anything happen to you," he said, his fingers moving over my cheek. "I promise that."

My chest swelled. "I know, it's just the idea of someone doing these things on purpose is really..."

"Scary?" he said, dropping his hand. "I know how to use a rifle. Like I said, if someone walks in here, they won't be walking back out."

I shuddered at that, but I was also relieved to know we weren't completely unprotected.

"It's probably just some jerk messing with us. Nothing to really worry about." He stood again, running his palm along his jaw. "I should probably try to get this room sealed off before we lose what little light we have."

Pushing to my feet, I ignored his frown. "I'm going to help."

"Syd—"

"Don't argue with me. I can help. What do we need to do? Gather some blankets? Make a bed fort?"

He cracked a grin. "Come on then."

We tacked a sheet from upstairs to the door leading to the sunroom, since some cold air was getting around the blue tarp. Then we gathered all the blankets and, along with a set of sleeping bags and a king-size mattress dragged down from upstairs, created one hell of a bed near the fireplace.

A makeshift bed we'd have to share—a makeshift bed with a shotgun tucked nearby.

Yikes.

As we put everything together, the tension between us

would evaporate and then return with a vengeance every time our hands or bodies brushed. When I looked at him, I would find him watching me, but he always looked away quickly. I didn't know what to make of that. We joked and made idle conversation to fill the silence. He avoided talking about anything that could lead back to what had happened between us or what could be happening outside.

By the time we had dinner (cold cuts again), I was wired tight and tense. I hit the liquor cabinet like someone coming out of forced rehab. After pulling out the bottle of Jack, I poured myself a shot and downed it. The liquid burned like hot coal, causing me to cough.

"Are you drinking again?" Kyler asked, setting his guitar case down in the living room.

I sat the shot glass down and refilled it. "Yeah."

He reached around me, taking the bottle from me before I could pour another. "I don't think that's a good idea."

I scowled at him. "I think it's a perfect idea."

"How about we stay away from the hard liquor tonight?" He bent and pulled two beers out of the tiny bar fridge. He popped them open. "And drink this?"

"I hate the taste of beer," I said, taking it.

He smiled as he went back to the guitar case and put the bottle down on the end table. "And I hate seeing you drunk."

I didn't know what to say to that. "Why?"

His shoulders rolled in a lazy shrug. "It's just not you, and don't take offense to that. I like that you're not like that. You're not a party girl, and that's okay."

My mouth opened, but nothing came out. He liked that I wasn't a party girl? But every girl he dated—and the word "dated" was used loosely—was a total party girl. My brain started to obsessively break down his words. What could he mean by that? It didn't make sense.

I was already annoyed with myself within a minute of him saying that.

Holding the bottle to my chest, I watched him pull out the guitar. Several candles had been lit throughout the room, casting soft shadows as soon as night had fallen. Pushing the air-dried hair back from my face, I averted my gaze when his eyes found mine, his fingers messing with the tuning pegs. I went over to our bed and sat, wishing I'd had the forethought to bring along some good old-fashioned paperbacks.

But a few moments later, Kyler started to play the guitar, and I wasn't thinking about books anymore. Twisting toward him, I was lulled into fixated silence. This wasn't a song I recognized, possibly something unique and original.

His long fingers slipped over the chords with a skilled ease I envied. The way he played was captivating, the lifting tune enthralling. As he played, a lock of brown hair fell over his forehead, and those impossibly long, thick lashes fanned the tips of his cheekbones.

When he stopped, he lifted his chin and his eyes met mine. My throat felt too thick to speak, but I couldn't look away. So much stretched out before us in the silence— words better left unsaid and truths that should've never been spoken.

Kyler put the guitar aside and reached over, picking up the bottle he had placed beside him. Only then did he look away, as he took a drink. After taking a deep breath, I let it out slowly. I wasn't sleepy. Actually, the exact opposite, but I wished I were. I sipped the beer, hoping it would knock me out. And that was the strangest damned thing. As much as I wanted to just sleep to avoid saying or doing something stupid, I didn't want to miss any time with him.

And then he spoke. "I shouldn't have given in."

KYLER

The words were out of my mouth before I could stop them. I didn't regret it, though, because it needed to be said. I shouldn't have done what I did in the sunroom, treating her no better than some random chick getting a quickie against the wall.

Syd was better than that, and she deserved more. And even though quick hookups were all I'd ever been capable of, I would've given her more if she had wanted that.

I would've given her everything if she had asked.

It would probably never be enough, and I knew I couldn't undo everything I had done in my past. I couldn't go back and change the fact that I'd been with all those girls, that Syd had seen me take home one girl after another, but damn, if she had asked, I would've told her that my feelings for her ran deep.

But I couldn't change any of that, and now Syd looked at me in the same way every single one of those girls in my classes and the ones I met at the bars did. She expected what they expected—a night of sex and nothing else. And I felt like a total shitbag for that.

Syd coughed on her beer and blinked rapidly. "Excuse me?"

I ran a hand through my hair. "Earlier in the sunroom—I shouldn't have given in to what you were asking for."

Her hands balled into tiny fists, and I had enough experience to be thankful she wasn't still holding the beer bottle because there was a good chance she would've thrown it at my head. "I was trying to avoid talking about this, since you made yourself painfully clear earlier."

"We need to talk about this," I said. "We need to clear the air between us. You—"

"I don't want to, Kyler." She stood swiftly. "I don't see the point. I think I've embarrassed myself enough over the past couple of days to last a lifetime."

I shook my head. "I'm not trying to embarrass you. That's the last thing I want."

"Then we don't need to talk about it. You don't want me. I get it." She stared at me for a moment, her lower lip trembling in a way that was a sucker punch straight to my chest, and then she turned to the curtained window. "There's nothing else to say."

"There's a hell of a lot to say, Syd." My voice hardened, and I swore to God, if she got closer to that window after what'd happened earlier, I was going to tackle her. "Why didn't you say something before? Or did you just wake up a few days ago and decide you wanted *that* from me?"

She let out a strangled laugh. "Yeah, that's how it works. I just woke up one morning and was like, 'Gee, I want to screw Kyler.' Seriously, you have no clue."

"Then tell me." I sprang to my feet and crossed the room. She backed away, putting the recliner between us. "I need to know why you wanted me to do that. Why you thought that would be okay."

She gripped the back of the recliner. Her throat worked. "You make it sound like it would be such a chore for you."

151

My eyes narrowed. What in the hell? "That's not what I said or am saying."

"Okay. You want to talk about this. Why are you so against it?" The words seemed to burst from her like a dam overflowing. "I've been your best friend since I can remember. I *watched* you start paying attention to girls, and I *watched* you start dating them, and I don't think you've ever turned down an offer from any girl before."

I jerked back. "I'm not a goddamned sex robot, Syd."

Her eyes widened. "You *will* fuck anything that walks and smiles at you, but not me!"

"Yes! That's what I'm saying." I took a step forward. Her eyes were as dark as tumultuous waves in the soft glow of the candlelight. "I don't want to fuck you, Syd. That's not what you and I are about."

She took a shaky breath. "You wanted me. I could *feel* that you did."

I looked away, grinding my teeth together so hard, I was surprised my molars didn't break. "You don't get it."

Wrapping her arms around herself, she backed away from the recliner and started toward the door leading to the rest of the house. Oh, hell to the no, where did she think she was going? We were *so* not done with this conversation.

"I do get it," she continued, her eyes taking on a sheen that made my entire body lock up. "I'm not good enough—or whatever enough—for you. It doesn't matter that I've been in love with you for—" Blood drained from her face. "Oh my God…"

The fucking world stopped. People said that shit happened when you heard something completely unexpected and shocking, and I thought it was just people being melodramatic, but hell if it wasn't true. The fucking world really did stop for me right then.

Syd was *in* love with me? She'd *been* in love with me?

"Oh my God," she whispered again.

I was in front of her so fast, I didn't remember moving. Clasping her cheeks, I tipped her head back so she had to look me in the eyes. "What did you just say?"

She looked like she was about to be sick. "Nothing—I said nothing."

"Bullshit." My eyes were wide. "You're in love with me?"

"Of course I am." She laughed, but it sounded like it was forced. "We've been best friends since forever, and I would be in—"

"That's not what you meant." My voice dropped low, and my heart thundered in my chest. That couldn't be what she'd meant. "Come on, Syd. That's not it."

She shook her head. "It doesn't matter. You don't—"

"You. Don't. Get. It." I wanted to shake her. She wasn't good enough? Was she insane? I was beginning to think so, because it was the other way around. "You're better than a one-night stand, Sydney. I can't do that to you. You deserve more than that. You mean more to me than anyone else."

Her eyes flared wide again. As close as I was, I saw the tiny tears well up and spill down her cheeks. Getting punched in the nuts would've felt better than seeing her cry and knowing I was the reason.

And it struck me then that this wasn't the first time I'd made her cry. There had been other times. Little dots on the map of us that hadn't seemed like big deals then, but looking back now, they'd meant everything to her. Each memory felt like getting cut with a rusty butter knife.

I was a bigger asshole than I could've ever imagined.

In the ninth grade, when I'd ditched movie night with Syd for the junior varsity cheerleader who'd had an extremely talented mouth. Syd's eyes had been red and swollen the next day in class, and she'd told me it was allergies, except... Syd didn't have allergies. Then, during the summer of our sophomore year, I'd constantly broken plans with her to spend time with girls. Our senior year, I'd promised her a dance at the prom, but I'd left early. Had a hotel room with a girl whose last name I couldn't even remember. Syd would always smile and say it was okay, but later...later she'd have something in her eyes—or have just read a sad book, or watched a depressing movie.

The same thing in college, even when she was with someone. Even recently—I remembered the look on her face when she'd seen Mindy coming out of the bathroom the morning we'd left for Snowshoe. I'd been wrong and I'd been right. It hadn't been disgust, but it had been crushing disappointment. All those times I'd broken her heart, and she was still here.

She was *still* here.

A sound came from the back of my throat. "Don't cry, baby. That's not what I wanted." I leaned in, catching the tear with my lips. "You have no idea how much you mean to me." Another tear snuck out, and I caught that one with my thumb. "I didn't sleep with her," I blurted like a total fucking idiot.

Syd blinked. "What?"

My cheeks heated. "I didn't sleep with Mindy—the chick who was at my apartment. I didn't sleep with her, Syd. I know that doesn't change much of anything, but I didn't."

That only made her cry harder, and I didn't really know what to do. I'd fucked up more than I'd realized and bigger than I'd feared. She tried to turn her head, but I held her face in a gentle yet firm grip. An ache formed in my chest.

The same ache I'd felt when she'd started dating Nate in high school.

So I did the only thing I could think of—the only thing I wanted.

I kissed her.

Chapter 14

SYDNEY

At first I didn't know if he was kissing me to get me to stop crying or if there was another motive behind it. A really strange way to do it, but it worked—I stopped crying because I just stopped thinking. He was kissing me. Years of wondering what this would be like and yearning for this moment had passed, and now his lips were on mine.

And it was such a soft, tender kiss that it reached deep inside me and stole my breath, then my heart. But Kyler had always had my heart.

His lips brushed mine once and then twice. I sucked in a sharp breath, and my hands fell to his waist. A deep sound emanated from him, and it rumbled through every part of me, eliciting a series of shivers that skated over my skin. The pressure against my lips increased, and his hands slid off my cheeks, delving deep into my hair. He slanted his mouth as he tipped my head back, his teeth tugging on my lower lip, coaxing my mouth to open.

My heart sped up so fast, I thought it would come out of

my chest. My fingers tightened around the soft material of his hoodie, and a small moan escaped me as his tongue flicked over mine. The kiss deepened, and I'd never been kissed like this before—like he was thirsting for the very taste of me. It left me spinning. An ache blossomed deep within me, starting in my heart and spreading like the sweetest fire possible.

Kyler pulled back as his hands slid down to the sides of my face again, cradling my cheeks. His lips brushed mine as he spoke. "Do you get it now?"

I could barely breathe as my eyes fluttered open. "Get what?"

He slanted his head, lining up our mouths once more. "You."

"Me?" I shuddered as our lips brushed again.

"This is what you deserve." He pressed a kiss against my lower lip, and I knew at that point I must've cracked my head on something and was dreaming because this couldn't be real. "And this," he added, his hands drifting to my shoulders. He pulled me against him, until I was pressed so tightly, I could feel every inch of him. "You don't deserve what you wanted in that sunroom, baby."

His tongue swept past my parted lips, and I kissed him back like I had dreamed of doing for years. He groaned as his hands snuck to my hips. When he lifted his head again, I was panting. "What else do I deserve?"

One side of his lips tipped up. "Everything, Syd. You deserve everything."

My heart swelled so much that I thought I'd float right up to the ceiling, but confusion trickled in, threatening the happy bubble building inside me. "Kyler, I…I don't understand." A dimple appeared in his right cheek as his smile spread, and my heart flopped over heavily.

157

"Then you really don't get it yet. I think I'm going to have to educate you."

A thrill coursed through me. The old saying "never look a gift horse in the mouth" was screaming at me right now. *Go with it*, I told myself. *Just go with it. Don't freeze up. Don't mess this up*—whatever this was. I didn't want to look back and regret that my mouth and endless questions got in the way. "Educate me?"

"Mm-hmm," he murmured, angling his body so our hips pressed together. "By the time I'm done, you will completely understand what I mean. And I think we'll start with this sweater."

"The sweater?"

Kyler nipped at my lower lip, and I gasped. "I like the sweater. The color is good on you. Perfect." He picked up a strand of my hair that had fallen across my chest and draped it over my shoulder. "But you know what I like best about this sweater?"

"What?"

His lashes lifted, and his stare pierced me. Tension stirred and coiled tightly within me. The heat in his intense gaze told me I was so, so out of my league with him. The dimple disappeared into a knowing smirk as he slid his fingers under the hem of my sweater. "Figure it out yet?"

I shook my head.

"Hmm…" That low grumble of his had me wanting to knock him flat on his back. His fingers spread across the bare skin of my stomach, and my breath caught as they pressed into my ribs. His head cocked to the side, and his brows lowered. "Syd, are you not wearing a bra?"

Before I could answer, his hands drifted up farther, until the fingertips brushed the swells of my breasts. "You're not. Very naughty, Syd."

My lips twitched. "Not like I need—"

"Don't say it." His lips captured mine in a long, searing kiss. "Back to the sweater."

"The sweater?" I repeated dumbly.

He nodded, and for a moment, the only sounds in the room were my pounding heart and the crackling of the fire. "The best part about this sweater, other than the fact you look fucking hot as hell in it, is that it comes off."

Oh, hot damn.

Kyler tugged the sweater off and dropped it on the floor. There was something much more intimate about this than earlier. Even in the shadowy room, I felt more exposed.

His gaze traveled from my face and down my throat to my breasts. The tips hardened under his gaze.

He scooped up my hair, framing my chest with its long strands. "Now that we're past the sweater, let's talk about these." His voice was gruff and thick. "These are absolutely perfect."

With him staring at me like that, I'd never been prouder or happier about my breasts in my life. True story.

He bent his head, and the edges of his hair tickled my chest. His lips were so close that I thought I'd die from the anticipation. He kissed one of the small cuts and another, and then his lips closed over the tip of a nipple. Pounding need took root. His hands splayed across the small of my back as he moved to the other breast and suckled deep.

"Perfect," he said again, and his tongue flicked over the tightened nubs, teasing until I grasped his shoulders, my back arching. He straightened, staring down at me. "You know what's next?"

My imagination had many answers for that, but I hooked my fingers under the hem of his hoodie. His wide smile, the kind that showed off the dimples in both cheeks, was my reward. He lifted his arms, and off went the hoodie and the shirt underneath.

His chest seemed more flawless now than I remembered. The hard planes of his chest and the dips of his stomach and all that golden skin beckoned me. I leaned into him, biting down on my lip as our skin touched. The cuts were a little sensitive, but it was nothing compared to the other sensations. A shudder rolled through me, and his head dipped to my shoulder. He placed a kiss there, and emotion clogged my throat.

"You're learning fast. I'm not surprised." He trailed kisses up my throat, stopping just below my ear. His hands moved between us, his thumbs smoothing over the tips of my breasts. "You've always been so damned good at everything you do."

"Not everything," I admitted with a blush. "This…I'm not good at this."

Kyler pulled back, one brow arched. "You are *amazing* at this."

"No, I'm not." I laughed, feeling sort of dumb. Sometimes I really just needed to keep my mouth shut. "I've only… well, you know, and it was…"

"It was that way because that punk-ass didn't know what he was doing." He dropped a kiss against my temple. "And trust me, I know *exactly* what I'm doing."

I had no doubts about that.

He took a step forward, forcing me back until I hit the edge of the makeshift bed, and the warmth of the fire traveled along my back. "Now about these…" He touched the waistband of my sweats.

"What about them?"

He winked, and damn if he didn't look good doing it. "They've got to go."

I took a breath, but it got stuck. Holding my gaze, he found the drawstring on my sweats and undid it with amazing quickness. Again, this was nothing like before in the sunroom. There wasn't an ounce of anger in his gaze or actions. There was just arousal and affection and something I was too afraid to acknowledge. And it wasn't like with Nate, where there had been a lot of awkward fumbling and pushing and then it had been over.

This was slow and sweet and perfect. God, *he* was perfect.

Kyler slipped the sweats down my hips. He steadied me as I stepped out of them, and I was just in my panties—cute ones, thank God. He brushed his lips across my forehead as his thumbs caught the strings along my hips. "So, do you get it now?"

"You want me?" My voice sounded strange.

He laughed. "Oh, you were so close, baby."

I started to frown, but in one unbelievably smooth move from Kyler, my undies joined the rest of my clothes on the floor. "Good God, if taking off panties were an Olympic sport, you'd have a gold medal."

His next laugh was deep and rich. "The sport only counts when it's something you really want to win." Then he stepped back, his gaze moving over me in a way that made me want to hide myself and let him look his fill at the same time. "You are beautiful, Sydney. You know that? You're so beautiful, and you don't even know."

My throat closed. Before I started bawling and completely killed the moment, I reached for the button on his jeans, but he caught my wrist. I raised my brows.

He shook his head. "I'm still educating you, Syd."

"Oh?" I said. The teasing quality to his voice was relaxing, except I was still buck-ass naked, and my skin was on fire for a multitude of reasons. I'd never been this naked with a guy, not even with Nate. When we'd had sex that one time, I'd been topless, and my skirt had been pushed up. That was all. But now there was no way for me to hide. I would have thought I'd be more uncomfortable, but as his gaze traveled over me, lingering on some areas longer than others, I felt like a goddess standing before him.

Taking my hand, he tugged me down onto the pile of blankets with him. The moment my back hit them, every muscle froze as I stared up at him. My throat seemed to seize, and although I should've felt warm, I went ice-cold on the inside. Where had my sexy goddess gone? She'd run for the damned hills.

Kyler hovered over me, supporting his weight on a hand planted beside my head. His body wasn't touching mine, and he was still half dressed, but I knew where this was heading. It was what I wanted—had wanted for so long—but I had such little experience in this, and I couldn't bear it if Kyler discovered I was as frigid as Nate had claimed.

And to think Kyler would've ended up with a broken nose for nothing.

"Hey," he said, touching my cheek gently. "You there?"

I nodded.

Kyler stared at me intently. "We don't have to do anything, Syd. We can stop right here if that's what you want."

Cursing myself for being such an idiot, I swallowed. "No. No, I don't want to stop."

He moved his hand to my shoulder, and my body jerked at the contact. His gaze lifted, and he didn't say anything.

Instead, he brought his mouth to mine. The kiss was slow and gentle, and it kept going until the tightness seeped out of the muscles in my arms and then my legs. A different kind of tension built again, turning my blood into molten lava. My hand shook as I placed it on his stomach's hard slab of muscle.

"That's good," he said huskily. "I like when you touch me."

And I liked touching him. Exploring the dips and rises of his muscles, I marveled at how smooth and tight his skin was.

Running did a body good.

I ran my hands up his chest and over his broad shoulders. His muscles flexed under my touch. His weight came down on me, inch by torturous inch, until my legs tangled with his. The material of his jeans against my bare skin brought forth a sweet rush. My hips tilted up, and he groaned in a way that made me yearn for more. His lower body pressed against mine, and I could feel him.

Kyler's lips left mine, and before I could mourn their loss, they were on my throat, trailing a heated path to my chest. He took his time there, his hands and mouth leaving me breathless. I moved against him, my fingers digging into his back. And then he went farther south, his lips making their way down my stomach, around my belly button, and then on to the flare of my hip.

"Starting to understand yet?" he asked, grinning as he slid a hand under my hip, lifting me slightly.

"I…I think so," I said, watching the shadows dancing over his face. A chill spread along my skin as his lashes lowered.

With one hand, he gently spread my legs. I fought the urge to close them as he made the sexiest sound ever known to man. "I have to do this," he said, and I knew what he meant. His eyes flicked up, seeking permission. "I *really* have to do this, baby."

Pleasure shot through me, but so did trepidation. "I haven't…I mean, no one has done that before."

"I know." He sounded proud and possessive. "It'll be amazing. I promise."

I nodded and let my head fall back against the blankets. I knew what to expect. I wasn't that naive or dumb, but when I felt his finger brush over me, I nearly came right then from the barely there touch. Just a brush of one finger and my body started shaking and my hips rose to meet his touch.

"So responsive," he murmured, slipping one finger inside, causing my back to arch as a soft cry was wrenched from my throat. Then his head dipped, and my back came clear off the covers.

The slight stubble on his jaw was tantalizing against my inner thighs. My entire body went rigid, and my senses overloaded the moment his mouth touched me there in the sweetest kiss possible.

"Do you get it?" he asked again.

My fingers dug into the blankets as he did something truly wicked with his finger. "Kyler…"

"You don't deserve to be fucked like a one-night stand." He kissed the inside of my thigh, and I melted. "You deserve pleasure. It should be all about you, always about you."

And then his mouth was on me again, joined by his tongue and his fingers. Pleasure coiled tight, and the first pulse was sweet and sharp. My hips rocked shamelessly against what he was doing, and his growl of approval sent me right over the edge. My body shattered, broke apart into thousands of little pieces as I cried out his name over and over in a way I might actually have been embarrassed about later. It was the most amazing, most complete thing I'd ever felt. It was like flying and falling at the same time.

He rode out the storm, not stopping until the last shudder rolled through me and my breathing began to return to normal. He kissed my thigh again and then rose over me, planting his hands on either side of my head. I opened my eyes, dazed.

His grin was partly smug. "Told you it would be amazing."

"It was…completely amazing." I reached up, running my fingers over his jaw and then down his throat, his chest. My gaze dropped, and I could see the bulge in his pants. I slipped my hand down his stomach, but he caught my wrist before I could reach what I wanted, and he rolled onto his side. I turned my head to him, confused. "Don't you want…?"

His brows rose.

Heat swamped my face, which was so stupid considering what he'd just done. "Don't you want to go further? I mean, you didn't come and…" And I just wanted to stop talking altogether. This was so embarrassing.

Kyler chuckled as he gathered me in his arms, fitting my back against his front, and I could feel him, still sprouting a raging hard-on. "I'm okay. This was about you."

"You don't feel 'okay.'" I wiggled my behind, and he groaned. A smile pulled at my lips. "See?"

"Yeah, I see and I *feel*."

I tipped my head back so I could see him, and I bit down on my lip, hoping my next question wouldn't sound incredibly lame. "Don't you want to?"

"Don't I want to?" Disbelief colored his voice. His hand fell to my waist as he pushed his hips forward, grinding against my rear in a way that had me aching all over again. "I want nothing more than to get inside you and stay there."

A shudder worked its way down my spine. "Then why aren't you?"

He smoothed my hair off my cheek, tucking it back behind my ear. "I wanted to do that for you, and I...well, I usually don't do that with other girls."

My stomach soured at the mention of other girls, but I ignored it. "Are you blushing?"

"No." He huffed. "I don't blush."

"Uh-huh, must be the shadows then." I folded my arms across my chest. "So you don't do that? Because it felt like you really had a lot of experience."

He laughed again as he sat up, reaching for a blanket. He pulled it over us, tucking it around me. "I didn't say I *never* did it." I considered that. There were a few girls over the years that he had hung out with for a while. I could imagine that he must've done that for them, but that still didn't answer why he hadn't gone further with me. I wished my brain would shut up because it was really starting to get on my nerves.

Kyler's hand slid around my waist. "I want to, Syd. I really do. So don't start filling your head with bullshit. I just wanted to do that for you." He paused, pressing his lips against my cheek. "And there's the fact the condoms are upstairs and walking is going to be difficult for me right now."

I giggled, unable to help myself. "I'm on the pill."

He groaned. "You're *so* not helping."

"You always use condoms, right? Please tell me you've used condoms."

"I've never *not* used a condom."

Relief washed over me. "So…"

"Syd, baby, you are killing me."

I grinned as I rolled onto my back. "There are other things I can do, you know. I've done other stuff."

His chest rose sharply, and he stilled. "You don't owe it to me, Syd. That's not why I did that."

I thought about the few times I'd given head or hand jobs. All of them had been with Nate throughout those years in high school and whatnot. I'd done it because I'd felt like I had to, or Nate would've moved on. Such a stupid thing to worry about, and I honestly would've been better off if he had, but all that was beside the point. I wasn't sure if I'd do it as well as everyone else, but it wasn't because I owed Kyler.

Wiggling onto my side, I tipped my head back and met his gaze. The blanket slipped past my shoulders, but I barely even noticed. "I want to do it. Not because I feel like I need to, but because I want to."

A muscle ticked in his jaw as he lifted himself on one arm, and I thought he might run away. Taking a deep breath and mustering my courage before I lost it, I placed my hand between his legs and cupped him. His entire body jerked as if he'd been shocked. I forced my eyes up, meeting his. "Are you going to tell me no?"

His eyes looked almost black, and what felt like forever passed before he reached down, placing his hand over mine. He didn't say anything, but he rocked his hips forward, pressing himself into my hand.

That was answer enough for me.

Chapter 15

KYLER

Honest to God, this hadn't been my intention when I started this. Hell, I wasn't sure I had even known *what* I was starting when I'd kissed her, except that I'd wanted to and I'd wanted her to stop crying, to understand that she deserved so much more than what she'd been asking for.

But now?

Yeah, all thoughts of pleasing her and then going to sleep—albeit uncomfortably—jumped right out the window the second she gripped me in her small hand. Even with my hand over hers, I knew I shouldn't let her do this. I'd lost count of how many times I'd gotten a hand job, and it seemed to go against nature to refuse one, but Syd…?

It was like my wildest fantasies coming true all over again, and with her taste still lingering in my mouth, I'd never been harder in my life. No one, no girl I'd ever known, compared to how she'd felt around my finger and against my mouth.

But this was Sydney, beautiful-as-fuck Syd.

She peered up at me through those dark lashes and, aw

hell, I was always a sucker for those big blue eyes of hers. A small, tentative grin appeared on her swollen lips. "I'll take that as a yes?"

The eagerness in her gaze was my undoing, and my self-control broke faster than an egg hitting the floor.

Probably made me the biggest asshole in the country, but fuck the whole gentlemanly thing. I was seconds away from coming already, and I still had my pants on. How awkward would that be?

I removed my hand from hers. "Take it however you want, baby."

Her grin spread into a smile that was so bright, it was almost too hard to look at. Pressure clamped down on my chest, unexpected and intense. I moved to stop her, but then her hand slid down the length of me and...and yeah, she had me. I was all hers.

In reality, even though I'd been with everyone else, I'd always been Syd's.

Putting my weight in my shoulders, I lifted up so she could tug off my sweats. I figured she'd hesitate with the boxers, so I wasn't surprised when she stopped, her fingers wrapped around the band.

She glanced up, her brows raised. "Christmas elves?"

I gave a lopsided shrug. "I'm sticking with a theme."

"I can tell." She bit down on that damned lip, and that made me want to kiss her again, but then she pulled my boxers down carefully, freeing me, and the air punched out of my lungs. She didn't stop until they joined my sweats, and then she sat up, the blanket pooling around her waist.

Damn.

Staring at her, my entire body twitched. Damn it, she was sexy as hell with her dark hair tumbling over her shoulders, partially obscuring her breasts. Whoever had said men were visual creatures had been totally on point.

Reaching up, I brushed the heavy locks over her shoulder, baring one of her perky breasts. She stilled, looking incredibly adorable as she squirmed. I could watch her forever and a day.

She ducked her head, and her hair fell back on her shoulder as she wrapped her fingers around my base, and *holy shit*. My back bowed as her hand slowly slid up and then back down. I squeezed my eyes shut because I knew if I kept staring at her, I'd lose it in seconds.

Not that I was far away from doing so anyway.

Her hand moved in determined, slow strokes, the movements a little clumsy, but there was something even sexier about that. She was unsure of herself, but that hadn't stopped her. Nothing stopped Sydney, and I bet if I opened my eyes, that little jaw of hers would be set in concentration. I had to see, and damn if I wasn't right. My entire body tightened as her grip became more confident and faster. "Uh, baby, I'm not…"

She looked up, her lips slightly parted and cheeks flushed. Her chest moved rapidly, and pleasure built at the top of my spine, about to power down. "Am I—"

"You're fucking perfect—too perfect."

She smiled again, and I had to close my damned eyes again, because if I fell into her eyes, I'd never resurface. Her hand slowed at the top, her thumb crested the head, and I groaned as my legs stiffened. I wasn't—

Holy hell!

The hot, wet warmth of her mouth closed around me, and that sent me right over the edge. My back jackknifed. I tried to pull her away, but she was latched on to me and not going anywhere. I kicked my head back, my fingers clenching in her hair. The explosion rolled down my spine, and there was no stopping it. The release shook me from the inside, and she stayed there, her mouth and hand working until I stopped pulsing. I was utterly destroyed in a way I'd never been before—that amazing, perfect kind of way.

Breathing raggedly, I gripped her by her upper arms. I pulled her over me, laying her across my chest. Our legs tangled, and her weight was nothing on me, but I felt her in every bone.

An unexpected tremor got me as she rested her cheek just above my heart. I wrapped my arms around her, holding her close. I knew she'd get cold soon, but I was too much of a selfish bastard to let her go long enough to find that damned blanket.

Feeling her softness all around me, I held her until my heart slowed, until I could open my eyes again, and that felt like forever.

———————

A languid peace invaded my body after I retrieved a blanket for us, but I didn't fall asleep easily. There was a part of me that didn't want to fall asleep because I didn't want to miss a second of her soft breaths. She'd passed out atop me, and with a smile pulling at my lips, I placed her on her side and nestled her against my chest with the covers pulled snug over us. The fire would last until the morning, but a chill had already seeped into the room.

I'd never slept with a girl before—like, shared the same bed or even the same blanket after sex. The other girls had usually left, and if they'd fallen asleep afterward, I'd slept wherever they hadn't. Syd had always been the only woman

I'd ever spent an entire night with, so I wasn't surprised that it didn't feel weird to do so now, even though everything was different between us.

Starting with the fact she was curled up against me—completely, beautifully naked. Her bare back rested against my chest, and the fantastic curve of her ass pressed against me. I hadn't put any clothes back on, so I was hard. Actually, I didn't think I'd lost the hard-on.

I was propped up on my elbow, my cheek against my fist. I'd been like that for at least an hour, watching her. She had the thickest lashes I'd ever seen. Not the cosmetically enhanced kind that were clumpy or spidery. They fanned the tops of her cheeks—cheeks lightly dusted with pale freckles. Her lips were slightly parted and plump. Swollen from *my* kisses. A surge of masculine pride came over me, and I leaned down, pressing a kiss to her temple.

Syd murmured something and shifted. My hand stilled against her stomach. I'd been tracing circles around her belly button, but every time she moved that sweet ass, it antagonized what hung between my legs.

She settled down pretty quickly, not waking at all.

My gaze traveled over her face. There was no need to commit each delicate, beautifully crafted line to memory because I already had ages ago.

The blanket had slipped off her shoulder, and I pulled it back up. In her sleep, a smile graced her lips, and my chest tightened.

Sighing, I stretched out beside her and tightened my hold, repositioning Syd so her head fit under mine. Didn't take long to drift off to sleep. I might've only slept a couple of hours before a noise woke me, but it was the best damned sleep I'd ever had.

My eyes snapped open. Pale gray light slipped in through the gap in the curtains, and the fire was almost out. Immediately on guard, I held my breath as I listened. The noise came again—a deep howling of wind. I released my breath slowly. I hated being jumpy as fuck, but after everything that had happened, I would rather be paranoid.

Tipping my head down, I checked out Syd. She had turned in her sleep, snuggling close. One leg was thrown over mine, and her head rested on my chest. Her hand was curled above my heart. And I was still so damned hard, I was beginning to wonder if it was going to become a permanent fixture.

Damn.

My hand shook as I reached up, brushing the hair off her cheek. I loathed getting up, but I didn't want her to wake up to a freezing room. As gently as I could, I slid out from underneath her. The girl had to have been worn out, because she barely stirred as I rose and pulled another blanket over her.

I tugged on my sweats, ignoring the urge to get back under those covers and wake her up in a way I doubted Nate ever had. Throwing the hoodie on, I padded out of the room. I immediately winced.

Hell's bells, it was *freezing* in the rest of the house.

I peeked out around the Christmas tree and saw the snow was still falling, but it was lighter. Everything was covered to the point it looked like Antarctica outside. Man, I had no idea how long it was going to take them to clear the roads up here or even if the plows could get out now.

Moving around the house, I checked the doors and windows obsessively. Everything was fine—locked and secured. As I headed down to the garage for firewood,

173

my brain replayed everything like it was stuck on the Syd channel. In the early morning hours and in the silent house, I couldn't believe last night had happened. Cursing as my feet hit the ice-cold cement of the garage, I hurried around the SUV and snowmobiles and gathered some of the dried-out logs. *Shoes would've been smart, dumbass.* That was how bad my brain was stuck on her. Fuck, when she'd said the "love" part, I had been completely lost in her.

I had been lost in her for a while now.

It wasn't like my feelings for her were new or that I'd discovered them when I'd had my mouth on her or when she'd blurted out that half-finished sentence. Shit like that didn't happen. Maybe some people woke up one day and fell in love. Not me. This had grown over time, kicking off when she'd gone out on her first date with Nate. Till this day, I still remembered that bitter bite of jealousy when she'd told me she was dating him. Before then, I really hadn't understood how I'd felt for Sydney. Fuck. We'd still been kids in a lot of ways, and I had been just discovering the happy, happy times to be had with women.

Not until after Syd had told me that Nate had ended things had I realized the extent of what I felt for her. Because I hadn't been sad or upset—I had been *glad*. I had felt *relief*. That alone made me so undeserving of Syd, but it was the truth. I had been a bastard. Still was.

I had known in that moment, while we stood outside the science building on campus, that I loved her. Not in the best-friend kind of way. Not in the almost-like-a-little-sister kind of way. I loved her in a way that transcended those things. And I was *in* love with her.

None of that had changed anything. My feelings for her were just something I hadn't acknowledged. I'd refused to

174

let them grow into something more than a yearning that couldn't be quenched. People did that all the time. I was just one of many. Syd had always been too good for me. Never once had I thought she could've possibly felt anything more than friendship when it came to me, and I still wasn't 100 percent sure because I couldn't understand how she could be in love with me after watching me—her words exactly—"fuck anything that walks" for years. How could she? I didn't get it.

And I also didn't want to question it, at least not right now. I had, what? A day or two of living out what I'd always wanted before reality bitch smacked me in the face, because I did know one thing for certain: There was a really good chance that when she left this place, got back into the real world, she'd realize she could do better than me. Find a guy who wasn't about to turn down a career guaranteed to make money—and who hadn't spent the past seven years going after every girl except her.

SYDNEY

I woke to the smell of freshly brewed coffee, which didn't make sense because I was sure we'd lost power. Maybe I'd dreamed that.

Rolling over, I didn't feel Kyler or his warmth. Maybe I'd dreamed everything from last night. My eyes flew open as my stomach twisted. Flames were going strong in the fireplace, and tucked under the covers, I was pretty toasty.

I was also very much alone on the makeshift bed.

My heart sank faster than the *Titanic*. I squeezed my eyes

shut. The likelihood of last night being a dream was highly unlikely because I was naked under the blankets, which meant Kyler had probably woken up this morning and been close to chewing his arm off to get away.

He regretted it. I knew it.

Regretted what we'd done, and we hadn't even had sex.

"You can stop pretending to be asleep." Kyler's deep voice drifted over to me. Amusement colored his tone. "I know you're awake."

I pried an eye open. "I'm not pretending."

"Uh-huh."

Fighting the urge to pull the blanket over my head and pretend I wasn't here, I took a deep breath and rolled onto my back. Kyler was sitting at the foot of the recliner, holding a thermos in his hands.

One side of his lips tipped up. He put the thermos on the floor and reached down on his other side, picking up a cup. "I know how you need your caffeine, so I found some instant coffee and boiled water over the fire. Got some sugar for you, too."

I sat up, holding the blanket to my chest. Our eyes met, and I felt my breath stall. His were so dark, nearly black. I couldn't gain a lick of anything from his expression. I searched my brain for something to say. "You boiled water over the fire?"

His smile spread, revealing those deep dimples that always got to me, as he unscrewed the lid with a twist of his wrist and poured the coffee. "You sound so surprised."

I just couldn't picture him doing it. Casting my gaze down, I didn't know what to do or how to act. What he had done last night had only ever existed in my fantasies and never in my reality. I couldn't reconcile the two. Just because he'd made me coffee and toiled over a fire to do so didn't mean he was about to pronounce his undying love for me or jump my bones.

"Syd?"

As I forced my gaze up, heat swept across my cheeks. I scooted over the bed of blankets and reached for the cup. "Thank you."

His brows rose as he pulled the cup back. "No. Not yet."

Cocking my head to the side, I frowned. "Why?"

"You'll see." After placing the coffee down, he stood and came to the edge of our makeshift bed. He knelt in front of me. Slowly, as if afraid he'd startle me, he cupped my cheek in his palm. "Good morning."

Lost in the simple feel of his hand on my cheek, I stared at him for a moment. "Good morning?"

He came down on his knees and leaned in, pressing his forehead against mine. "I think we can do better than that."

My heart tripped up. His closeness was a good sign, right? I tried not to wonder if I had morning breath as I swallowed. "We can?"

He nodded, and his nose brushed over mine. My grip on the blanket tightened as my stomach hollowed. "Very easily," he said. "Want to see?"

"Yes." That word came out as a whisper.

Tilting his head to the side, he kissed one corner of my lips and then the other. A tremble coursed through me as his thumb smoothed over my cheekbone, and then he deepened the pressure on my lips, kissing me for real.

"How about that?" he asked, dropping another kiss on my lips, a quick one. "Was that a better 'good morning'?"

No longer able to speak, I nodded.

Kyler chuckled as he leaned back and picked up the cup.

Handing it over, he settled down beside me where I'd turned into girlie mush in a split second.

The first gulp of coffee went a long way toward my finding the ability to speak. "How long have you been awake?"

One shoulder shrugged. "A couple of hours. The fire was dying, so I had to put more logs in."

I took another sip. Instant coffee wasn't bad. "I slept through all that?"

"Yep. Well, you were talking a little in your sleep."

My mouth dropped open. "Oh no. Was I? What did I say? Oh, my—"

"I was just joking." Laughing, he glanced at me sideways. "You didn't talk in your sleep, but by your reaction, I'm wishing you had."

I narrowed my eyes. "That was mean."

He grinned. "Did you sleep well?"

"I think that was my best sleep since the last time I took NyQuil." I blushed again, realizing what it sounded like, and I hastily dipped my head, letting my hair shield my burning face.

Kyler was silent for a moment. "Same here. Best sleep I've had in years."

"Really?" I dared a quick peek at him. I didn't know why that seemed so important, but it did.

He was staring straight ahead. "I've never slept with a girl before."

My brows rose. "Come again?"

His lips twisted into a wry grin. "I've never slept with a girl after doing anything with them. You're actually the only girl I've ever shared a bed with overnight."

A rush of giddiness swept through me, and I hid my smile by taking another sip. I remembered what he'd said about Mindy, and I almost jumped up and did a happy jig naked. "Not once?"

He shook his head as he twisted toward me. "I never wanted to."

Our eyes met again, and I wouldn't have been able to look away if Santa had run through the room with a rifle. "Never?"

Leaning back, he planted a hand behind me. "Never," he said, his voice low. Tipping his head down, he pressed a kiss against my bare shoulder and then rested his chin there.

I was afraid I was going to spill the coffee everywhere. He didn't regret last night. That much was obvious. Relief was like a sweet drug clawing at me, but I still didn't know how to act, and I was petrified of saying the wrong thing.

Luckily, Kyler had way more experience than me at all this. "The snow isn't falling as heavy now. The plows should be able to get out here at some point."

A twinge of disappointment hit me, and I hid it with a smile. Funny how, a day ago, all I'd wanted was to go home. "Do you think they'll get to us today?"

"I'd be really surprised. Probably tomorrow," he replied. "It's like the North Pole out there right now."

"Sounds good for Santa."

His eyes glimmered. "I think even he'd get lost in that mess."

I finished off the coffee, and Kyler took the cup from me. Gathering the blanket around me, I mumbled something about the bathroom, and he told me to use the one downstairs. I shuffled out of the room, hitching the blanket close as I hit the chilly temps in the rest of the house. It probably would've been smart to pick up my clothes—wherever they were—so I could change, but I rushed to the bathroom, my bare feet slapping against the cold wood floors.

I discovered Kyler had gathered up some personal items and placed them in the bathroom so I wouldn't have to go upstairs. Due to the thoughtful gesture, I smiled as I went through my morning routine. Butterflies had nested in my stomach and were about to take full flight. Using what I had, I washed up the best I could without killing myself with the frigid water.

Those damned butterflies were fluttering around, bouncing off my insides as I left the bathroom. My cheeks were warm in spite of the cold. I stopped by the Christmas tree— only for a few seconds because of the windows and the danger they presented. My gaze dropped to the two presents under the tree, the ones with our names on them. A smile fluttered across my lips as I dragged my eyes up to the shiny star perched atop the tree. We hadn't even thought to turn the lights on.

If I had my days right, Christmas was a week and a few days away. I knew what I wanted for Christmas, and it seemed like I'd gotten it. I hoped the holiday had come early for me and this wasn't some wild fluke.

When I returned to the living room, Kyler had spread out a buffet of breakfast food across the dark oak coffee table. The noncooked kind—bananas, breakfast bars, dry cereal, and whatnot.

I stopped just inside the room, my heart in my throat or maybe in my mouth at this point.

He glanced up and grinned. "This is the best I can do for breakfast."

"It's perfect." My words sounded thick, and I realized I was close to tears. The good kind, but really, bawling like a baby wouldn't be attractive. Ducking my head, I went over to the side and sat on an unoccupied pillow, keeping the blanket close.

"Looks like chips and raw vegetables for lunch and dinner," he said, sliding another cup of fresh coffee my way. "We're eating healthy today."

I laughed. "Like I eat differently any other day."

He scoffed. "You're such a red-meat kind of girl. Don't lie." That part was true.

"Thank you for putting this together."

"My pleasure." He elbowed me gently. "Eat up. I have a big day planned for you."

My brows rose. "You do? Planning on getting me outside to shovel the driveway?"

"No." Picking up an apple, he leaned back in an arrogant sprawl. "Doesn't involve the outside, but it does center some physical activity."

Heat zinged through my blood. "Really?"

He regarded me with a wicked glint. "Look around the room, Syd. There's something you're missing."

Scanning the room, it took me a couple of moments to catch on. "My clothes? Where are my clothes?"

His answering grin was pure sin. "You're not going to need any clothes today, baby."

Chapter 16

SYDNEY

Oh my, my, my...

My eyes widened to a size that was probably seriously unattractive. Under the blanket, my body warmed deliciously. "So all I have is this blanket?"

"Most of the time."

A thrill went through me. "Okay. And you get to wear clothes?"

Kyler winked as he took a bite of the apple. "Most of the time."

"Doesn't seem fair, does it?"

Heat simmered in his gaze. "Oh, it will be equally fair."

Was it possible to turn into goo? I believed so. His deep chuckle caused me to flush, and I turned back to our little buffet, busying myself with eating. So many questions rose to the tip of my tongue. I wanted—no, I *needed*—some sort of confirmation of what was happening between us, but to be honest, I was too afraid of saying something that would bring all this crashing down on me, shattering like a fragile snow globe.

It was weak, probably even a little wrong, but I kept my mouth shut.

After a few moments, we started talking…talking like normal. About the next semester and what classes we had left. How he planned to talk to his mom about veterinary school during the break, and I really hoped it would go better than what he dreaded. Kyler needed to do what would make him happy, not what his mother expected.

Hours passed. Every so often, he'd check the window and return to my side. We talked about Andrea and Tanner, about how I imagined Tanner had to be bummed about not getting to snowboard. We just talked like we always did, but there was something more to it. Kyler would touch me at the most random moments, and I came to anticipate those seconds. He brushed his fingers over my cheek as he spoke about his mom attempting to cook turkey again this year. I'd been an unwilling participant in many of his mom's cooking adventures, so I didn't envy him. When I admitted that I still nibbled on raw stuffing, he tucked my hair back behind my ear. And as he talked about wanting to make a gingerbread house when we got home—and he said "we"—he slid his fingers over my bare shoulder, eliciting a series of shivers from me.

Kyler stood, extending a hand. I had no idea how much time had passed when he did this. "It's time for some of that physical activity I promised."

For a while I'd completely forgotten that I was naked under the blanket. Not so much now. I swallowed hard. I had a pretty good idea of what that physical activity was. My nerves unraveled suddenly and frayed at the edges, and

I couldn't find enough air to breathe. I locked up. I wanted him so badly. I'd always wanted him, but I had no idea what to do. What if I did something wrong? What if he felt the same way Nate had afterward?

But I trusted Kyler, and that made a huge difference.

Holding the blanket to my chest, I gave him my free hand. His fingers threaded through mine, and he pulled me to my feet with astonishing ease. He slipped an arm around my waist. With a soft smile, he bent down and pressed his forehead against mine.

"Do you remember our senior prom?" he asked. His hand tightened around mine, but he didn't pull me any closer.

I blinked at the unexpected question. "Yes."

"I promised you a dance." His eyes drifted shut, and his fingers splayed across my back. "I didn't keep that promise."

Shaking my head slightly, I stared up at him. "Kyler..."

His eyes opened. "We never danced. I was a douche."

My heart started thumping at the memory. I'd gone to prom with Nate, but Kyler had promised me a dance. As wrong as it had been, I'd spent most of that prom looking forward to that one dance instead of paying attention to Nate, but Kyler had left with Betty Holland. They'd had a hotel room. I'd overheard her talking to her friends in the bathroom.

I shook my head again, at a loss for words. I couldn't believe he even remembered that.

"So I'm making up for it right now." He straightened and graced me with one of his full smiles. "We don't have the music, but I think we can make it work."

Tears burned the back of my throat, and I dipped my head. Taking a deep breath, I nodded. "We can make it work."

"Good," he said, his voice huskier than normal.

Kyler lifted me so my bare feet were atop his, and I laughed at the act. His dimples deepened in response, and he pulled me close. My hand was pinned between us, holding my blanket, but our legs were pressed together. Humming under his breath, he swayed slowly, moving in a small circle. I didn't recognize the song, but the lilting sound and the deep vibrations coaxed my eyes closed.

Placing my cheek against his chest, I smiled as we danced. In a matter of moments, I forgot that I was wearing nothing but a blanket, that the only music besides his humming was the wind outside, and that we weren't in some glamorously overdone ballroom. This—being in Kyler's arms—was breathtakingly perfect. There was no other way to describe it. My heart swelled to the point that I thought it'd burst into an ooey-gooey mess. He was making me into a giant toasted marshmallow, turning me into nothing but goo on the inside.

This dance was better than any dance at prom could've been.

Lifting my head, I opened my eyes, and my gaze immediately latched on to his. His eyes were almost black, and they became my whole world.

Kyler lowered his chin, and the slightest touch of his lips against mine sent a shivery rush through my veins. He whispered my name, and it thundered through me. One hand slid up my back and fisted in my hair. He took over, nipping at my lips until I opened for him, and the kiss deepened, causing the air to catch in my throat. He kissed me until I felt like I'd drunk too much, until heat flowed through me and I was swimming in raw sensations.

"I want you," he said roughly, his lips brushing mine. "I

want you so bad, I can taste it. Tell me you want the same thing."

A shudder rocked me. I was snared in his heated stare. I was sure I'd already made it clear what I wanted, but I still felt compelled to speak aloud. "Yes."

"Say it." His lips brushed mine, and he kissed me once more, twisting my insides into delicious knots. "Tell me, baby."

"I want you," I said, dizzy. "I want you, Kyler. Only you."

With a deep sound that made me tremble, he lifted me off his feet and then loosened the blanket from my fingers. It slipped away, falling to the floor in a soft hush. Liquid fire poured into me as his gaze traveled over me.

"Damn," he growled as he pulled his sweater off, tossing it somewhere. Hopefully not into the fireplace, but at that point, I didn't think either of us would've noticed.

My gaze got snagged on his stomach. He'd taken a six-pack and turned it into an eight-pack. God. I wanted to suck in my breath, to hold my belly in, because standing naked next to someone who was the epitome of fitness was a little unnerving, but then he grasped my upper arms. He pulled me to him hard, our chests flush. The contact fried my senses. Capturing my lips again, he kissed me as he started to move. We were dancing again. One hand on the nape of my neck, the other against my lower back, he kept kissing me as we swayed to the sound of our pounding hearts and the wind. His hand slipped down over the curve of my rear, and I gasped against his mouth.

I felt his lips curve into a smile as they slipped over my chin. He guided my head back, exposing my throat. The kisses he trailed along my neck spun me so high with anticipation that I whimpered. I didn't realize he'd even turned me around until my feet brushed the blankets.

My fingers dug into the taut skin of his sides as he lowered me to the blankets, his body almost, but not quite, covering mine. I sucked in a shrill breath as I slid my hands along the hard ridges of his stomach. My fingers tingled, and my entire body felt strung too tight in a delicious sort of way. Old insecurities crept in, threatening the heady bliss he'd created as he reached into his back pocket and pulled out *several* foil packets.

I tensed under him.

His grin was sheepish. "I'm prepared this time."

"I see that," I croaked, my stomach twisting and dropping at the same time. How could I feel so good and so nervous at the same time? It seemed impossible to feel so much.

Kyler stared down at me, his chest filling and brushing mine. "We don't have to do this, Syd."

"No." I clutched his arms. "I want this—I want you."

"Relieved to hear that because I..." He trailed off with a little shake of his head and dropped a kiss against the hollow of my throat. "You need to relax. Let me help you relax."

Before I could respond, he swept me up in a kiss that was so soft, so tender, that tears filled my eyes. I didn't know I could be kissed like that. That kisses could be so heartbreakingly perfect, they could shatter you forever. My muscles relaxed, and I placed my hand on the drawstring of his sweats.

Kyler groaned, and his hands...well, his hands were everywhere, paying homage to my curves and sensitive areas.

He took his time, seeming to commit every inch of my body to memory. I didn't know how he could go so slowly. I was burning with need. I was so ready that, when his fingers brushed me between my legs, my entire body moved into the touch, arching and aching.

"Damn, baby, you make it so hard to stay in control." His body shuddered as I slipped my fingers inside his sweats. "So fucking hard."

I didn't want him to stay in control.

His breathing quickened as I tugged down his pants. He was totally commando underneath, and for some reason, I found that sexy as hell. He sat up, sliding out of his sweats, and then his mouth traveled down, following the path his hands had traveled. Every brush of his lips, flick of his tongue, or tiny bite felt like he was branding himself into me.

My fingers clawed at his hair as he dipped his tongue into my belly button. A strangled sound escaped me, and then he went lower still, kissing me in my most sensitive part. It didn't take long before I was thrashing under him, crying out as he nuzzled and nipped and licked. He drew every breath out of me, every moan and whimper. I shattered apart, my body buckling and my heart racing.

Aftershocks rocked me as he sat up, grabbing a foil package. I hadn't realized he'd slipped a condom on until his body covered mine—chest to chest, hips to hips. I expected him to flip me over—the way he'd said he liked it—but he didn't. He settled between my legs, and I could feel him hard and ready.

"Are you sure, baby?" he asked, his voice deep and husky and so damned sexy. "We can stop right here."

"I'm sure." I slid my hands to his hips and hooked a leg around his, bringing us closer together. "Please, Kyler. I want this. *Please.*"

KYLER

That one word broke me.

"Please." Like she had to beg me to do this when I'd been dying to get inside her? I should have been the one begging her.

I reached down, plucked her trembling hand from where it rested over my heart, and pressed a kiss in the center of her palm. The way her body shivered against mine had me almost coming right there. My gaze flicked up, meeting hers. Pressure seized my chest. Her eyes were so blue, they almost seemed unreal.

Lust, rife and powerful, slammed into me. The kind I'd never felt before. My body demanded I thrust into Syd, fall all the way into her. I ached to do so, to lose myself in the rush of pleasure I knew was coming, but I forced myself to slow my roll. She'd only done this once before, and I didn't want to hurt her. I didn't want there to be one moment that wasn't sublimely perfect for her.

Slipping a hand under her slim hip, I lifted her until I was poised at her entrance. My heart stuttered a beat and then sped up. She pulled her hand free and cupped my cheek.

I was fucking lost.

Capturing her mouth, I slipped my tongue into her warm recess as I slowly thrust into her, and holy shit, I felt each inch in every nerve ending. Amazing. Sliding into her felt like the first time. And in a way, it was. I'd never done it this way before—face-to-face. I was like a damned virgin all over again. Didn't even think it was possible to feel that way, but I did. My body shook with the effort it took to stop myself from plunging into her and from the feeling, from the emotion behind it. Lifting my mouth from hers, I pushed in farther. She was so incredibly tight. Every inch gained was a fucking beautiful miracle. An eternity passed, and I was all the way in and completely surrounded by her. Overwhelmed. Completed. My hips rolled, and I groaned as acute sensations pounded through me.

Syd whimpered, and I stilled, my heart tripping up. "Am I hurting you?"

"No," she whispered, her eyes so bright and so wide. "It's just, you're…" A sweet flush covered her cheeks, and God damn, the feels. "You're big, and I haven't…"

I bit back a grin and a surge of dumbass pride. "I know." I smoothed a thumb along her jaw. "It'll take a couple of moments for you to get used to it."

She nodded and smiled, but the hue of her eyes was too clear, too sharp. She was wet and she was warm, but her body was rigid. Shit. She wasn't enjoying this. Not as much as I was.

Determined to fix this, I kept my hips sealed to hers as I lowered my head, kissing her softly. Syd kissed me back, but I could feel her trembling underneath me. I bit back a curse, knowing I should've taken it even slower.

I slid a hand between us, moving it along the fragile line of her collarbone and then down, over the swell of her breast. I cupped her, skimming my thumb over the tip. Her nipple pebbled, and that was a good sign. Her reaction sent an immediate pulse through me.

Deepening the kiss, I stayed still inside her, letting her take the next step. And she did. Her hips twitched, just a tiny movement at first, but I felt it like a shock wave. Moving my head down, I captured a rosy tip and suckled.

Her hips moved again, and I lifted my head, grinding my teeth together. Her fingers curled in my hair as her eyes unfocused, and she wrapped her leg around mine, a silent urge. Her hips rose again, and I let out a harsh gasp. Syd moaned, and my blood simmered.

Now that was a damned great sign, but I needed to make sure. "You're okay?" I asked, barely recognizing my own voice.

She wrapped her arms around my neck. "Yes. It…it feels better."

"Better?" My lips twitched into a half smile. "We can do better than 'better.'"

"We can?" She sounded breathless.

"Uh-huh," I murmured, sliding my hand along her thigh and guiding her other leg around my hip. Her gasp of pleasure was what I needed to hear. "How about that?" I kissed her as I pulled out slowly and then slid back in. She shuddered as I pulled halfway out. "And that?" I asked.

Her eyes were only half-open. "That's…that's good. That's…oh…" Then her eyes drifted shut, and she rocked her hips up, reclaiming the inches. "Oh, wow."

"Yeah." I grunted. "Wow."

Syd did it again, and I slammed my hand into the pillow beside her head. I let her set the pace, and dear God, once she got the hang of it, she curled those damned legs around my hips, and my restraint broke. I thrust into her deep, over and over. Her soft moans rose as the intensity and pace became feverish. I moved faster, grinding my hips against hers and lifting, getting leverage and going deep. Her movements became frantic, and I was mindless, swept away as she cried out my name and her body spasmed around mine in tight, sensual waves. I couldn't hold back. Not any longer. With two more thrusts, I buried my face in her shoulder and pounded into her as I came.

As I shuddered inside her, I finally got it. Hell. I got in that moment what had been so elusive to me this entire time. Sex mattered—oh, holy shit, it mattered—when it was with a person who meant something.

It mattered with Sydney.

Chapter 17

SYDNEY

My body ached in all the right places in a really, really great and unfamiliar way. God, I got why everyone freaked out over sex now. What we'd done had been amazing. I wasn't so naive that I didn't know it wasn't always that sublime, but I'd never felt that way before, never come like that or felt so—*God, I can't believe I'm thinking this*—full and complete.

I'd had no idea sex could really feel like that.

It took forever for my heart rate to slow down, and I knew it was the same for Kyler because when he'd pulled out, he'd rolled onto his back and tugged me along with him. I was half on him, half off. One arm and leg were thrown over his body, and my cheek rested over his heart. We stayed like that, his hand moving in a slow circle over my lower back. I was snuggled as close as I could be, more content than I could remember.

Everything seemed unreal. To be lying next to a fire on a snowy day after doing something so wonderful. How many romance novels featured passionate sex by a fireplace? More than I could count. I almost laughed, but...

But Kyler hadn't spoken yet.

Opening my eyes, I watched the flames wrap around the logs and told myself to not freak out and ruin this, whatever this was. Of course, my brain didn't listen to me at all and started spewing questions like an annoying child. Why hadn't he said anything? Did he regret it? Had he enjoyed it? Had I come across as frigid and he couldn't wait to get the hell out of here? On and on my thoughts went until I was ready to punch myself in the face, but the truth was, Kyler had said *nothing*, and shouldn't he have said *something*? Even Nate had spoken afterward, telling me he'd enjoyed it, which had turned out to be a lie, but he still had opened his mouth.

Oh God, what if this had been a mistake?

I squeezed my eyes shut. I'd never see what we had done as a mistake. No way, but Kyler...? His hand stilled along my back, and I realized I'd gone completely stiff.

"Syd?"

Part of me wanted to bury my head, but the blanket was tangled along our hips, and I would look real awkward shoving my head down there. I forced myself to lift my head and look at him. His eyes were lazy slits, but I knew he saw me—saw everything.

"What are you thinking?" he asked.

Heat swamped my cheeks, and I started to sit up. "Nothing. I mean, I'm just thinking about everything. What we did? It was awesome. Really. And I hope you feel—"

"Hold up." His arm tightened around my waist, keeping me in place, and his eyes were wide open now. "You *hope* I thought it was awesome?"

Feeling way too exposed, I crossed my arms over my chest and nodded.

"Are you insane?"

My brows shot up. "Excuse me?"

"Did I think it was awesome? No. It wasn't awesome. It was the fucking best thing I ever felt, baby."

I gaped at him.

"And that's the truth. So don't go filling your head with bullshit. Being with you? Yeah, nothing has *ever* compared to that." In one fluid motion, he sat up and pulled me into his lap. "You feel me?"

Gripping his shoulders, I gasped. Oh, I *felt* him. A ball of molten lava formed in my belly. "I...I feel you."

"Good, because it's the truth." His hands slid to my hips, and my heart fluttered in response. There was a glint to his deep-brown eyes and a mischievous tilt to his sensual lips.

He couldn't be...

Kyler shifted slightly, and he pressed against my core, hot and ready. Holy crap, he was inhuman. He chuckled when he saw my expression. "What? You look surprised, babe."

"You're ready to...um, go again?"

His lips tipped up in a half smile. "I'm always ready when it comes to you, but I don't—"

"You don't what?" I'd been stuck on the whole "always ready when it came to me" thing. "Want to do it again?"

He tipped his head back, his eyes searching my face. "There's nothing I want more than to do it again, but we don't have to." He cupped my cheek, sliding his thumb along my lower lip. "We can just chill."

I didn't think I was capable of just chilling, not when I could feel him, and I was a little surprised that I was so ready to go again, too. And I *was* ready. I was drenched, and he had to know that.

My heart was thumping fast once more as I lowered my lashes. "I want to."

His cock jumped. "Syd…"

Turning my head, I felt his thumb slide over my lower lip again, and in a move of boldness I didn't know I was capable of, I sucked the tip of his thumb into my mouth.

Kyler's entire body jerked, and he made the sexiest sound ever. "Damn, baby…"

Fueled by his response, I took his thumb deep into my mouth as I leaned into him. His chest was smooth against my sensitive skin, and I moaned around his thumb, my eyes drifting shut as my body quaked.

"Fuck." He grunted, clutching my hip as he pushed up. "God. I can't get enough of you."

"You have me." I lowered his hand to my chest, moaning the moment his fingers covered my breast. "All of me."

He rose up, kissing me. Slow. Deep. An ache pulsed between my thighs, in tune with my racing heartbeat. Sliding his hands down my sides, he moved my legs so I was straddling him, and he prodded at my entrance. I may have started this, but he took complete control. He palmed my breasts and my head fell back, my body arching.

His mouth closed over a rosy tip, and I lost the ability to breathe. What he did with his lips, his tongue, and his teeth sent stinging jolts of pleasure through me, and in that instant, I knew Kyler could be a lot rawer than he was. And that excited me even more.

I reached between us, gripping his throbbing cock. His answering groan sent a wave of shivers through me. Stroking him slowly, I pressed my forehead against his. "Please," I whispered, my eyes closed.

"Baby, you don't have to beg me." He caught my lower lip and nipped. "Just tell me what you want, and you'll have it."

My grip tightened, and I forced the words out. "I want you. I want you to make love to me." My eyes flew open at the last four words. I wanted to take back those words. Oh God, I shouldn't have—

Kyler moved so fast, it felt like the world was spinning. He snaked an arm around my waist, lifted me, and then laid me on my back. The moment my head hit the cushions, he was on me.

I jerked as he parted me and dove in like a man starving. I dug one hand into the blanket and threaded the other through his silky hair, holding on as his tongue plunged in. I thought I'd come apart right that instant. I was close, but his caresses were too breathtakingly soft.

"You taste so good," he said, working a finger inside. "And you're so fucking tight. You're perfect, you know." His lashes swept up, his eyes locking with mine. "And I love when you look at me like that when I'm doing this." To punctuate this, he hooked his finger, finding a spot I hadn't even known existed, and I cried out. "And I seriously fucking love *that* sound."

Beyond words, I thrashed my head from one side to other as he licked, swirled, and thrust. Then his lips clamped down on that bundle of nerves, wringing a moan from me. Kyler moaned against me as my body started to shake. He worked another finger inside, and I flew apart, shattering into oblivion.

Kyler had a condom on by the time the last cry left

my swollen lips. Things seemed to blur around the edges as our eyes locked. His searing stare lit me up all over again. An array of emotions flickered over his striking face as he gripped my hips and pulled me onto my knees. Boneless, I placed my hands on his chest. It moved with each ragged breath.

Holding me to him, he sat back and pulled me above his lap, his legs stretched out behind me. "Ride me," he said, his gaze on fire.

I moved my hands to his shoulders as I spread my thighs wider. "Another first?"

"Oh yeah," he said, holding himself ready. "It's another first."

That made me all kinds of insanely happy, and as our gazes collided again, I was unprepared for the feral, possessive stare in them. Gripping my hip with his free hand, he guided me down.

The initial bite of pain as he slid into me quickly dissipated into a wondrous feeling of pressure and fullness.

It took a couple of moments to catch a rhythm, but soon he was pushing up as I was sliding down, our bodies moving together in perfect sync. He caught my mouth as he wrapped an arm around my waist, pulling me flush against his chest as his tongue matched the thrusts of our hips.

"Sydney," he growled, his big body trembling.

I twisted atop him, writhing, but it wasn't enough. A whimper escaped me, and in one fluid motion, Kyler had me on my back, his hips slamming into mine. He gripped my hips, lifting me as he went deeper and deeper. He got an arm under my waist and placed a hand on my lower belly, holding me in place. I couldn't get enough leverage to move at all.

It was what he wanted. "Damn, I don't want this to end. I want to feel this—this right *here*—" He ground his hips, and my whole body shuddered. "I want to feel this forever."

"Yes. Oh my God..." The tension built so rapidly, I couldn't breathe. I tossed my head back, my eyes wide and unseeing. Words tumbled out of my mouth. "Faster. Please. Kyler, *please*. I love—"

He slammed into me, cutting my words off, and I blew apart, shattering so deeply that he shouted and came immediately, his body spasming. The things that came out of his mouth almost tumbled me over the edge again. They were prayers. Curses. Incoherent words that somehow all made sense to me. When he collapsed on top of me, he buried his face in my hair and managed to keep most of his weight on his arms. I wouldn't have minded if he'd fallen on me.

I realized at that point that my legs were wrapped tightly around his waist still. I eased them down, moaning as it triggered an aftershock.

He mumbled something, then said, "I don't want to move."

I smiled into the sweat-slick skin of his chest. "Don't."

His deep chuckle rumbled through me. "How are you feeling?"

"Mmm."

"Same here, baby. Same here."

KYLER

We went a step up from chips and raw veggies, settling on cheese and crackers for a late lunch/early dinner.

"We're in the big time, baby." I placed the platter between us.

She giggled, arranging her crackers in a row of five. "Aren't we sophisticated?"

Loving the sound of her laugh, I pulled my eyes away from her crackers to her and nearly tossed the food aside to tackle her like an animal. I'd slipped my hoodie over Syd's head, and she looked so damned edible sitting with her legs tucked under her with the edges of my U of M sweatshirt skimming the soft skin of her thighs, wearing nothing else.

Truth be told? I just liked her in my clothes...and half naked.

Easy access and all—access I'd be using in no time.

And I also loved how her gaze kept dropping to where my sweats hung low on my waist. Every time her eyes fastened on the area between my hips, she'd flush and bite down on her lip or press her thighs together.

I couldn't believe what Nate had said about her. I wanted to break his jaw all over again, and maybe some ribs. Frigid? This girl was the opposite of frigid—a hot little minx who blew my mind.

She took the paring knife I was using to cut the cheese and carved out Mickey ears. Giggling, she plopped them on a cracker and fed it to me.

Yeah, I could get used to this.

After feeding ourselves, she brought the guitar over to me. Stretched beside me, with her bare legs near the fire, she listened to me play, and I played for hours, stopping every so often to just touch her, kiss her, stroke her.

I couldn't get enough of her.

She was like a drug I wanted to keep going back to. I was addicted to the way she felt and the sounds she made. I thought maybe, just for a few seconds, that things would be awkward between us after having brain-cell-destroying sex, and there had been a moment or two when neither of us had seemed to know what to say. Or maybe both of us had wanted to say something but couldn't. Either way, that had passed quickly. Everything was like it normally was, except it seemed brighter and better. Yeah, that sounded completely lame, but it was true.

Every look, every touch, and every word meant something deeper now.

Syd fell asleep as I played the guitar, and though I was hesitant to leave her, I checked the doors and windows again. Nothing was amiss. No one was peering in our windows or trying to break through the doors. If it weren't for the cut wires on the generator, I wouldn't have been so damned paranoid. The good news was the snow had almost tapered off. Tomorrow I'd dig out the snowmobile and head to the main lodge to find out what kind of condition the roads were in. The plows had to be out on the main roads by now, and I really would need to check my cell to see if I had service, but right now? I just didn't want to.

I returned to the room and felt my heart do some kind of damned flutter when my gaze landed on Syd. Lying on her back, with the quilt spread across her legs and her rose-colored lips parted, she was the most fucking beautiful and seductive creature I'd ever seen.

Yeah, I didn't want to think beyond Syd.

Because I had no idea how things would be for us once we got back to the real world and were surrounded by friends and family. Was this the beginning of a relationship or some fling? I honestly didn't know. I'd heard what she'd been so close to saying when she came, but I'd been known to spew some crazy shit in the heat of the moment. The first time was a fluke, and whispering sweet nothings during sex could never, ever be taken seriously. You loved just about everyone, including your bio professor, when an orgasm was barreling through you.

And Syd—innocent, lovely Syd—didn't have a lot of experience when it came to sex, but even if she did, it was always hard to decipher feelings once sex was added to the equation.

I knew she cared for me deeply. Obviously. But did she really love me? The kind of love my parents had shared before my dad had passed? The kind of love I felt—

Fuck.

Kneeling beside her, I closed my eyes. It was funny how you thought if you didn't finish a sentence in your thoughts, it somehow wouldn't be true. That was so fucking stupid because the brain might take a la-la land vacay, but it didn't change a damned thing.

I was *in* love with Syd.

Like totally, madly, irrevocably in love with her—had been for years. I thought about the tattoo I'd gotten after high school, the one on my back, and shook my head. Maybe I hadn't wanted to acknowledge it before, and maybe I was a total shitbag for being with those other girls, but I couldn't ignore how I felt for Syd any longer.

Reaching over, I brushed a strand of hair off her cheek, and my hand lingered as my gaze traveled across her face. Would we have gotten to this point if we hadn't been snowed in together? I didn't think so. I would've kept fucking random girls, and she would've found someone who didn't parade other chicks in front of her. The guy would have been good to her. He'd have had his shit together. He'd have treated her like she was the most cherished thing in this world. He'd have been one lucky son of a bitch.

I wanted to be that man.

I *could* be that man, if she'd have me.

It took a hell of a lot for me to stretch out beside her and not wake her up, especially when she turned on her side, thrusting that ass against me. Fuuuck. But like the night before, I fell asleep pretty damned quickly and woke up before her, strangely refreshed for sleeping on a damned mattress on the floor and rocking a hard-on to end all hard-ons.

I woke her with my mouth between her thighs.

Syd rose onto her elbows, her hair tumbling over her shoulders and her chest rising raggedly. "Kyler, what are you...?"

I pressed a kiss against her thigh. "Should I continue?"

"Yes and please." Her voice was husky with sleep and arousal. I loved the sound. "Oh God..."

Smiling against her, I slipped a finger into her hot wetness as I circled her clit with my tongue. I loved the taste, smell, and feel of her. Could spend an eternity between her legs. I watched her as I added another finger and sucked deep. Her weight went on her elbows, and her head kicked back. The low breathy moan almost had me losing my shit right then. Syd raised her hips and made little rocking movements against my hand and mouth. It was the hottest thing ever.

"Oh..." she gasped. "Kyler, I'm gonna..."

"You're gonna come?" I flicked my tongue, and her movements amped up. "Yeah? That's what I want, baby. Let go."

And she did.

Syd fell back, her body arching, causing the borrowed hoodie to slide up her stomach. A stream of words came out of her as her inner muscles clamped down on my fingers. Her brows were pinched, and her throat worked. I watched her come like a dirty bastard, but I loved it.

Fucking beautiful.

I didn't even remember moving, but I somehow got that damned hoodie off her, and my sweats were clear across the room. Lust rode me hard, digging in deep. Gripping her slender arms, I stretched them above her head, pinning her wrists down.

I was inside her in one deep, powerful roll of my hips, all the way in. Her body exploded around me again, and I caught her scream with my lips. I pumped in over and over, losing myself in her once more. Something about this time felt so different. Raw. Animalistic. Her slick tightness clenched me like a satin glove as my tongue plunged into her mouth. She was in every pore, soaking through my muscles and bones, occupying a place deep within my chest.

My own release was beginning to power through me, lighting me up until my hips pounded against hers, and I was distantly aware of her muscles clenching and unclenching again. I'd never felt this before, so goddamned connected and—

Holy shit, the impossible had occurred, something that'd never happened to me before. I'd forgotten to use a condom.

Chapter 18

SYDNEY

It took me a few moments to realize the reason why Kyler felt so incredibly good inside me, hot and throbbing, the sensation breathtakingly intense. Every inch of him was a delicious torment, and every thrust was a heady tug and push.

He didn't have a condom on. Oh my God…

Shock rippled through me. I had believed him when he'd said he always used a condom. Kyler wasn't stupid, but he hadn't this time, hadn't even stopped to consider it. Panic rose for the briefest moment but then gave way to an overwhelming tide of pleasure. The knowledge that this was another first for him, combined with the way he held me down, the way he felt with nothing between us…well, it swept me headfirst into another powerful orgasm.

"Sydney," he growled, and he pulled out at what I knew was the last second. His mouth was on mine as he pressed against my stomach, his body spasming. Only then did he let go of my wrists.

Wrapping my arms around his shoulders, I held him tight

as aftershocks rocked him. He didn't move until his breathing slowed and his heartbeat returned to normal. Then he eased most of his weight onto one side.

He looked down between us. "Shit. Sorry about all that."

I grinned as I turned, pressing a kiss against his chest. "It's okay."

"I *always* use a condom. I just…" He let out a soft laugh. "Hell…"

"It's all right." I threaded my fingers through the hair curling against the nape of his neck. "I'm on the pill," I reminded him. "You could've…you know."

His lips brushed the side of my face. "I remembered, but I'm so used to wearing a condom. Kind of a hard habit to break." He leaned back, clearing his throat. "Not that I'm trying to break that habit or anything."

My lips parted, but my mouth was suddenly dry. What had he meant by that? Was he not planning to break the habit because he was still planning on sleeping around? I closed my eyes, mentally stringing together a sailor's vocabulary of cuss words. He hadn't meant anything by that other than he wasn't making a habit of not wearing a condom. That was all.

I hoped.

But what if nothing changed once we left here? God, I couldn't…

I tried to push the troubling idea away, but it settled in my belly like week-old food. We needed to talk, but every time I opened my mouth, nothing came out. I didn't know what to say or how to start this conversation. *Excuse me, do you plan on being a man-whore still?* Yeah, that wouldn't come out right. Even though Kyler had told me I deserved more than a hookup, I hadn't asked for more, and he hadn't offered.

We really needed to talk.

Opening my eyes, I tilted my head back. Kyler was watching me with a slight smile on his face. He looked so... so relaxed, more than I'd ever seen him before, and now would be the perfect time to say something.

"I need to shower" was what came out of my mouth.

Kyler's gaze dropped to my belly. "Yeah, sorry about that. I made a mess of you."

That was so not what I'd wanted to say. My cheeks burned, especially when his grin spread. "It's all right. I mean, sex can be messy sometimes, and these things happen and...I really need to stop talking."

Kyler chuckled deeply, and then he kissed the tip of my nose. "Have I told you how adorable you are?"

Adorable? I'd been aiming for sexy or hot. I shrugged one shoulder.

"You're fucking adorable." Dipping his head farther, he kissed me. It was quick and soft, but it curled my toes nonetheless. "I think we both need a shower. It's going to be cold, though."

Remembering the icy drenching I'd gotten when the generator had gone off, I winced. "Yikes."

"I guess it depends on how badly you want to shower."

I considered it and decided I wanted a shower that badly. Sighing, I wiggled free and sat up. Grabbing for the blanket, I held it to my bare chest. The flames were low in the fireplace, almost out. I listened for a moment and realized I didn't hear the wind. My gaze went to the thin slit in the curtains, and I wasn't sure if I should be happy or sad about the fact the blizzard was over.

Kyler's lips brushed my bare shoulder, and I turned my head toward him. His hair flopped over his forehead, a complete mess. My heart tumbled over when he gave me his lopsided grin. "Shower?"

"Yeah," I said.

"Together?"

Heat pooled in my lower stomach. "Yeah?"

That boyish grin turned wicked. "Maybe we won't even notice the water is cold."

A minute later, we noticed that the water was ice-cold. No amount of sexy Kyler nakedness could change that fact.

"Holy shit," he said, dunking his head under the stream of water. "Holy shit balls."

I laughed as I hobbled in front of him, my arms wrapped around myself. He was taking the brunt of the icy deluge, and I was just getting sprayed every few seconds by it. Little bumps covered every square inch of my flesh, and as crazy as it was, I was freezing, but I was also oh-so hot.

Kyler had lathered up, and soapy suds traveled down that impeccable stomach of his, following the ropy muscles and disappearing between his legs. I couldn't stop staring. It was embarrassing. It was thrilling. He turned at some point, and I was staring at the tattoo down his spine. What language was it in? Then he faced me again.

"Okay," he breathed, shaking his head. "You ready for this?"

I dragged my eyes up and nodded, but then said, "Not really."

"I'll try to make it as fast and painless as possible." He wrapped his arms around me and pulled me against the front of his body. His skin was warm in some areas, cold in others, and I knew he could feel how hard my nipples were against his chest. I wasn't sure if it had to do with the cold or Kyler.

Mostly Kyler.

"Get ready," he murmured, turning slowly.

I jumped as the water hit my back, almost climbing straight up him. Keeping an arm around me, he grabbed the soap. My teeth chattered as he helped wash me. I couldn't stay still, and all the movement was not lost on Kyler. I could feel him thickening against my belly. His chest was rising and falling pretty fast, and even though my skin felt like an ice cube, heat simmered in my veins. When his hand slipped between my thighs, I bit down on my lip. He really took his time there.

It was the coldest and hottest shower I'd ever had.

Afterward, he wrapped me in a fluffy towel and plopped me down in front of the dying fire. He changed quickly and went into the garage, bringing back wood. Once he had the fire crackling again, he turned to me. Tension had seeped into him after the shower. He hadn't said much, and when he looked at me, his eyes were as dark as shards of obsidian.

I squirmed, uneasy.

"I'm going to head down to the lodge and see if they know anything about the main roads." He crouched in front of me, his damp hair curling around his ears. "I shouldn't be long. Okay?"

I nodded, already starting to stand. "I can go with you. Just let me—"

"You should stay here." He put his hands on my shoulders, gently pushing me down. "And stay warm. It's not snowing anymore, but it's way below freezing out there. I'll be back before you even realize I'm gone."

I felt like he was already gone.

But I said nothing as I watched him bundle up like he was going snowboarding. He didn't kiss me before he left, and even though I was sitting in front of the roaring fire, I felt inexplicably cold.

Kyler stopped at the door leading to the basement, sliding his cell into his jacket pocket. "Don't go outside while I'm gone. Okay? I know nothing has happened since the generator, but I don't want to risk it."

"All right." I twisted toward him, wanting to say something—anything—but my ability to form sentences was completely gone.

He turned and stopped once more. Looking back at me, he opened his mouth, but then he gave a little shake of his head and disappeared downstairs.

I didn't know how long I sat there staring at where he'd stood, telling myself not to overreact, but I was, like, the queen of overreacting. I should have had a crown for it. In the short period of time between when he'd left and when I heard the snowmobile fire up outside, I already wanted to punch myself several times for not talking to him about everything. I realized then that I really didn't have my shit together like I'd previously thought. I was twenty-one years old, and I couldn't have a serious, heart-to-heart conversation with Kyler and speak the truth. If that was the case, then I probably shouldn't be having sex with him.

I needed to grow up.

Telling myself that it would be the first thing I did when he got back, I stood and hurried upstairs to get clean clothes. Once I was changed, I tugged my boots on over my jeans and sat on the couch, tapping my fingers on my knees.

Okay. Maybe the first thing I would do when he returned wouldn't be to jump on him about our questionable relationship status. I'd let him tell me about the roads first, and then we were going to talk.

Unable to sit, I left in search of my phone. It was still in the bowl of rice in the kitchen. Taking it out, I brushed off the rice with high hopes. It powered on, but the screen was nothing more than pretty waves of green and blue.

"Shit," I moaned, fighting the urge to toss it across the kitchen like a football.

I glanced at the wall clock. Half an hour had passed since he'd left, and I was already going stir crazy. I wanted to get out of this house. Without him here, I was developing a mad case of cabin fever.

Stopping by the Christmas tree, I huddled down in my sweater and stared out the large window. I felt…different. It was strange that only a handful of days had passed since we'd arrived in Snowshoe, but it felt like a lifetime.

A small smile pulled at my lips, and I closed my eyes as I remembered telling Kyler that I wanted him. I did a little wiggle out of residual embarrassment and then laughed, because seriously, I never in my life had thought I'd have the courage to put myself out there like that, and until that moment, I really hadn't realized how afraid I'd been. That wasn't any way to live, I realized sort of dumbly.

It didn't have anything to do with the sex—the different way I felt. Well, I did ache in a wholly pleasant way in areas I hadn't thought I could ache in, but it was more than that. I never really went after anything I wanted. I'd always been too cautious, and ever since the way things had ended with Nate, I'd been even more afraid of letting go—of not being in control and of doing things that could potentially end in a world of hurt.

In a way, it was like a childish security blanket that I'd wrapped around me. Telling Kyler I wanted him had been like shedding that blanket. Now I just needed to follow through and tell him everything.

I needed to tell Kyler that I loved him. The other times didn't count.

My heart skipped a beat even thinking about doing that. I was going to be afraid. It was going to be painfully awkward, and I'd rather kick myself than do this, but I would.

When I'd been alone with those thoughts for over an hour, then another twenty minutes, I couldn't take the waiting anymore. What was taking him so long? He should've been back by now. With all the strange things that had happened, it was impossible not to worry. I had no way to contact him. I made up my mind without really thinking about it. Pulling my coat on, along with gloves and a hat, I headed down to the garage.

Dragging the other snowmobile into the heavily packed snow was a huge pain in the ass. Since the power was out, it took a few moments for me to pull the garage door down by hand, and I didn't close it all the way, leaving a gap a couple of inches high so I could open it when I got back. I climbed on the red-and-white snowmobile and let out a happy sigh when it kicked on with no problems. Temps were brutally cold, so I hurried as I slid the helmet on.

I wasn't a pro at driving a snowmobile, but there was so much snow, it glided smoothly, kicking up a fine dusting. Even with the gloves, my fingers felt like frozen fish sticks by the time I slid to a stop in front of the main lodge.

People stood in front of their businesses along the street, shovels in hand, starting the massive dig-out process. In some areas, snowdrifts covered cars, and only thin slices of metal peeked through. It was amazing and crazy to see what Mother Nature was capable of when she was pissed or bored. Many snowmobiles were parked by the shoveled walkway, and I couldn't tell which one belonged to Kyler.

They all looked alike to me. As I headed up the pathway, I could hear machinery off in the distance, most likely plows.

The main lodge was all kinds of nice and toasty, illuminated by lights and TVs; it was like paradise. I pulled my helmet off and looked around. They obviously hadn't lost any power here. Lucky bastards.

But honestly, I couldn't be that upset about the electricity thing. Cuddling with Kyler totally made up for eating crappy food and freezing showers.

There was a game room and sitting area off to the side, and the smell of fresh coffee and bacon. Hot damn, I bet that was where Kyler was, shoving food in his mouth. Not that I could blame him. I would do bad things for some scrambled eggs right about now.

A lot of people were clustered around the games and couches. Some of them were talking about how long they'd been out of power or when they were planning to leave. I scoured the crowd but didn't see Kyler. I did, however, recognize the bartender from the first night here.

He turned and smiled when he spotted me. "Hey, good to see you survived the blizzard of the century."

Holding my helmet to my hip, I approached his side. "Yeah, we survived without power."

"That's what I heard." He took a sip from his coffee, and my taste buds started drooling. "Your friend told me a tree took out the power lines."

My brows rose. "Kyler?"

He nodded. "Yeah, he was down here not too long ago. He was telling me that he thought someone had been messing with the house during the storm—something about shooting out a window and cutting the wires to the generator?"

"Yeah, I was hoping it…" I trailed off, replaying his words in my head. "Wait. You said Kyler *was* here?"

Scratching his jaw, he nodded again. "Yeah, he was asking about the roads, too. He seemed eager to get out of town. Not that I can blame him. Snow is fun when you can get out and do stuff in it, but when it dumps on you like this, not so much."

"Oh." I shifted the helmet. "I must've just missed him then." As soon as I said that, though, I knew that didn't make sense. There was only one way to get from the lodge to the house, and I would've seen him. Dread turned the blood in my veins to slush. What if he'd veered off somewhere and was hurt? "When did he leave?" I asked.

His brows knitted in concentration. "Ah, maybe about forty-five minutes ago?"

My heart stopped. I swore it totally missed a beat.

"Yeah, that sounds about right. He and Sasha left around nine forty-five."

"What?" I didn't—I couldn't have heard him right. There was no way. My ears were little fucks and were messing up words. There was no way he meant Sexy Sasha, the statu-esque brunette bombshell Kyler knew from *way* back. "He left with Sasha?"

"Yeah." The bartender grinned, and I did not like that grin. It was an "attaboy" grin. "Seemed real happy to see her, too, but they always hang out when he comes here."

I stared at him. Kyler came up here a lot during the season, sometimes alone and other times with Tanner and others. I only did the Christmas trip, so it took no leap of imagination to think the bartender was familiar with Kyler.

Familiar with Kyler and Sasha together, apparently.

The bartender shook his head, grinning. "I think they

were heading back to her place. She's been without power, too, but I doubt he's checking *that* out."

Yeah, I doubted that too because—*oh God*—because Kyler didn't know shit when it came to electricity. He was with Sasha.

He was fucking Sasha.

I took a step back, my mouth open, but I didn't know what to say. My stomach roiled as a deep ache exploded in my chest. I was going to be sick.

"Hey," the bartender said, putting his hand on my shoulder as I bent down. "Are you okay?"

"Yeah." My voice sounded reedy and far away. "I'm okay." But I wasn't. I was far from okay. That ache in my chest was crawling through my veins and up my throat. My eyes burned and my body felt numb.

"Oh shit." The bartender let go of my shoulder and cringed like he'd just told me I had some incurable disease. "Oh shit, shit, shit. You're with Kyler, aren't you? Like, *with* him?" He didn't give me a chance to respond. "Look, I'm just talking out of my ass. I'm sure he just went over there to check out the power thing and nothing else."

I really didn't hear any more of his backpedaling. My heart was thumping in my ears. The floor seemed to have moved out from under my feet, and even though I was still standing, it felt like I was falling. Part of me wanted to kick the messenger. Jump on him and slam my fists into his stomach and make him take back what he'd said, but it wasn't his fault. I had to keep telling myself that.

"I'm not with him," I blurted.

He frowned. "What?"

"I'm not with him," I repeated, and it hurt. It *physically* hurt.

Like someone had stabbed a rusty knife in my chest and twisted, because it was the truth. I wasn't with Kyler. I'd had sex with him, but I wasn't *with* him. There'd been no labels between us, no promises. He'd said I deserved better than a hookup, but that was what I was. I was nothing more than a hookup when all was said and done.

And this—*this* was typical Kyler, going from one girl to the next. It wouldn't even be the first time he'd been with two girls in one day...or at one time. He'd been so quiet after the shower, so tense. Had he decided he'd had enough?

I knew him better than anyone else on the planet. Sex didn't mean anything to him. Time and time again, he'd said it was only about two people getting off. Why would I think it would be any different with me? Just because he'd fucked me face-to-face and had forgotten to use a condom once? Holy shit, had I really thought *that* meant something?

I had. God, I really had thought I meant more.

"Hon," the bartender said. "I'm really sorry."

Without saying another word, I turned and headed out of the large room. I started for the door, then stopped and backtracked to the main area. "Can I use the phone?" I didn't recognize my own voice as I put my helmet on the counter.

The lady behind the desk nodded and placed the handset by me. I almost called Andrea, but I couldn't talk to her. She'd know the moment she heard my voice. It rang twice before it was picked up.

"Mom?"

There was a static-filled pause. "Sydney? Is that you?" Unless she had another child I was unaware of...

"Yeah, it's me."

"Oh, thank God. I've been worried with this storm and

all, and you haven't answered your phone. Kyler's mom said you did something to it and you two were okay, and I knew you'd be fine with him, but…"

I winced at the sound of his name and almost lost it right then. "Mom, how are the roads back home?"

"Main roads are pretty much clear. Your father said the highways are fine."

"Okay." I squeezed my eyes shut against the burn. "Do you…do you think you guys can come get me?"

"Yes. Of course, but what about Kyler? Is he staying up there longer? Or is something wrong with his car?"

My mom, the queen of questions I couldn't even begin to answer. "His car is fine. I just…I just want to come home. Please."

There was another pause, and I swore I heard my mom's sharp inhale. "Are you okay, honey?"

"Yeah," I croaked out, forcing my eyes open. The lady behind the desk was staring at me like I was deranged. "I think I'm coming down with something."

Mom said something about being sick for Christmas, then got off the phone in search of Dad. I felt terrible for asking them to drive more than an hour to come get me, but I couldn't be in the house with Kyler after this. I didn't think I could be anywhere near him ever again.

Thanking the lady, I handed the phone over and headed out to the snowmobile. I didn't remember the ride back to the house. Only that when I slid off the snowmobile, I realized I'd left my helmet back at the lodge. I hadn't even felt the whipping wind of the drive here. I was numb as I stumbled through the snow.

I saw the tracks first. Not snowmobile tracks, but two separate sets of slashes that came from around the side of the house, like the kind made by using skis or dragging your feet through the snow.

My stomach flipped.

Had Kyler come back while I'd been at the lodge? And had he brought Sasha with him?

I stared at the marks in the snow. No. No way would he be that bold. Unless he just didn't care. Oh God, I couldn't even think about that. I pressed a mitten-covered hand against the front of my jacket. If he was in there with Sasha, I was going to kick him in the junk.

The back of my throat burned as a sharp pain sliced across my chest. Blinking back tears, I turned to the garage door. It wasn't closed all the way, and the gap in the bottom was a lot bigger than I'd left it.

I briefly considered going back to the lodge and waiting however long it took my parents to get here, but since I was a complete idiot, I hadn't told my parents I'd be at the lodge. They'd come here first, and besides, I had to pack up my stuff.

I could do this. I wasn't going to be a baby and run. It was bad enough that I'd called my parents. I could do this.

Forcing one foot in front of the other, I hastily wiped at the tear sneaking onto my cheek. With my luck, the sucker would freeze on my face, and the whole world would know I was seconds away from bawling like a kid being told Santa wasn't real.

I'd cried then.

I was about to cry again.

As I reached the garage door, I wondered why Kyler had parked out back. That part didn't make any sense, but I really didn't give a crap at this point. The ache in my chest got worse. Lifting the door, I took a deep breath, and it got caught in my throat.

I blinked slowly, thinking I'd stumbled into an episode of *Law and Order*.

Two men were kneeling at the back of Kyler's SUV, by the rear tire. Black ski masks covered their faces. One held a wicked-looking knife, dragging it through the thick black tire, and the other held a baseball bat. Both were staring at me. They started to rise.

Oh crap.

Chapter 19

SYDNEY

Everything seemed to move in slow motion. Part of me couldn't believe what I was seeing. My brain refused to digest what was happening, but my heart and body were already on board. Instinct kicked in as my pulse went into overdrive.

The man raised the baseball bat. "Shit."

Backpedaling, I opened my mouth to scream, because screaming would be really good at this moment, but my foot hit the edge of the snow by the door opening. I went down, my arms flailing as my foot slipped out from underneath me. My back and legs hit the hard cement, knocking the air out of me.

One of the guys laughed, and I wasn't sure if I should be pissed or terrified by that.

The one with the baseball bat loomed over me, his head cocked to the side. "Shit," he said again, turning back to the other guy. "We need—"

I let loose an earsplitting scream as I scrambled backward

through the snow. Twisting at the waist, I pushed up. I had to get to the snowmobile, head back to—

An arm circled my waist, snatching me clear off the ground. A hand smacked over my mouth, stifling another scream. My heart jumped against my ribs. I started struggling, kicking my legs.

"Well, well, what do we have here?"

The voice sounded familiar, but I was too panicked to give it much thought, especially when the guy with the baseball bat appeared in front of us. That meant the knife-wielding dude was the one holding me. Terror dug in with razor-sharp claws.

"Whoa, man, what are you doing?" Bat Guy demanded.

Knife Guy kept walking backward, alongside the SUV, completely undeterred by my struggling. "What? We're just going to have a little fun. Nothing serious."

My heart thumped against my ribs. This couldn't be happening. Horror hit me, and I twisted my head, trying to dislodge his hand. Every safety video the campus police had forced us to watch warned not to let someone get you in a car or out of sight. And we were already out of sight enough, considering where we were. This wasn't good. Oh God, this wasn't good at all.

"This wasn't part of the plan," Bat Guy said, and he dropped the bat. It clanged off the cement as he held his hands up. A different kind of panic punctuated his voice. "You said we were just going to screw with the tires. I'm not—"

"Shut up! Jesus." Knife Guy wrenched my head back against his chest, and needles of pain shot down my neck. "Don't be a pussy. We aren't going to do anything serious."

I pleaded with Bat Guy with my eyes. He didn't seem

like he wanted to be part of this, whatever this was. He was my only hope.

"Serious?" He gestured with his hands at us but refused to meet my stare. "What the fuck do you think this is? What are you planning to do to her? This is fucked up."

"Man, come on." Knife Guy shifted. "Just open the fucking door, you pansy-ass. We're just going to scare her. That's all."

My heart stuttered and my eyes were wide, filling with tears. *This isn't happening.* Those words were on repeat. I couldn't process how my morning had started one way, so full of hope and love, and had gone to Shittyville in a nanosecond.

Bat Guy cursed under his breath as he moved around my flailing legs and opened the door to the basement. My stomach dropped. As I was carried through the opening of the basement, I froze for a second. The rush of dread was paralyzing. It sank deep, threatening to drown me.

The familiar landscape of the covered pool tables, the air hockey table, and the picture of Kyler as a small boy with his father snapped me into action.

Twisting my head sharply, I dislodged my attacker's hand far enough that I was able to bite down on his fingers. Clamping my teeth onto his skin, I pressed down until I felt his skin pop and a metallic taste exploded in my mouth.

Knife Guy howled and yanked his hand away. His grip on my waist loosened enough that I tore myself free. He blocked the only exit, and while every horror movie in the world replayed in my head, I had no other choice but to run farther into the house.

I ran faster than I ever had. The soles of my boots were damp and slick from the outside as they slipped over the wood floors. I entered the stairwell at breakneck speed. A weight hit me in the back, throwing me down on the stairs. I caught myself before I face-planted on the steps.

"You little bitch." He grunted, grabbing a fistful of my hair as his knees pressed into my hips. He yanked my head back, and a wave of sharp pain rolled down my spine as he pulled me up. Twisting onto my side, I kicked out, catching him in the shin.

I didn't see the blow until it landed. Pain burst across my face, hot and stinging. Crying out, I clawed at the hand in my hair.

"What are you doing?" the other guy yelled. "Holy fuck, are you out of your mind?"

Knife Guy ignored him, dragging me up the stairs. My scalp was on fire as we hit the living room, and my gaze landed on the bed Kyler and I had built. It was messy from what we'd done that morning, and seeing that right at this moment caused nausea to rise in my gut.

This isn't happening.

"I fucking hate stuck-up bitches like you," Knife Guy said, pushing me forward.

I stumbled and lost my balance, falling to my knees near the coffee table. Desperation clouded my senses. Full-blown panic set in.

"Why?" I winced as my lip pulled. "Why are you doing this?"

"Why?" he mimicked my voice. "You little shits come up here every year and think you own this place, acting like you're better than us. You're not. You aren't anything."

I blinked against the tears filling my eyes. A chord of familiarity rang inside me.

He dragged me past the coffee table, toward the blankets.

"And that fucker Kyler? He thinks he's the shit, right? Thinking he can boss me around."

It hit me then, and for a second, I couldn't move as realization sank in. I knew who was behind the mask. I almost blurted it out but clamped my jaw shut. If he thought I didn't know he was Zach, then I probably had a better chance of walking away from this. At least, I hoped I did, and I clung to that.

"Come on, dude. This is enough," Bat Guy said from somewhere behind us. "She's scared, okay? We need to get out of here. You fucked with their stuff enough already. This has gone too far."

"Too far?" Zach hissed in my ear, and I shuddered in revulsion. "Like it was too far when Kyler fucked my girlfriend? Or the fact he's with her right now?"

Holy shit—did he mean *Sasha*? Kyler had mentioned that there'd had been something between Zach and Sasha, but Kyler had said nothing had happened between himself and Sasha. I suddenly got the animosity between the two at the bar.

Kyler had lied to me, actually lied to me. And now Kyler was with Sasha, and I was with Zach. How unbelievably fucking twisted; Kyler *had* slept with Zach's girlfriend, once upon a time.

The rusty knife that had been planted in my heart when I'd heard where Kyler was twisted deeper and then broke off. I was in this situation because of Kyler and his inability to keep his dick in his pants. Plain and simple. The emotional pain slicing through me was just as potent as my stinging lip and aching muscles, and the bruises on the inside would take a hell of a lot longer to fade than the ones that no doubt blotted my skin. The hurting went to a whole new level, cutting in so far that I knew there was no chance of our repairing this.

That was, if I actually made it out of here alive.

I struggled to get control of my breathing to think around the soul-shattering hurt and panic. "I'm sorry," I mumbled. My lower lip was numb, causing me to stumble over my words. "I'm sorry that he slept with your girlfriend. I'm so—"

"*You're* sorry?" Zach laughed harshly as he shoved me forward. "That little bastard should be sorry."

Okay. Obviously sympathizing with the psycho wasn't going to work. Scrambling off my knees, I spun around, aiming for the doorway to the foyer. I could get out the front door, and then what? Run like hell.

I made it halfway across the room before he got hold of my jacket. In a frantic attempt at escape, I tore the zipper down and slipped out of it. I'd almost made it to the door when he tackled me from behind. I hit the floor hard. My cry was lost in Bat Guy's shouts. Zach roughly flipped me onto my back, and the terror amplified, bursting through me. I swung at him, my knuckles glancing off his jaw. He caught my hands, easily pinning them beside my head.

"God, you're fucking feisty, aren't you?" Zach laughed, and through the slits of the ski mask, his eyes held a scary gleam. "You and Kyler are just friends, huh? Fuck buddies by the look of it. Yeah, I saw you two in front of the window. Would've got you out of the bar sooner if I'd known you were just another one of Kyler's whores."

Just another one of Kyler's whores.

Rage swamped me, a fiery burn that slithered through my veins like poison. I bucked my hips, trying to throw him. "Get off me!"

225

"Hey!" Bat Guy shouted, his voice a high-pitched squeal. "This is going too far! I didn't sign up for this shit! Fucking with the house is one thing, but this? Hell no. I'm not a part of this."

"Whatever," Zach growled. "Get the fuck out then."

Breathing heavily, I locked eyes with Zach. How far was he going to take this? Obviously, what was happening wasn't part of any plan. Bat Guy was way too freaked out for that to be the case. They must've been watching. Saw Kyler leave, and then me. They probably hadn't expected me to show up in the middle of them vandalizing Kyler's car. But now? My brain couldn't go where this kind of stuff ended. This couldn't be happening to me.

A door slammed shut somewhere in the house, and the last of my hope dwindled. Bat Guy was gone. I was alone with Zach, and revenge glittered in his stare.

KYLER

Coasting over the snow, I cursed under my breath. Way too much time had passed since I'd left for the lodge. Syd probably thought Bigfoot or something had eaten me. I hadn't intended on taking so long. The good news was that I learned progress had already been made on the town's roads, and the main ones were clear enough for slow traffic. Man, my head was still spinning from what'd happened when Sasha had strolled into the lodge. It had solidified two age-old sayings—the past always comes back to bite you in the ass, and no good deed goes unpunished.

Jesus. H. Christ.

All I wanted to do was gather Syd up and get as far away from here as possible. Coasting to a stop beside the other snowmobile, I frowned. What the hell was that doing out? Had Syd gone somewhere and come back?

Irritation bit deep as I turned the engine off. God damn it, would she ever listen to me? The last thing I wanted was her running around by herself, especially after what I'd learned from Sasha.

Fucking Zach—fucking backwoods asshole—had been behind the shit going on at the house. Apparently, he'd busted out a couple of her windows, too. That little punk still couldn't get past the fact Sasha had moved on. You'd think by the way Zach acted over a year later that Sasha had a golden vagina or something. Shit.

It took everything in my power not to find my way to where Zach lived and beat the living shit out of him. His screwed-up obsession with Sasha could've gotten Syd hurt—or worse.

It would've been your fault, whispered an insidious voice. Fuck.

That was true.

Whipping my helmet off, I hopped off the snowmobile just as someone came running out from under the half-closed garage door.

First thought: What the fuck?

Second thought: Fucker was wearing a ski mask and was coming out of my house, where Syd was? Oh, hell to the motherfucking no.

Throwing the helmet down, I caught the son of a bitch around the waist as he tried to dart around the house. I took him down in the snow, planting my knee in the dude's stomach.

"Who the fuck are you?" I demanded, gripping the guy by the shoulders. "Answer me!"

The man held up his hands. "I don't have nothing to do with this. I swear. He said he just wanted to fuck with the house and your car. That was—"

Grabbing the edges of the ski mask, I yanked it up over the fucker's head. It was one of Zach's cronies. He'd been at the bar a few nights back. Without even thinking twice, I slammed my fist into the guy's face. "Where is he?"

The guy looked like he was about to piss himself as he jerked his chin toward the garage. His bloody lips trembled. "I'm sorry. It wasn't supposed to go this far, but Zach, man, he hates you for that shit with Sasha. He's inside, man."

I went stock-still for a second. It was like the world had just fucking crashed on top of me. Fear exploded in the back of my throat, and it tasted like I'd swallowed a mouthful of blood.

After springing off the douche, I tore through the snow and skidded across the cement. I hit the side of my SUV and rebounded. My head shut down as I flew through the open door, my eyes scanning the room for Syd.

Footfalls thudded upstairs, and a cry rang out, stopping my heart. Shit, that sounded like Syd. Oh my God, that sounded like her. My hands were already forming fists, and pure rage boiled my blood, turning to ice at the sound of a fucking gunshot from above. Oh God—Syd. If she was hurt, I swore to fucking God, I'd kill the bastard. There'd be no stopping me.

Racing around the pool table, I made a beeline for the stairwell as feet pounded over the floor above and down the stairs. A second later, another fucker in a ski mask rushed out of the dark stairwell, drawing up short when he saw me.

I knew it was Zach. It was his build. Half his face showed through the torn lower half of the ski mask. My gaze dropped to his hands. There was blood all over them.

I fucking lost it.

Launching myself across the room, I slammed into Zach and took him down. Punk-ass swung on me, but I dodged the strike. Grabbing the collar of his sweater, I pulled him up by one hand. My arm swung back and shot forward, connecting with his jaw. Once. Twice. Three times. He didn't get one punch in. Fuck no. The blows blurred into blood, split skin, and flares of dull pain. It wasn't enough. I wanted to pummel him into an early grave, but when Zach's head flopped back on his neck, I dropped him on the floor and forced myself to stand.

My hands were shaking, my knuckles busted and raw.

Taking the next breath was hard, but not as hard as it was to step back from Zach. The only thing that made me do it was that I needed to get to Syd. *Gunshot—oh God.* If she was hurt or...I would never forgive myself. It was as simple as that. I shouldn't have left her here alone.

As I stepped over Zach, he rolled onto his side, moaning. I resisted the urge to kick him upside the head. While I raced up the stairs, my heart was throwing itself against my ribs. "Syd!" I thought I yelled, but I choked on her name, choked on the possibility of what could've happened to her.

Barreling through the half-closed door, I skidded to a halt when I saw her.

She was sitting on the edge of the coffee table, staring at the dying fire, her arms wrapped around her waist. Dark hair fell forward, shielding her face. My stepdad's shotgun lay across her knees.

"Sydney?"

I walked around, easing my hands open. Stopping in front of her, I knelt and felt my heart crack. Splinter. The collar around her neck was torn, the skin along her chin red and blotchy. Her lower lip was split and an angry red. Fury slammed into me with sickening force. I wanted to go back downstairs and beat Zach into a nice little head injury.

"Syd, baby, look at me." I reached out to her, wanting to pull her into my arms, needing to do so.

"Don't." She jerked away and stood, clutching the gun and backing up rapidly. "Don't touch me."

Chapter 20

SYDNEY

Standing next to the Christmas tree, I watched the state vehicle ease down the road, its plow scraping up snow and pushing it aside. Sirens blared in the distance. Kyler must've called the police. That was smart, really smart. I honestly hadn't even considered that. It was like my brain wasn't working right.

My jaw and lip ached, but I felt detached from it. Residual terror and adrenaline sent a shudder through me. I wasn't really hurt. Other than the one blow Zach had landed, I was okay. By the looks of Kyler's knuckles, I bet Zach was worse off than me. And the wall of the living room had taken the bullet.

Zach had wanted to scare me, and he'd succeeded. I honestly didn't know what would've happened if I hadn't been able to pull away and grab the gun from where Kyler had propped it against the wall. And what if Zach had gone for it? Right now, I couldn't really consider all that could've happened. If I had learned anything in my psychology courses, it was that humans were capable of doing anything, and Zach...yeah, something was definitely wrong with him. The gun had shaken so badly in my hands when I'd turned and pointed it at Zach. I'd seen the hesitation in his eyes: *Does she have the guts to pull the trigger?*

I'd wondered that at the time, too.

My knees shook so badly, I was surprised I was still standing and hadn't fallen into the Christmas tree yet. I knew it was shock. Not the deadly kind, but shock nonetheless.

"Syd?"

At the sound of Kyler's voice, my eyes stung. I didn't turn around.

"The police are almost here. They're going to want to know what happened." Another stretch of silence, and when he spoke again, he sounded closer. "Are you okay?"

"Yeah," I croaked, wishing he'd just go away. I wasn't ready to deal with him yet. I didn't think I'd ever be ready. My chest ached worse than any other part of my body.

There was a pause. "Did he...did he hurt you? I mean, more than what I can see?"

I shook my head, swallowing hard. The sirens were closer. I dreaded talking to the police.

"Syd, will you...will you look at me?"

I didn't want to, but I forced myself to turn toward him. He was as pale as I felt, his eyes wide and dark like chips of obsidian. I steeled myself, because looking at him hurt in a deep, unforgiving way. "What, Kyler?"

He looked like he was about to take a step forward but stopped. "What...what's going on? Why won't you let me touch you?" His head tilted to the side, and a chunk of brown hair fell across his forehead. "I really want to hold you right now. You have no idea how scared I was when I realized he was in here. I never—"

"Stop—stop right there." I held up a hand, realizing I still had the gun in the other. I lowered it to the floor, the lump in my throat the size of a golf ball. Everything rushed to the surface at a dizzying speed. This *so* wasn't the time for this, but I couldn't stop myself. "You don't think I know where you were?"

His brows rose as he took a step back. "Syd, I—"

"I went to the lodge looking for you. Yeah, I know I was supposed to stay here, and maybe this shit wouldn't have gone down the way it did if I had, but I went there and you *weren't* there." The back of my throat burned. "You were with Sasha, who, from what I heard, seemed *really* happy to see you, and you didn't think twice about going back to her place. Not even after we—" My voice gave out, and I shook my head, blinking back tears. "You lied to me."

Kyler opened his mouth, but I cut him off, on a roll. "You told me that you and Sasha weren't like *that*, but that was obviously not the case, was it? All this—the stuff with the window, and the generator, and Zach? This was because of you and her. Zach came here because you slept with his girlfriend!"

He flinched, and my stomach tumbled. I hated that I actually felt sorry for that. "Oh God," he said. "Syd, baby, I'm so—"

"Don't say it!" My voice cracked. A tear snuck out, and I wiped at it angrily. "You have never lied me to before. Never! But you lied about her, and he came here because of your inability to keep your dick in your pants for five seconds!" That was a low blow. I knew that. I also knew that what Zach had done really wasn't Kyler's fault, but I was hurt. I was destroyed, and I wanted him to hurt as much as I did. "Tell me this. Did you use a condom with her earlier? Did you fuck her face-to-face? Or is 'doing it from behind' just another lie? God, you must think I'm the stupidest chick alive because I believed that."

Kyler looked like I'd kicked him in the junk. "What? No. I don't think that, and that wasn't a lie, Syd. I—"

"It doesn't matter." I drew in a sharp breath, and it hurt as it scorched my throat. "I'm a lot of things, but I'm not *that* stupid."

Before he could say anything else, a stranger's voice rang out from downstairs—a police officer's—and I stepped forward, my entire body trembling. "You were right, Kyler." Tears clogged my throat. "I *do* deserve better than this."

KYLER

I would've preferred a kick in the junk than to be standing before Syd, to see her in so much pain, and to know I was the cause of it. Some of it was my fault. Hell, a lot of it was, and I would have gladly walked through a pit of rattlesnakes to take back those things.

Zach had come here because of what'd happened between Sasha and me well over a year ago. The psychotic SOB had taken his issues with me out on Syd, and fuck if that didn't slaughter me. I wished I'd told Sasha no when she'd asked me to help her tarp up her windows. I should've been here to protect Syd, not fucking around with broken windows and avoiding Sasha's nonstop innuendos. Yeah, Sasha would've been down for a quickie. That girl would always be down for anything, anytime, but that hadn't happened. Hell no.

But had it happened before? Yeah, it had. A long time ago.

I desperately searched my memories for what I'd told Syd. Had I lied about Sasha, or had I skipped around the question? Either way, I hadn't come out with the whole truth. The damage was done. It was too late. I saw it in Syd's eyes, heard it in her voice.

Syd turned away at the sound of approaching footsteps. The police were yelling something. I barely heard them. The world that'd crashed down on me outside was still falling apart. She was quiet, but her shoulders shook, and I knew if she faced me now, tears would streak her face. I wanted nothing more than to go to her. I started toward her because I couldn't bear to see her like this. No matter what fucked-up shit I'd done in my past, I couldn't stand this. There had to be a way to make this better.

I made it about a foot.

Then I was tackled from behind, my arms were yanked behind me, and I was in handcuffs in less than a second. Probably had to do with the fact there was a half dead guy downstairs and the cop had no idea who had done what here. With my cheek smashed into the floor, I cursed under my breath.

"Wait!" Syd's shocked voice erupted, and I forced my chin up. Confusion poured into her pale face. "He's not the one who needs to be handcuffed. He's—"

"Just stay back, ma'am, until we have this situation under control." The officer yanked me up, and the muscles in my arms and back protested, causing me to grunt.

Syd's teary eyes went wide with panic. "You're hurting him! Oh God, please stop. He's the one who called you."

235

This really didn't feel good, but in a sick way, I welcomed the pain. It dulled the burning in my gut. Another officer barreled into the foyer, causing Syd to jump. Silver ornaments on the tree rattled. A bulb fell to the floor, shattering. The second officer spotted the gun where Syd had left it on the floor. He hurried over, pushing it away from Syd with his booted foot.

The first officer barked orders, and the story came out in a rush of words—Syd coming home to find two guys messing with the tires on my SUV, the one guy running off and Zach telling her that he wanted to scare her. She left out the part about Sasha and how her lip had ended up split, but those answers came out when the officers took the handcuffs off me and the EMTs rolled into the house.

Apparently Zach was moving around. Too bad.

I tried to keep an eye on Syd as an EMT checked her out while I told the officers about Zach, but when she winced at the guy probing at her lip, I didn't think twice. I started toward her.

"She's fine, son." The officer clamped a hand down on my shoulder. "She's being taken care of. The best thing you can do for her is to give me all the information you can. Start from the beginning."

I was seconds from telling the officer to go fuck himself, but my gaze locked with Syd's. A moment stretched into eternity, and then her lashes lowered. Tears clung to them like crystals—tears I knew weren't from the busted lip.

I hated myself in that moment more than I ever had before.

"Son?"

Rubbing my palm over my jaw, I turned back and focused on the officer. I started from the beginning, with the snowmobile. So many officers moved in and out of the house—too many, it seemed—that I lost sight of Syd for a little while. I knew she hated my guts right now, rightfully deserved, but it made me itchy not to know where she was and if she was okay.

She reappeared with the EMT, a bag of ice pressed to her lower jaw. An officer blocked her from my view, getting her official statement.

That...hell, that was the worst part of all this, listening to her tell the officer what'd happened. And when her voice wavered, it was like a punch to the chest. Syd was so incredibly strong and brave, but she should have never had to face something like this.

I'd never thought I'd be the one to put her in danger. For years, I'd been the one always looking out for her—keeping her away from trouble. I just hadn't thought I'd be the cause of any.

I didn't know how much time passed as we were interviewed. I did hear that Zach would be carted off to jail after making a pit stop at the hospital. He had also given up his friend. The officer assured us that both of them would be charged with breaking and entering, vandalism, and assault, and it could even go as far as attempted murder with the buckshot-through-the-window thing. Served the stupid bastard right if he ended up spending most of his life behind bars.

The officers were still milling around, making it impossible to talk to Syd. I didn't think I could explain myself in any way that would make things better, but I needed to apologize for this mess and to let her know I never meant for her to get hurt in any way.

I caught sight of her in the kitchen, walking side by side with a young cop. He had a hand on her shoulder, and she was without the ice bag. I doubted she should've gotten rid of the ice that quickly.

"Sydney!"

Startled by the sound of her father's voice, I whirled toward the living room. What was he doing here? A second later, a bear of a man came through the door. Syd's father had scared me shitless as a kid. Mr. Bell was the kind of man who shopped in the big-and-tall section and could give someone a look that made most guys want to run for the hills. He drew up short, midway through yanking off his wool gloves, when he saw his daughter. A look of horror flashed across his face, and then his cheeks went red with anger.

His gaze moved from his daughter to me, and I wanted to crawl into a fucking hole. I was a big motherfucking letdown. I'd let his daughter get hurt. I couldn't be more of a fuck-up than that.

A second later, a smaller figure darted around Mr. Bell. Syd's mom looked like a child standing next to her husband. Syd's "vertical challenge" was all from her mom, as were the thick, dark hair and heart-shaped face. The startling blue eyes were her father's, though.

"Baby," Mrs. Bell cried out, nearly knocking an officer over in her rush to get to her daughter. "Oh my God, what happened? Look at you. What happened?"

Syd broke away from the cop and met her mom halfway, throwing her arms around her.

"Kyler."

The sound of my name was like dropping steel down my spine.

I turned to her father, and in that short period of time, Sydney and her mother were gone.

Mr. Bell took a step forward, and he was one of the few men in this world who made me feel about an inch tall. "What in the hell happened to my daughter?"

Chapter 21

SYDNEY

Being home was a relief, standing in my **heated** *old bedroom,* surrounded by all my things from childhood straight up to my teen years. But I'd been in a funk since we'd arrived in Hagerstown three days ago.

I needed to get peppy or something. Christmas Eve was in two days, and it'd always been my favorite holiday—the food, the family, the presents—everything about it.

Meh.

My bedroom was weird in a way, like a time capsule. It had never bothered me before, but right now? I wanted to take a sledgehammer to the room. I was embarrassed by the various teddy bears stacked near the pillows. I picked one up, a red bear Kyler had given me for my eleventh birthday. Pain sliced my chest, and I placed the bear back down and turned away from my bed. I was bored with the overstocked bookcases. I couldn't care less about the ribbons Mom had tacked on the wall above my desk, hanging in a line next to the academic awards I'd accumulated throughout high school. There were newspaper cuttings of the dean's list. I started to straighten one of the frames, but stopped and left it the way it was. Crooked. Unbalanced. Imperfect.

Turning away from the awards, ribbons, and clippings, I picked up my old cell phone off the bed and slipped it into my pocket. I headed downstairs to find Mom in the kitchen. Dad was still at the office. Some things never changed, including his late nights.

The whole lower floor smelled like apple pie and cinnamon—usually my favorite. Mom looked up from the magazine she was poring over as I dropped into the seat in front of her. "Are you still going out with Andrea tonight?"

Dropping my elbows on the table, I put my chin in my hands. "Yeah, she's driving up from Frederick and picking me up in a little bit. We're going to grab dinner." And I had a feeling she'd be visiting Tanner later, who was home in Smithsburg, about ten minutes away.

"Good." Mom winked. "I didn't put enough chicken in the oven to feed you *and* your father."

"Nice."

She laughed softly as she flipped a page. "Has your lip been bothering you?"

"No. It's fine." And it practically was. Just a little mark was on it, near the corner, and my jaw didn't hurt anymore. "I hope you're not worrying about it."

"Of course I'm worrying about it. What you went through?" She took a deep breath and closed the magazine. Looking up, she fixed her dark eyes on me. "Honey, I—"

"I really don't want to talk about it." I placed my hands on the kitchen table. "I'm fine. It's over. In the past."

"Until the case goes to court," she reminded me gently.

"He might plead guilty, and then I won't have to testify

or anything." God, I really hoped that was the case. "Anyway, if I have to do it, I'll do it."

Mom didn't say anything for a moment as she watched me.

I sighed as I sat back, knowing she was about to say something I didn't want to hear. She had that "Mom" look about her.

"Honey," she started, and my suspicions were confirmed. "I was talking to Mrs. Banks about what happened. You know, she's the school counselor."

Oh. Dear. God.

"And she suggested what I thought would be best," she continued carefully. "I think you should talk to someone about what happened to you."

"What?" My jaw hit my lap. "You're kidding, right?"

Mom frowned. "Honey, you're going to school to be a psychiatrist—"

"Psychologist," I corrected.

Her frown deepened. "*Anyway*, you know how important it is for people to talk things out and not hold them in."

I resisted the urge to roll my eyes. I did know how important that was. And while those moments with Zach had been the scariest in my life—and there were still moments where they haunted me—I didn't need to talk about it and soak up a therapist's time that could be better spent helping someone who needed it.

"Mom, I don't need to talk to anyone. I'm okay. Really, I am. I promise."

Her eyes narrowed. "Then why have you been moping around this house like someone kicked your puppy into the street?"

I made a face, but my stomach dropped. "That's real nice, Mom."

"You know what I mean."

Tracing the grain in the wood of the tabletop, I shrugged. "I haven't been moping around."

"Yes, you have." She picked up her cup and stood, taking it over to the sink, where she washed it out before slipping it into the dishwasher. When she finished, she faced me and crossed her arms. "I have never seen you so listless and unhappy this close to Christmas before. So if it wasn't what happened to you, then what is it?"

"It's nothing. I'm just in a mood or something."

Mom sighed. "Honey, you know you can talk to me, right? About anything. You're not too old for that."

"I know." But what was bothering me was something I was *so* not talking to my mom about.

Her lips pursed. "Is it Kyler?"

Ah, there it was. That horrible sinking feeling expanded through me at the mention of his name. My entire body locked up, and a hollow feeling poured into my chest. It was like being punched and knocked down. Kyler. Kyler. Kyler. I'd tried not to think about him since I'd left Snowshoe. That was as easy and fun as playing *Frogger* on the interstate.

Kyler consumed my thoughts no matter what I did. And the worst part? Two out of the three nights, I'd dreamed about him. God, it made me lamer than normal.

But I did know something I'd never really known before. This was what a broken heart really felt like. Silly me, thinking I knew what it felt like every time I'd seen Kyler with a new chick. That had nothing on this.

I tucked my hair back and decided on saying, "Why do you think it has to do with Kyler?"

"Well, for starters, I'm not blind."

My brows rose.

"Kyler hasn't been here once since you got home. That boy practically lives in this house when you're home from school. And not once has he stopped by, and that is like the sign of the apocalypse."

I would've laughed at that, but it was true, and it made my throat burn.

"I thought it was strange how you left without saying goodbye to him, but I chalked it up to the shock of everything that'd happened." Mom walked over to the table and sat across from me. "And then there's the fact I'm pretty sure he hasn't even called you."

Wow. *Thanks for reminding me.* Not that I'd believed he'd call. I'd made things pretty clear in Snowshoe, but the fact he hadn't called stung like a hornet. And that was stupid, because I wasn't ready to talk to him, but if I were being honest with myself—which sucked, so who wanted to do that?—I knew what I really wanted.

Kyler to come begging and pleading for forgiveness— forgiveness I wasn't even sure I could give.

"So I'm assuming something happened between you two," Mom said.

"You know what they say about assuming things…"

Mom's expression looked like she'd swallowed something sour. "Funny."

A sigh shuddered through me. I didn't know what to say or how to begin. What could I tell her? "Mom…" My phone buzzed with a message from Andrea saying she was outside. I flew from the table, relieved. "I've got to go. Andrea's here."

"Sydney—"

"Mom, I'm okay. Everything is fine with Kyler." I gave her a quick hug. "Really."

I darted from the house before Mom could stop me,

grabbing my jacket off the back of the couch. After nearly breaking my neck on the iced-over driveway, I joined Andrea in her toasty Honda.

"Hey, girl, hey…" Andrea chirped, studying me in the dim light like I was some kind of science experiment. "You don't look too busted up."

I rolled my eyes. "Gee, thanks, I think."

She tossed a red curl off her forehead. "I'm glad you don't. Holy shit, girl, I still can't believe it. You could've died! Or worse."

I wondered what was worse than dying.

"Or you could've ended up on *Dateline* or something." She shook her head as she slipped the gear into Drive. "Maybe had an episode of *Law and Order* based on what happened."

I laughed then. "You're nuts."

"But you love me," she replied as she coasted into the street. "And I love you. So, on a serious note, I want to drive to Snowshoe and stab that asshole in the eyeball."

"Me, too."

Andrea flashed me a quick grin. "Where to?"

Since there wasn't a huge selection around here, I told her to hit Route 11 and head toward 81. "What are you in the mood to eat?"

"Hmm." She tapped a gloved finger on her chin. "I'm in the mood for…meat."

"Go figure."

She smacked my arm. "Whatever."

I listed our choices, and we settled on Outback. The drive was a little slower than usual, with the shoulders of the highway still covered in snow and the wind tossing flurries everywhere.

As we got out of the car, she caught me in a squeeze-worthy hug. "Sorry," she said, leaning back. "I was really upset when you told me what happened. I don't know what I'd do…"

"It's okay. Look, what happened was messed up to the max, but I'm totally okay."

She turned away quickly, and I swore she wiped under her eye, but I had to be seeing things because I had never seen the girl cry. Not even during *The Notebook* or those terrible Humane Society commercials that always made me tear up.

The restaurant was pretty packed with last-minute Christmas shoppers from the nearby mall, and I went to the restroom while she asked for a table.

We didn't have to wait too long. After the waiter took our drink orders and plopped down fresh bread, Andrea picked up the huge knife and pointed it at me. "Okay. So now that I'm not driving and am paying attention fully, you and I need to talk."

I leaned back against the cushion. "Do you need to be holding a knife when you do it?"

"Oh, yeah, probably not the greatest thing to be waving in your face. Sorry." She placed it down on her napkin slowly. "All right, we need to talk about Kyler."

I blinked, not expecting that. I hadn't told her a thing about Kyler. I hadn't told *anyone*. "Wh-what do you mean?"

"You're stuttering. That alone tells me a lot." She picked up her glass and took a sip. "I know something went down between you two because Tanner called me this morning."

My eyes practically popped out of my head. "*Tanner* called you?"

"Oh yeah," she replied, looking like she was carrying a bucket full of secrets.

I gripped the edge of the table. "What did he say?"

"More like what he didn't say." Andrea cut a slice of bread and dropped it on my plate, but my ball of nerves was taking up too much room for me to even think of eating. "He called to ask me if I knew what happened between you and Kyler in Snowshoe. I assumed he meant all that other stuff, but when I said that, he was like, 'Oh, hell no.'"

My mouth opened, but I didn't have a clue what to say. Heat swept across my cheeks, which was a dead giveaway.

Andrea's eyes narrowed. "Oh, you dirty hussy, something *did* go down, and you've kept quiet. I should disown you!"

The older couple across the way looked over at our table, and I wanted to hide under it. "Andrea, come on."

"I'm your bestie," she said without a trace of shame. "You're required by the laws of feminism to tell me these things."

I snapped out of my inability to speak. "Whoa. I think you have the idea of feminism wrong."

"Whatever." Her eyes rolled. "You need to tell me what happened because Tanner said Kyler looks like he's done died and went to hell and hung out there for a while."

My heart spasmed. "Really?"

She nodded. "Supposedly has been on a two-day bender, and today is the first day the guy has been sober. So whatever went down obviously didn't end with a Disney happily-ever-after. All I have to say is that you need to tell me what is up, and it better include some rated-R stuff."

My brows knitted.

"What?" She raised her hands. "A girl can live vicariously, right? I mean, every chick out there wants to star in a porn video with Kyler, so I'm dying to know if he's that good."

247

"He's that good." The words were out of my mouth before I could stop them.

Andrea smacked her hands on the table. "Oh my God, you slept with Kyler?"

I looked around, my cheeks burning. "Okay. Can we keep the volume down?"

"Sorry, but I'm just excited to hear about this. Not that I'm excited that he obviously fucked up because I know it wasn't you that screwed this up. It was him—it's always the guy's fault."

Shaking my head, I released my breath. In a weird way, it felt good to unload this. Things still felt raw and abrasive, and I prayed to God I didn't start crying like a freak in the restaurant, but it was a relief to finally put some of these things into words. I gave her the quick and not-so-dirty version of what'd happened, glossing over some of the details that I'd die before I spoke out loud. Andrea waved the waiter away when he returned to see if we were ready to order, leaving me to tell her about Sasha and why Zach had started messing with us in the first place.

When I finished, I slumped in my booth, absolutely exhausted. "So…there you have it."

Andrea opened her mouth and closed it several times like a fish out of water. "Holy shit…"

I took a sip of my Coke. "Yep."

"Whoa, okay, let me get a grip on this." She tugged her curls off her face. "You got drunk and tried to come on to him. He turned you down and then later said you deserved better than a one-night stand while he was feeling you up? Then you two caved to your wild-monkey lust and had sex several times, doing it in a way he claimed he'd never done it before?"

Thank God she kept her voice low on that one. "Sounds about right."

"And you guys spent over a day in pure sexual bliss, eating crackers and being all lovey-dovey, and it wasn't awkward or anything?"

I shook my head.

"Hmm…" She fiddled with her straw. "And he didn't act weird, right?"

"No. The exact opposite, Andrea. He was…he was perfect. I thought that he must've really wanted to be with me, you know? And that morning, we even took a cold shower together. He was…he was so sweet and then…" I sighed, feeling stupid. "He did seem off that morning, but then all this happened."

Andrea's lips pursed. "So he obviously went over to Sasha's, but how do you know he did anything?"

I gave her a bland look.

"Okay." She raised her hands. "It *is* Kyler, but you don't know what he did over there. Sure, it looks suspicious, and I can see why you'd think that, but you really don't know."

It wasn't like I hadn't considered that maybe Kyler hadn't had sex with Sasha that day. Once I'd gotten home and calmed down a little, that had crossed my mind every five seconds. I shook my head again. What if my initial suspicion had been true, but I convinced myself otherwise and then found out I'd been right the first time? My heart would be broken all over again.

"But he lied to me, Andrea. I asked him about Sasha, and he said they weren't like that." I picked up a piece of bread, wanting to throw it. "He's never lied to me before."

"There is that," she agreed as she pulled on a coppery curl, straightening it all the way out. "And the fact that guy hurt you because of Kyler's never-ending sexual escapades. That's hard to get past."

"Yeah," I mumbled and popped the bread in my mouth, wondering where our waiter had disappeared to. Andrea had probably scared him away.

"But..." Andrea let go of the curl, and it bounced back into a perfect spiral. I was jealous. "That's really not his fault, right? I mean, yeah, he might've slept with a chick and pissed off a boyfriend a year ago, but do you really think that's the first time he's done that?"

"I hope so." Then I rolled my eyes. "No. That's probably not the first time."

"And I know it bothered you before—I'm not saying it didn't—but you still cared deeply for him." Her eyes met mine. "I guess what I'm getting at is that he really needs to make it up to you for putting you in that position, but I don't see any of this as being insurmountable."

A tiny flare of hope kindled in my stomach, and I smashed it. "Okay. Let's say that he didn't sleep with Sasha a couple of days ago, and I can get over the fact he didn't tell the truth about his past with her, and the shit with Zach, but I don't think what we did meant that much to him. That's the problem."

"I don't know if I agree. Look, it's been obvious to everyone that you've been madly in love with him. And it's the same for him."

"Really," I said dryly. "It was so obvious with the bus terminal that is his pants?"

Andrea snorted. "Guys are totally stupid when it comes to unrequited love. We women pine away and keep our thighs closed for the most part when we love someone we can't have. Guys swing their shit around at anything that has a hole, trying to forget the one they want."

"Wow." I laughed. "So eloquently put."

She flashed a quick grin. "It's true. Sort of like the laws of physics. It's just the way it is, which brings me to a very important question. Do you still love him?"

My heart tumbled through my chest. "I never said I loved him."

Her eyes rolled. "Okay. Stop the bullshit. Like I said, it's been obvious since I've known you. Listening to you tell me about what happened, I can hear it in your voice. Answer the question."

I was pinned by her steady stare. Andrea really needed to look into law enforcement or something. She'd never do that with her past—I got that—but damn if she didn't have the detective hardness in her voice. I had a choice right then. I could tell her what I wanted to say, or I could tell the truth. Sometimes lying was the easiest thing to do, especially when I was lying to myself. And speaking the truth out loud meant I could never take it back.

"Okay," I said. "I still love him." Once those words came out, I expected balloons and glitter to fall from the ceiling or something. Of course, that didn't happen. "I'm *in* love with him."

Andrea nodded slowly. "Then what do you want, Sydney?"

I dumped the half-eaten bread on my plate. "I don't know. Like, I guess I thought he'd try to repair the friendship or something."

"But you don't want just a friendship."

"No."

Her brow rose. "But you don't want a relationship?"

I opened my mouth.

Andrea leaned forward. "I get that you're mad, and trust

251

me, you have every right. Kyler has spent how long being the universal bicycle that had no training wheels? And he has a lot to make up for because his actions *hurt* you. And I'm not saying you even have to forgive him. Honestly, I'd totally understand if you didn't. Guys suck, Kyler among them, but…" She tapped her fingers. "But if you *are* in love with him, and *not* forgiving him hurts more than forgiving him does, Syd, and he wants to make it up to you, you'd be a fool to walk away from that."

Knots formed in my belly as I stared at my friend. Not forgiving Kyler would hurt worse in the end, even if we only remained friends. Holding on to the anger would create nothing but bitterness. But I also didn't want to be the person who gave so much of herself to someone who didn't deserve it and ended up never being whole again.

I sighed, unsure of what to do or say. "I don't know, Andrea. Maybe after some time passes, things will go back to normal." I felt stronger for saying that. Hopeful. Maybe we could move past this, eventually. That seemed more likely than Kyler professing his undying love for me. "I guess we'll just see."

"You're right. We will see."

I raised a brow at her.

Andrea leaned back, dropping her hands on her legs. "All right, well, don't hate me."

Suspicion blossomed and spread like a weed through my mind. "Why would I hate you?" A sheepish look crept into her expression. "Andrea."

She bit down on her lip and cringed. "I sort of invited guests to our dinner."

My stomach roiled. "What?"

"Well, I sort of told Tanner that we were going out to

dinner, and he made the suggestion that it would be a good idea to invite Kyler, so it's really Tanner's fault, not mine."

All I could do for several seconds was stare at her while part of me started doing squealing jumping jacks and the other part wanted to get up and run for the door. "You didn't."

"Ah…"

"Andrea!" I whispered.

She smiled tentatively. "I sort of texted them where we were, and they should be here any minute."

Chapter 22

KYLER

"This is probably the worst idea you've had in a long time." I killed the engine and sat back, clutching the keys in my hand until the jagged edges cut into my palm.

"Seriously?" Tanner snorted. "I can come up with an entire list of worse ideas, but hey, you're sober for the first time in two days. And just in time for the holidays."

Leaning my head back against the headrest, I groaned. "It still feels like someone is slamming an ice pick into my temples."

"You *were* pretty drunk," Tanner commented, reaching for the door. "Which is why I think this dinner is the best idea ever."

I rubbed my palm along my chin, frowning at the growth of stubble there. I hadn't shaved since the first night at Snowshoe. "Yeah, you'd think that, since Syd doesn't hate your guts."

Tanner rolled his eyes. "She doesn't hate your guts. I don't think that would ever be possible."

"Oh, it's possible. Trust me."

"Look, I don't know what really went down between you two, but something did. It's not the end of the world." Tanner opened the passenger door, and a wealth of frigid air streamed into the SUV. "So stop being a pussy and get out of the car."

I shot him a dirty look, but I climbed out. As I joined him on the other side, I asked the question I'd already asked a dozen times. "She's knows I'm going to be here, right?"

"Yep." Tanner opened the door and motioned me in. Once we got past the hostess, he glanced at me. "Okay. I lied. I don't think Syd knows."

"What?" I stopped in the middle of the aisle, nearly causing a waiter to slam into me. I glared at Tanner. "Are you fucking kidding me?"

Tanner clamped his hand on my shoulder, steering me away from the packed round table in my path. "Nope. Chill out. I'm sure she knows by now."

Easy for him to say "chill out," but I felt like I was walking in front of a firing squad. So many times since Syd had left Snowshoe, I'd fought the urge to call her. I wanted nothing more than to hear her voice and to see her. And yeah, my fucking stupid-ass heart was bouncing all over the place, but Syd had made herself pretty damned clear.

"You're a bastard," I grumbled, running a hand through my hair. Man, I wished I'd shaved. While I had showered, I was sure I still smelled like whiskey. That shit would be bleeding out of my pores for days to come.

I saw Andrea before I saw Syd, and my heart pounded like I'd run up and down the quad, and I was sweating like a whore in church on Sunday. Tanner got in front of me somehow, proving that I was dragging my feet.

The bastard took the seat next to Andrea, who had the biggest, fakest smile known to man on her face. Of course, I *wanted* to sit next to Sydney. I also wanted to touch her, hold her close, and kiss her. There were other things that I wanted to do to her, things that had kept me up late at night in a drunken stupor with my hand between my legs.

But I was also sure she might punch me in the balls.

Needing to pull it together, I told myself that the best thing to do was to act normal. With that in mind, I stepped beside the table and looked at Syd.

A heartbeat passed and she looked up, her large blue eyes fixed right on me, and it was like seeing Jesus. Okay. Maybe not seeing Jesus, but it was definitely like being socked in the chest and hearing angels harking.

God. Damn. She was beautiful. It wasn't that I had forgotten, but after things had ended so fucked-up between us, it felt like years instead of days since I'd seen her. Those eyes...they were astonishingly blue and clear. Stunning. There were dark smudges under them, a shade darker than her skin. I wanted to smooth them away but managed to keep my hands to myself. But then my gaze dropped to her lips, and they parted on a sharp inhale. A faint flush spread across her cheeks, and I wanted to chase it with my fingers, my mouth, my tongue... Everyone was staring at me.

Clearing my throat, I forced myself to sit and placed my hands on the table. I glanced at Syd. "Hey."

Her face was bloodred. No one blushed like she did. "Hey."

Across from me, Tanner raised a brow. Andrea started playing with a piece of bread like she was two. No one spoke, and Syd was so stiff, I thought she'd break in half.

Wow, this was awkward as hell. I needed to leave.

"So, is everyone excited about Christmas?" Andrea chirped.

Tanner looked at her and said in a deadpan voice, "I am so excited."

Her eyes narrowed shrewdly. "You don't sound excited."

"Well, I'm not twelve." Tanner cocked his head to the side. "Christmas ain't that interesting once you grow up."

"What?" she gasped, her eyes wide. "Christmas *ain't* that interesting once you grow up?"

He shrugged.

"You're un-American," she accused.

Syd's lips pursed.

Tanner looked unaffected. "Man, I just like the time off from school, and the food. That's it."

"But it means more than that." Andrea shook her head, and curls flew everywhere. "What about the presents?"

"Yeah, I don't think that's what Christmas is about," he commented.

Andrea huffed. "That *is* what Christmas is about. Anyone who says differently is trying to make themselves look all spiritual and shit. I keep it real."

My gaze slid over to Syd, and she looked at me, her brows raised. Our eyes locked, and for a moment, a sweet fucking moment, it was like it used to be. Us sitting back, listening to Andrea and Tanner annoy the living shit out of each other. We should've had popcorn when those two went at it.

But then Syd cast her eyes at her glass and started fiddling with her straw, and that was a cold reminder that things weren't normal. Syd was never this quiet, and things were rarely strained between us.

I couldn't say I regretted the time with her, though,

because I didn't. I just hated how it ended. Looking back, there were a lot of women I wished I'd kept my dick in my pants with, but Syd would never be one of them.

The waiter showed up and got our drink and food order. Small talk was made, mostly on Tanner and Andrea's end. They kept it going so there wasn't an awkward lull in conversation, but sitting here, not talking to Syd, was wrong on so many levels.

Leaning back, I looked over at her. She tipped her chin up at the same moment, and our gazes collided for another second. I sort of felt like an inept schoolboy. It was that bad. "So your lip looks a lot better."

She blinked. I was a dumbass.

"It healed up pretty quickly," she said, training her gaze on her glass. "Just a little mark."

That was good to hear. "Your jaw?"

"It doesn't hurt at all."

It seriously was a relief to hear that. Even drunk off my rocker, I'd been going out of my mind with worry for her.

"Your knuckles still look a little raw," she said, causing me to look up.

Our eyes locked and held this time. "What?"

"Your knuckles," she said in a quiet voice as she reached over to the hand I had on the table. I held my breath as she ran her fingertips over my knuckles. It was a featherlight touch, but it traveled straight through me, and I jerked. She pulled her hand back, casting her gaze to the table. "Do they hurt?"

"No." My voice sounded thick. "They don't hurt at all, baby."

Her lashes swept up, and her eyes darted across my face like she was looking for something, but then she looked across the table.

Andrea cleared her throat. "Did you guys hear that they're calling for another snowstorm next week, on New Year's Eve?"

And so that was how the conversation went for a while. Andrea or Tanner would smooth over the tense silence with some random statement, Syd and I barely said more than an entire sentence, and then the food came.

Syd had ordered a steak, but she just seemed to cut it into tiny pieces and push it around her plate with her fork.

"You're not hungry?"

She glanced up, tucking back her hair with her free hand. "I guess I ate too much bread."

My gaze went to the half loaf that remained, and I arched a brow. "Doesn't look like you ate that much."

Her fingers tightened around the handle of her knife, and I wondered if she was fantasizing about stabbing me with it. "How do you know that's not our second or third loaf?"

"It's our first," Andrea announced, stopping a deep conversation about the differences between the zombies from *The Walking Dead* and *28 Days Later*.

Syd shot her friend a look, and I hid a grin.

Andrea shrugged and turned back to Tanner. "The infected are not the same as the zombies in *The Walking Dead*."

Tanner shook his head. "Is there really a difference?"

I shook my head as she went into a deep description of the differences.

Out of the corner of my eye, I saw Syd grin as she speared a piece of steak with her fork. She glanced at me. "The infected *are* different," she whispered.

A smile pulled at my lips and tugged at my heart. "I believe you."

She met my stare for a moment and then attacked another piece of steak, dipping it into her mashed potatoes.

"Are you going to your grandparents' for Christmas?" It was a stupid question to ask. She always did, but I wanted to say something.

Syd nodded. "My parents want to leave Christmas Eve and stay the night with them. How about you?"

"Grandpa is coming down this year, doing the Christmas-morning thing with us."

"Wow. He's driving down from Morgan County by himself?"

"Yep." Pride filled my voice. "The man is as old as dirt, but he's still running around like he's twenty."

"Your grandpa is so funny. Remember when he tried to build a playground in your mom's backyard with the crane?"

I laughed. "Yeah, Mom wasn't too happy about that."

"Neither were the neighbors." Out of habit—and I knew that was what led to this—she pried half the shrimp off the skewers and placed them on my plate. She didn't even seem to realize she'd done it until she was done, but then her brows knit, and she fell silent.

I already missed the ease of conversation and felt the chill like a harsh arctic wind. "I told Mom about going to vet school."

"What?" She dropped her knife as she twisted toward me. "You did?"

Thrilled with having her full attention, I ignored Andrea and Tanner, who'd stopped arguing for five seconds. "Yeah."

"Well?" Excitement turned her eyes into shining sapphires. "What did she say?"

The dreaded conversation had happened about fifteen minutes after I'd walked through the door when I'd gotten back from Snowshoe. And approximately fifteen minutes after that, I'd started drinking. "Ah, she wasn't too thrilled about it. There were tears, but I think in the end, she knows it's what I want."

"She cried?" Syd winced. "Oh no."

I nodded. "She seems better with it now, but I think it's going to take a little bit for her to get used to it." Leaning back, I spread my legs until my thigh pressed into hers, totally on purpose, and she didn't shy away. I took that as a good sign. "I'm glad I finally got it out in the open. It's really because of you."

"Me?" she squeaked.

Tanner tilted his head to the side, his brows raised.

I was going to punch him in the face later. "Well, you know, after we talked about it, I knew I had to say something to her soon. You...you gave me the courage to do it."

Tanner choked.

I was seriously going to spin-kick him in the balls, but Syd smiled—smiled so widely and beautifully that Tanner's balls might have been safe. "That's great," she said. "I'm happy for you. Really. I know that's what you want, and you'll be great at it."

Pressure clamped down on my chest, and there was so much I needed to say. Now wasn't the right time, but I had to say something because I was two seconds from climbing all over her. "What are you doing after this?"

"Nothing," Andrea answered for her. "She's doing absolutely nothing."

Syd slowly turned to Andrea with bugged eyes, and I wanted to hug the damned girl.

"So you have nothing to do," I cut in before Syd could say anything. She turned back to me, and I felt like everything came down to this minute. If she said no, then I knew it was done. My muscles seized like I was about to hit a high slope. "Can we—"

"Kyler Quinn," a smooth, throaty voice interrupted. "Hot damn, it's going to be my lucky night."

SYDNEY

The dinner had started off in seven different circles of hell, but over the course of the meal, I'd relaxed. Not completely, because sitting next to Kyler was a true test of self-control. I was torn between wanting to crawl into his arms and wanting to kick him out of the booth.

But with him looking at me like I was the only thing he needed in his life? I was starting to side with the crawling-into-his-lap side when a voice made to get guys to drop their pants slithered over my skin like snakes.

Forcing my gaze away from Kyler's dark brown eyes, I saw a girl I barely recognized. It took me a few moments to remember her name was Corie. We'd gone to high school together. I had no idea what she'd been up to over the years, but I remembered who'd been *up* her several times in high school.

My gaze traveled over her skintight red sweater. Corie had boobs dreams were made of. She looked at me, and I knew she dismissed my presence outright. Like there was no way the fact that Kyler was sitting next to me at a table meant anything.

Any other time, this probably wouldn't have bothered me. If anything, I was used to random chicks approaching

Kyler everywhere we went. The boy was well traveled, but right now, after everything? Yeah, it did not make me feel warm or fuzzy.

Andrea muttered something under her breath as Kyler turned slowly. "Hey," he said evenly. "How've you been, Corie?"

Corie popped a hand on her hip as her red-painted lips spread into a smile. "I've been good. Haven't seen you around lately. Guess you're home for Christmas?"

"No shit," Andrea muttered under her breath, and I was sure Corie hadn't heard her.

Tanner pressed his lips together as he suddenly became invested in the food on his plate.

"Yeah, I'm home for a little while." Kyler dropped his arm along the back of the seat behind me. "Then *we're* heading back to school."

If "we're" was a hidden code for something, no one got it, especially not Corie. She tossed lovely blond waves over her shoulder and then crossed her arms. Even *my* eyes went straight to her cleavage. "I'm on break, too, from Shepherd, until the fifteenth of January. We should get together."

It was like I wasn't even sitting there.

"I don't know about that," Kyler replied diplomatically. "I'm going to be real busy, but it was good seeing you, okay?"

Corie blinked, and her lips formed a perfect O. I was doing the same thing. I couldn't even think of a time Kyler had shot down a pretty girl. Granted, it could have been because I was right there, and given our newly acquired history, he was being a little more discreet than normal.

My gaze caught Andrea's, and she had the biggest cat-that-ate-every-canary-in-the-cage grin, and I couldn't help the smirk that graced my lips.

"Well, call me. I'll make time for you, if you make time for me." Corie smiled, but it lacked the confidence of earlier. "See you around."

Kyler nodded.

After Corie bounced off somewhere, silence descended on the table, and the smirk slipped away from my lips. Unease turned the food in my stomach, and I wished I hadn't eaten what I had. Tanner was still studying his food like he was going to be tested on it. Andrea was remarkably quiet, which meant the apocalypse had started, and Kyler was staring off into the distance, a muscle working in his jaw. I didn't know exactly what made it all sink in then, but I suddenly realized, like *really* understood, that what had happened between us affected every aspect of our lives.

Even our friends.

Because right now, Tanner and Andrea were most likely experiencing a mad case of secondhand embarrassment, or they just didn't know how to handle the situation. Maybe they felt bad for me, or they felt awkward on behalf of Kyler. They were probably waiting to see how I'd react, if I'd get mad or jealous or run off in tears.

Even if Kyler and I got past this and moved on as friends, our other friends would always be uncomfortable. The weight of that knowledge settled on my shoulders, and I slumped, wanting nothing more than to go home and crawl into bed.

The truth, no matter what Andrea said or I wanted to believe, was that Kyler wasn't the kind of guy who was into commitment. And if he'd wanted to be with me, he would've called or done something after I'd left. Anything other than drinking himself into a stupor. Of course, he probably wanted to salvage our friendship. He was…he was a good guy like that.

Andrea smiled at me, and she seemed to sense how far my mood had plummeted. "You ready to get out of here?"

Ignoring Kyler's sharp look, I nodded. I didn't think at that moment there was anything I wanted more than to get the hell out of there.

Chapter 23

KYLER

The girls made a quick exit, leaving Tanner and me to our own devices. He ordered a beer, and if I weren't driving, I would've ordered an entire bottle of Jim Beam.

"That went brilliantly," I said, rubbing my temples.

Tanner snickered. "I didn't think it went that bad. Well, when Blondie showed up, that was about ten kinds of awkward, but…"

"That was just awkward?" I couldn't believe Corie had popped by our table. Syd and I seemed to have been getting somewhere and then *BAM*, a blast from the past. Perfect fucking timing. "I'm sure Syd enjoyed that."

He took a swig of his beer. "Buddy, you need to tell me what happened between you two, because a week ago, Sydney probably would've been irked about that, but she wouldn't have cared that much. So stop with the bullshit and tell me what happened."

I arched a brow at him.

Tanner winked. "Or I'll get the girl version from Andrea,

in which you will come across as a giant ass. Tell me your side of the story."

"I *am* a giant ass."

He tipped his chin down. "Do tell."

The last thing I wanted to be doing was talking girl problems with Tanner, but shit, I could tell by the way Andrea acted, she knew. He'd find out sooner or later. So I told him the basics. No way in hell was I going to go into detail, not about Syd, because that was just wrong. When I finished, I really didn't feel any better. I'd sort of confirmed how much of an ass I'd been this entire time—years of being the King of Assdom.

Tanner sat back, shaking his head slowly. "I think I need another beer to digest all that."

"Shit. You and me both." I ran a hand through my hair. "So yeah, I fucked up. Royally."

"Well, people have fucked up more than you have, bro. Trust me on that." He leaned forward, his expression serious. "The shit with Zach is fucking terrible, but you didn't know that stuff was going to happen. Sydney's a reasonable girl. She'll get over that."

"I don't think *I* can get over that." I paused, staring at the table. "The fucker *hurt* her because of what I did in my past. If it weren't for me, she never would've gone through that."

"But you didn't do that to her."

"Is there really a difference?"

"Yes," Tanner said adamantly. "It's not a huge difference. You did create the situation, but you didn't force that fucker to do anything. That's not on you, bro. It's not."

I got what he was saying, but it would take a lot to absolve me of that guilt.

"And that's not the big issue," Tanner said, eyeing me. "Did you lie to her about Sasha?"

"Shit." I raised my hands. "I really don't know. I mean, when Syd asked me about her, it was before anything went down between us. I didn't think Syd really thought of me any differently. All I said was that Sasha and I weren't like that. And we're not. We hooked up once over a year ago. I just wasn't thinking when I said it to Syd."

"Hmm, technicalities are a bitch." Tanner finished off his beer, his eyes narrowed. "Did you really think Sydney didn't have it bad for you?"

"No. I didn't. I couldn't think that, because if…"

"If she did, then it would ruin your friendship. I get that, but damn, that girl…you must've been rocking some serious denial." He shrugged. "Makes sense, though—you secretly wanting her and shit."

"It does?"

Tanner laughed. "Yeah, man, you didn't like it if a guy even looked in her direction. Hell, if *I* looked at her for too long, you'd get pissed. And when you went after Nate? That's some pretty hard-core 'friendship' right there."

"Shut up," I growled.

He smirked. "So what are you going to do? Be a pussy, or fix this?"

"Excuse me?" I shook my head. "Dude, you're lucky I like you."

"You're lucky I don't bullshit around." He winked as he pulled the sleeve of his sweater down, covering one of the intricate tattoos etched into his arm. "Look. I'm being serious. You love this girl, right?"

For once in my life, I didn't hesitate. "Yes. I love her, Tanner." Holy shit, that was the first time I'd said it out loud. It shook me up, and my voice was thick. "I love her more than anything."

"Then what's the deal?"

I stared at him. "I'm pretty sure I listed all the problems."

"You listed a bunch of unfortunate shit is what you did. Nothing unfixable. It isn't like you did something unforgivable. It's not like one of you two is dead."

"Damn…" And that was all I could say.

Tanner sighed. "A lot of people would kill to have the chance to be with the one they love. Don't mess it up."

He never really talked about his past, and other than the weirdness between him and Andrea, he didn't really talk to girls. Slipping in and out of their beds? That was more up Tanner's alley. "What about you?" I asked.

"Me?" He laughed again. "I am allergic to that shit. Love? Nope. All I've seen that do is tear people down and fuck up lives. I don't want any part of that."

My brows shot up in surprise. "Whoa. That's…that's positive."

"Whatever. We aren't talking about me, and we aren't going to, so get that look off your face."

I raised my hands. "Message received."

Tanner cocked his head to the side and gave me a tight smile. "Anyway, all I'm saying is, why are you still sitting here talking to me?"

Staring at him for a moment, I shrugged. "Who else is going to drive your grumpy ass home?"

SYDNEY

After changing into my pajama bottoms, I tugged a long, thick cardigan on over my tank top as I padded downstairs

269

in my slippers. Feeling incredibly in need of my mom, I was disappointed to find her already passed out on the couch next to Dad, the multicolored lights from the Christmas tree flashing over their forms. I resisted the urge to wiggle between them and demand attention.

I headed into the kitchen and grabbed the box of cocoa out of the cabinet, preparing it in a ceramic mug. Once done, I took my chocolate goodness upstairs and set it on my nightstand to cool down. I pulled my hair up into a messy bun as I shuffled over to the bookcase. What I needed was to lose myself in a good book—one with tons of sex and angst, complete with an unbelievable happily-ever-after that made me love and hate the book at the same time.

As my gaze traveled over the spines, some straight and others warped, my brain wandered right into annoying territory. It had a name—Kyler. God. I didn't want to think about him. I didn't want to think about how he'd looked at me when I'd left with Andrea, like I'd hurt his feelings or something.

Pulling out an old favorite, I headed back to my bed and plopped down. I dropped the book on the bedspread and picked up my hot cocoa, wishing I'd had the foresight to grab some of those tiny marshmallows.

I tried getting into the book, but I found myself reading the same paragraph two or three times and still having no idea what I was reading. Flopping onto my back, I placed my arms over my face and groaned. I wanted to cry, to scream, to rage, and to shove my head under a pillow.

In a weird way, it felt like a year had passed since I'd left for Snowshoe. So much had changed in such a short span of time. Had it really only been last week that I'd briefly considered seeing if Paul was interested in me? Only a week since my heart had been slightly bruised but completely whole? Now I couldn't even think about going out with anyone.

And my heart was utterly demolished.

What was I supposed to do from here? Try to pretend like nothing had happened? That wasn't going to work. Avoid Kyler? That would be so hard, almost impossible to consider. I squeezed my eyes shut against the tears. How could I avoid him when he was such an integral part of my life?

What if Kyler now thought I was as frigid as Nate had claimed?

Rolling over, I shoved my face in the pillow. I was going to drive myself crazy because I didn't have answers for any of this. And there'd be no—

Tap.

I lifted myself onto my elbows and frowned. Had I already gone crazy? Because I swore I'd heard a—

Tap.

Pushing onto my knees, I twisted, scanning the room. I didn't see anything that could have made that noise.

"Okay," I whispered, sliding off the bed. I walked to the center of the room and stood completely still.

Tap.

I jumped.

Oh my God, what if my house was haunted now? Or what if I was about to pull some *Black Swan* shit? What if—

Tap.

I whipped around. Aha! It was coming from my bedroom window…two floors off the ground. What in the world?

And then it hit me. The sound—oh, holy baby Jesus in a manger—the sound was familiar. It wasn't a ghost, but insanity was still an option because it couldn't be what I thought it was.

Years ago, Kyler had used to throw rocks before he'd climbed the massive walnut tree outside my bedroom window. So cliché and ridiculous, but he'd done it up until middle school.

It couldn't be.

My legs shook as I took a step forward and then two. I reached the window, and with trembling hands, I parted the filmy white curtains. A second later, a small rock smacked off the thick glass of the bottom part of the window, making me jump.

I froze as my heart sped up, and then I lurched forward, unlocking the tiny latch and lifting the window. I slid the screen up next and leaned out into the freezing December air.

And my heart skipped a beat.

Kyler stood below, next to the lit wire reindeer, a knit cap pulled low, one arm raised. He let go a second before he saw me. "Oh shit!"

I jumped back as a small pebble zoomed past my face. *Holy crap.* I put my hand over my racing heart and gingerly approached the window again. I leaned out.

Kyler waved his arm. "Sorry about that!"

"It's okay." This was really surreal. Maybe I was dreaming. "What are you doing, Kyler?"

"Talking to you."

"I can see that. Why…why didn't you call me?" Because that seemed like the easiest way to talk to me.

He shuffled from one foot to the other, huddled in his jacket. "I needed to talk to you face-to-face."

The porch light came on, and I winced. A face-to-face conversation was so not possible with him standing outside and with obviously one, if not both, of my parents awake. "Kyler—"

"Hold on," he called out. "I'm coming up."

I'm coming up? Then I realized he wasn't using the door. Oh dear Lord, he was climbing the tree. He was going to kill himself! I leaned out the window, my breath puffing small white clouds in front of my face as he shimmied up the trunk. "Kyler, are you insane?"

"No. Yes." He pulled himself up on the first thick limb. Straightening, he glanced down with a frown. "Well, this is harder than I remember."

My mouth dropped open. "Maybe you should just go back down and use the front door, like, I don't know? A normal person would?"

"I'm already halfway there." He got his foot in a groove and propelled himself up to the limb closest to my window. Wrapping his hands around it, he looked at me. His cheeks were rosy from the cold, and his eyes glittered in the moonlight. "If I fall and break my neck, will you say something nice at my funeral? Like, 'Kyler was usually more graceful'?"

"Oh my God…"

Kyler chuckled as he pulled himself up so he was crouched against the massive trunk, holding on to the tree above him. "Don't worry. I got this."

My gaze dropped to the snow-covered, *hard* ground below. I wasn't so sure about this. "Why didn't you just knock on the door?"

He cocked his head to the side, like he hadn't thought of that. "I didn't think you'd answer."

"I would've answered," I said.

"Too late now." He winked, and my heart tumbled. "You might want to move back."

Backing up, I held my breath as he eased out on the

limb, causing half the tree to rattle like dry bones. Oh God, I didn't want to watch this. I wanted to close my eyes as he crawled near the edge, stopped, and then peered down. He lifted his head, appearing to judge the distance.

My heart seized up. "Kyler, don't—" Too late.

Kyler half jumped, half threw himself toward my open window. I was a wuss. Closing my eyes, I balled my hands near my chest and let out a little shriek. There was a sound of flesh hitting wood, and my eyes flew open. He came through the open window, landing on his feet like a damned cat. He stumbled, though, and banged into my desk, causing my books and computer to shake.

He held his hands out to his sides and looked around slowly before his gaze settled on me. "I am awesome."

I could barely breathe. "Yeah."

A knock sounded on my bedroom door a second before it opened. Dad popped his head in, his eyes wide. "I'm just making sure he made it up here alive."

I nodded, and Kyler flashed a grin. "I'm in one piece."

"That's good to see." Dad started to close the door, then stopped. "Next time, use the front door, Kyler."

"Yes, sir," Kyler said.

Shaking his head, Dad closed the door, and Kyler and I were alone in my bedroom. It wouldn't be the first time. When we'd been home over fall break a few months ago, he'd been in here, but now?

It felt completely different.

Having him in here, so close to the bed—and with me not wearing a bra or panties under my clothes—made my skin flush. This spelled trouble.

Kyler pulled off his knit hat, and then he paused halfway through taking off his jacket. "Do you mind?"

I shook my head as I pulled the edges of my cardigan closed.

Lean muscles flexed as he stripped off the black jacket and draped it over the chair at my desk. Then he turned to me, and the air leaked out of my lungs. He had never looked so...unconfident and vulnerable. His throat worked several times, and then he sat on my desk chair and let out a long breath.

"We need to talk," he said, resting his hands on his knees.

"I know," I whispered because there was no point in lying or delaying the inevitable. I couldn't sit, so I stood. "I'm sorry about how I left Snowshoe without saying anything. I just needed to get out of there."

He nodded. "I can understand that."

I thought about what Andrea had said about Zach and what he'd done. Guilt burned like acid in my belly. "I...I shouldn't have said some of the things I said to you about Zach. That wasn't your fault. Not really, and it was low of me to put that on you, so I'm sorry."

Kyler blinked. "*You're* apologizing?"

The sound of disbelief in his voice unnerved me. Like he didn't want my apology, like it was too late for that. "Yes. I shouldn't have said that to you. And what you did a year ago—"

"Hold up." Kyler raised his hand. "You can't be serious."

I sucked in a deep breath, but it got stuck in my throat. My heart pounded fast, and suddenly I did need to sit. I sat on the edge of the bed, feeling like we were about to break up...except we weren't together.

Kyler toed himself forward, the wheels of the chair squeaking over the hardwood floor. "You have absolutely no reason to apologize, Syd. 'I'm sorry' shouldn't even cross your lips."

"I shouldn't?"

"No." He rubbed a hand over the scruff on his jaw. "All this is my fault. I fucked up, Syd. I fucked up so bad, so many times, that I shouldn't even be sitting here. You shouldn't even be talking to me."

"Oh?" I wasn't sure how to process that.

He let out a shaky breath, and then he straightened. I tensed because he had this look like he was steeling himself. Like he was about to rip off a bandage, and maybe that was why he was here. To tell me that nothing should've happened between us, that we should've stayed just friends, and he was sorry for allowing it to go any further. I didn't want to hear it, but I knew I needed to. It was going to hurt—hurt like hell. I thought of Nate and what he had said, and I wanted to crawl under the bed, but I forced myself to sit there. No more running. No more hiding. Life was imperfect. This was going to be one of those moments.

Our gazes locked.

"I'm sorry for a lot of things," Kyler started, holding my gaze. "I wish that you hadn't had to go through what you did with Zach. He hurt you. I know you say you're okay, but he put his hands on you, and it was because of something I had done. I'll never forgive myself for that."

"That wasn't your fault." The earlier guilt grew like a noxious weed. "Please don't think that. The guy was obviously unstable—"

"I know, but it's going to take me a lot to get over that," he admitted openly. "I keep reliving the whole thing, and every time I think about you getting hurt, it kills me a little. I'm serious and I'm so sorry, Syd. I am so sorry."

My heart hurt hearing him talk like that. "Kyler…"

"But that's not what I'm most sorry for," he continued,

and I thought, *Here it comes.* I tried my best to prepare myself, but a lump was already growing in my throat. Kyler ran his hands through his hair. "I'm most sorry for hurting you. I know I have. I know I've hurt you before with other girls. I hurt you by not being upfront about Sasha. I didn't mean to lie. I just wasn't thinking because Sasha and I aren't like that now, but I should've told you that we did hook up in the past. And I didn't sleep with her again. I sure as hell didn't sleep with her when I went to her cabin to help her with the busted windows—"

"Busted windows?" I repeated numbly.

"Zach had bashed her windows the night before. She lives on her own up there and needed help," he explained. "But I wish I hadn't helped her. I should have been there for you, and I wasn't. I can't forgive myself for that."

I closed my eyes, feeling so much that I didn't know where to start. Too many emotions whirled inside me to really digest all this. "Oh, Kyler..."

"And I don't expect my apology to make a damned bit of difference. Trust me," he rushed on, and I opened my eyes, blinking back hot tears. "I know there is a lot for me to make up for. There've been times I ditched you to go to the movies with another girl, broke plans to get laid, that kind of thing. Because that's all I was about—screwing, you know? And then there was prom. I didn't even dance with you. And this whole time, you were right there beside me, and I'm..." He shook his head. "I'm fucking rambling. I probably can't fix any of that. I won't blame you if you tell me to get the fuck out of this house, but just know there are a lot of things I wish I could do over, but there is one thing I'll never regret."

I stilled, my thoughts and pulse racing.

Kyler stood and walked over to me, kneeling. He tipped his head back so he looked me straight in the eyes when he said the next words. "I will never regret being with you, Syd. *Never*. And I wish I could go back and relive those hours. I wish I could go back in time, and instead of hooking up with some chick, I'd man up and tell you how I really felt for you, how I've *always* felt for you."

I opened my mouth and gasped, but there were no words. I searched his striking face, and he stared back, open and right there—finally, *right there* in front of me. My heart was swelling and bursting at once. Hope burned as bright as the North Star. "How you've always felt?"

"I've loved you my entire life," he said, his eyes locked on mine. "And I would love you for the rest of my life if you'd let me, Syd."

Chapter 24

KYLER

Once those words left my mouth, I knew it was the right thing to say. There was no doubt in my mind. It was what I should've said years ago, from the first moment I'd realized how deep my feelings for her ran. And there was a good chance it was too late now, but a weight lifted off my shoulders. I'd spilled the truth. I didn't expect my apologies to be enough right now, but telling her how I felt could open a door for later. At least that was what I hoped. But the longer Syd was quiet, the more worried I became. Syd looked a little dumbstruck. She didn't move. Her hands were limp in her lap, her palms up. She didn't say anything. Her pretty, rosy lips were parted. She just stared at me.

It felt like I'd been punched in the gonads. Had I messed up so badly that my declaration of love had blown her mind in all the wrong ways? Aw, man, I didn't like this feeling. Most likely I deserved it, but that didn't make it easier to swallow, especially when her eyes turned glassy, as if she were fighting tears.

I hadn't planned on that. Fuck.

"Syd, baby, say something, please." I dropped my hands on my thighs to stop myself from grabbing her. "*Please.*"

She gave a little shake of her head, causing a few shorter strands to slip free from her bun. Dark tendrils brushed her temples and the nape of her neck. Then she leaned forward. Before I knew what she was doing, she cupped my cheeks with trembling hands.

Okay. This was good. This was heading somewhere I'd—

"I want to strangle you," she said, her voice hoarse.

All right, that wasn't good. Not at all.

"You have no idea how badly I want to kick you right now," she added.

And that was worse. This wasn't—

"I love you," she said, and she swallowed. "I've loved you since you pushed me down on the playground. I swear—I've loved you since then."

"I...what?" I stared at her. "What did you just say?"

Syd kissed me.

Her lips were soft against mine; the touch was hesitant and breathtakingly *her* and so damned sweet. I inhaled her through the kiss, pulling her deep into me. My brain shut down as I reveled in her kiss, like a dog rolling onto his back for a belly rub. I rose without thinking, my hands falling to her hips. She grabbed my upper arms, her fingers digging into my sweater in a way that had my entire body throbbing.

"Say it again," I pleaded.

Her lips curved up at the corners. "I love you, Kyler."

A shudder rolled through me. I lifted her and set her down farther on the bed. I lay over her, kissing her back. In seconds our bodies were flush with each other. My tongue swept past her lips, and she moaned, sending a thrill through me. Her hands ran down my back, and mine found their way under the heavy sweater, against her camisole. She arched, as if willing my hand to travel farther north. I rose slightly, my gaze drifting over her sweetly flushed face, her long, graceful neck, and the hard tips of her breasts straining against the thin material. My body shook with the effort to not strip her bare.

Oh fuck.

My hand looked incredibly large splayed across her stomach, directly under her breasts. Whoa. I needed to slow it down, but I was aching to be inside her, to have nothing between us.

Syd reached up, running the tips of her fingers along my jaw. I pressed into the gesture, closing my eyes as I willed my heart to slow down. "You love me?" she asked.

"Always," I said, pressing my lips to the center of her palm. "I know I've had a shitty way of showing it, but I've loved you since you made me eat mud pie."

She trailed her hand to my chest, stopping above my heart. "Yeah, I'd say it's a pretty weird way."

I opened my eyes, ready to apologize more. Then I saw the soft smile on her face, and my heart actually jumped in my chest. I opened my mouth, but I was beyond words as my gaze traveled over her face. "Honest?"

"Honest," she whispered.

"I really didn't think you saw me as anything other than a friend." I lowered my head, kissing her lips because they looked like they were lonely. "And I didn't realize I wanted more until you got with Nate, and I figured by then it was too late. Even after you guys broke up, it seemed like I'd missed my chance."

Her brows pulled down. "Why didn't you ever say anything?"

"Why didn't you?"

She pursed her lips. "The same as you. I didn't think you saw me as anything other than a friend and the…"

"I know. The girls…" I pressed my forehead against hers. "I thought I couldn't have you, so I wanted to forget about how I felt. It was a terrible idea."

Her eyes narrowed. "Yeah, it was."

My past really took the "horn" out of "horny." "I wish I could go back and change those things. I wish—"

She placed a finger on my lips, a finger that smelled of cocoa. "It's in the past. There's nothing we can do about that. And hey, I could've said something. Developed some lady balls."

"Lady balls?" I raised my brows.

"Uh-huh."

I made a face as I eased onto my side beside her. "I really don't want to think of you with balls, Syd."

She giggled then, and the sound brought a smile to my face.

I caught the light, happy sound with my lips. "If you had, I would've…" I shook my head. "It doesn't matter. It's about what I'll do now. That's all that matters. I'll spend the rest of my life making up for it. I promise."

At first I thought I had said the wrong thing. Tears welled in her eyes quickly, and she rolled onto her side, burying her face against my chest. Oh shit, I had most definitely said something wrong. That quickly. Wow. That had to be a record. "Hey." I slid my fingers under her chin. "What's going on?"

She fought me but gradually let me lift her head. "I'm sorry. It's nothing you did. I'm just…really emotional right now."

That wasn't a good enough answer for me. Sitting up, I pulled her into my lap, and she settled against me. "Syd…"

Wiping at her cheeks, she laughed softly. "They're happy tears. I swear. It's just that I never thought this would happen. Not really, and I thought…I thought you regretted being with me, and that's why you wanted to talk. That you thought I was frigid, like Nate—"

"Whoa. Wait." I tipped her face toward mine. "You're the exact opposite of that, and I never once even thought that could be true. Man, I want to break his jaw all over again. I can't believe you still worry about that."

She sniffled. "I know it's stupid."

"It's not stupid." I brushed a lone tear off her cheek.

She leaned into me, wrapping her arms around my waist. "It *is* stupid. I let that get to me for how many years? And I guess that's why I was so ready to believe you were with Sasha, and I overreacted."

"You didn't overreact." I held her tight, resting my chin atop her head. God. I hadn't realized how good holding her would feel until I was doing it. "It looked bad. I deserved everything you said."

"Kyler." She sighed.

"I know." I laughed. "It's in the past, right?" When she nodded, I resisted the urge to squeeze her. "You know what else is in the past?"

"What?"

"These damned teddy bears on your bed. I think you've had the brown one since you were a kid. It's probably covered in your germs."

Syd pulled back, smacking me on my chest. "No, it's not, you ass!"

Laughing, I leaned back among the bears, knocking

283

most of them on the floor as I brought her down with me. I turned so we were face-to-face, lying side by side. "Hey." I reached around and picked up a ragged red one. "Is this the one I got you for your birthday years ago? You kept it?"

"Yeah." She snatched it away from me, holding it between our chests. "Of course I kept it."

A good dose of pressure filled my chest. I didn't say anything as I watched her.

"What?" she asked, her eyes on mine.

Sometimes words weren't enough—they couldn't cover the feeling. This was one of those times. So I closed the distance and kissed her, putting everything I felt for her, every promise I wanted to make, into that one kiss. When I pulled back, her eyes were glazed over, and I wanted to throw that bear across the room and get all over her.

Parents downstairs and bedroom door unlocked? Not going to happen. And besides, I was just fucking thrilled to be here with her.

"This is the best early Christmas gift I've ever gotten," I told her.

Her bright smile sucker punched me. "I think that's the smartest thing you've ever said, and I'd have to agree."

"Uh-huh?" I caught a piece of her hair and twisted it around my finger. "I'm so lucky. I know that. So damned lucky to have your love."

She wiggled closer, and the bear was smushed between us. She kissed me in a way no other person ever could because she was Syd. I cupped the back of her neck, holding her there as I took control of the kiss. It wasn't long before the bear ended up on the floor and our arms and legs were tangled. We were making out like two teenagers sneaking a few seconds. She was under me, her hips rocking against mine, urging me on. With how thin her bottoms were, it was like having almost nothing there. Need was driving me insane, pounding through my veins, and I didn't want to stop, even though I knew it couldn't go any further than this. And it was *too good* to stop, and the way her body moved against mine was too perfect, and her soft, barely audible moans were too sweet to pass up.

I didn't know how long we stayed like that, kissing and touching, whispering to each other and laughing. It was late when I looked at the clock.

"Can you stay a little longer?" she asked.

I doubted her dad would appreciate finding me in her bed in the morning, but I couldn't refuse her. "How about I stay until you fall asleep?"

"Perfect," she murmured, resting her cheek on my chest. "Just use the front door when you leave."

Smiling, I smoothed my hand down her back, loving the way she moved closer to me, fitting her body to mine like we were made for each other. Hell, I thought we really were, and it had just taken me a long-ass time to realize it. But I finally had, and that was what mattered.

I loved her. God, I loved her so much. I couldn't believe I'd made it this long without telling her. I was an idiot, but I was one hell of a lucky idiot.

Chapter 25

SYDNEY

Ever since I was a little girl, I'd always been more excited about Christmas Eve than Christmas Day. There was something about the anticipation, of knowing what awaited me the very next day, of wanting time to pass quickly and at the same time wanting it to slow down.

This year was no different, but it was.

I couldn't stop smiling, and I was sure I probably looked half-stupid to my mom and dad as I made pecan candies to take over to my grandparents' house. Several times I found myself not concentrating, daydreaming while I was placing the caramel candies on the pretzel squares.

Things seemed surreal. I guessed after spending so long wanting something—*someone*—when it finally happened, I almost didn't believe it. I kept waiting to wake up...but it was real.

Kyler loved me.

He'd been gone by the time I had woken up yesterday, but the slight scent of the cologne he wore and the outdoorsy scent that was uniquely his had lingered on my pillows. He'd left me a note, saying that he'd be back over and that he would use the front door when he left.

Right after lunch, he'd shown up, and he hadn't left until after dinner. My parents hadn't seemed surprised to see him, and they also seemed happy to see the change in our relationship. Mom had been pro-Kyler-and-Sydney since we'd been in high school, so seeing us together was probably making her year.

It sure as hell was making mine.

"Honey." Mom laughed, drawing my attention. "What are you doing?"

Frowning, I glanced down, and then I laughed outright. I'd stacked three pieces of caramel on top of one pretzel. Plucking them off, I set them aside. "Whoops."

"Uh-huh," Mom said with a knowing look on her face. "Your head is just not attached to your shoulders."

"Nope," I admitted, arranging the pretzels and candies on a baking sheet. "I probably shouldn't be doing this."

"You have to." Mom washed her hands. The kitchen smelled of the stuffing she'd made to take with us. "Your grandfather will hit someone with his cane if we don't have these candies."

Not doing this was almost worth seeing my grandfather chasing people down with a cane. I popped the candies in the oven, setting the time for three minutes, long enough to get the chocolate and caramel all gooey.

"So…" Mom began, staring out the window above the sink. Blue-tinted shadows grew longer across the snow as the sun set. We'd have to hit the road soon, since we had to drop some of the food off at church before heading to my grandparents'.

I arched a brow, waiting.

Mom grinned. "You and Kyler seemed awful chummy yesterday."

Here we go. "Mom, people don't say 'chummy' anymore."

She pinned me with a look as she wrapped tinfoil over the large bowl of stuffing. I was sure it wasn't sanitary to make stuffing for the turkey the night before, but my family had been doing it for years. "I use it, therefore people use it."

I grinned.

She sighed. "Are you going to fess up?"

"Fess up to what?" I asked innocently. Mom crossed her arms. I giggled. "Okay. Kyler and I are...together."

"I figured that much," she said dryly. "But I'd prefer to know the details."

The timer buzzed, and I grabbed a mitt. Opening the oven door, I pulled out the baking sheet. Moving quickly, I grabbed the bag of pecans and started placing them on the warm, semi-melted candies. "We're together," I told her, sneaking a pecan. "I'm not sure how else to say that."

Mom popped her hip against the counter. "Well, what made this come about?"

I *so* was not telling her how it had happened. Moving on to the second row of candies, I felt my face flush. "Things just sort of happened, and we both admitted we had feelings for each other. You know, more-than-just-friends kind of feelings. It was time."

She didn't say anything, and I glanced over at her. She was teary-eyed.

I paused with the pecans. "Mom."

"What?" She blinked rapidly and then laughed. "I'm sorry. It's just that I always knew you cared about that boy more than you let on and that Kyler felt the same way toward you. I'm happy you two finally recognized that in each other." She paused, then added, "Took long enough."

I frowned as I hastily added the rest of the pecans before the candies cooled. "I'm beginning to think Kyler and I were the only ones who didn't notice it sooner."

"I think so." She walked over and kissed my cheek. "He's a good boy, honey. I couldn't be happier for you."

My lips split in a wide smile. "I'm happy. I really am." And then I was happy-happy less than half an hour later, when Dad announced Kyler had pulled into the driveway beside their car. He hadn't texted, and I hadn't planned on seeing him tonight, but I loved how comfortable he was with just swinging by. I popped the lid on the plastic container I'd put the candies in, and then I raced through the house nearly knocking over my mom. I opened the door before Kyler could ring the doorbell and literally threw myself into his arms.

He caught me at the last moment, wrapping his arms around my waist as he stepped back to balance the unexpected weight. "Hey," he said, holding me tight. "You're happy to see me."

"I'm always happy to see you." I looped my arms around his neck as I slid down his front, and his hands dropped to my hips.

He made a sound deep in his throat as he pressed his lips to the sensitive spot under my ear. Then he said, in a low voice that simmered my blood, "You greet me like that more often, and we'll never make it into the house."

Heat swamped me, and it was an effort to pull away, but I didn't get far. He slid his arms around my waist, his half grin devious. "Whatcha doing here?" I asked, eyeing the backpack slung over his shoulder.

"I wanted to see you." Kyler kissed my forehead. "I have a surprise for you."

Excitement bubbled. "You do?"

"Yeah," he said, then looked over my head.

I turned in his embrace, finding my mom in the doorway, pulling on her jacket. Dad was behind her, his arms full of containers. We'd loaded the presents and our overnight bags in the car earlier. Disappointment filled me. "We're leaving now?"

"Your mother and I are." My dad winked. "We'll drop the food off at the church and set things up there. Kyler will bring you up to your grandparents'."

I faced Kyler, my brows raised. "Really?"

He winked. "I talked to your parents yesterday."

My disappointment vanished in an instant, but I couldn't help but tease him. "What if I want to leave now? Awful confident of you."

Kyler smirked. "You want to spend time with me. Don't even lie."

I rolled my eyes.

Mom eased past us, kissing my cheek and then Kyler's. "Be careful when you drive out. The roads are still icy."

"Get inside," Dad grumbled. "It's freezing out here, and you don't have a jacket on."

I barely felt the cold temps, not when I was standing this close to Kyler. We promised not to wreck and die on the way to my grandparents' house, and then we headed inside.

"I am happy you came by," I said as Kyler put the backpack on the floor and stripped off his jacket, draping it over the back of the couch.

He swaggered over to me, placing his hands on my waist. "I know."

"You're cocky."

"I'm right."

I rose onto my tiptoes. "Then again, it was between you and my grandparents, so…"

"Nice." He laughed, and then he kissed me—kissed me in a way that left me breathless, made me forget it was Christmas Eve, which seemed impossible but totally was with his lips moving against mine. I clutched his arms, wondering how we'd gone this long without doing this.

Kyler sat on the couch, by his backpack, and pulled me into his lap. "Mom wants to know if you'll come by tomorrow and say hi."

"I can come over tomorrow evening, if that works."

"Whenever." He slid his hands up my back, causing me to shiver. "Tanner called me this morning to see what I was doing for New Year's Eve."

I hadn't even thought about that. My mind was too occupied with the present.

One of his hands traveled over my hip, resting on my denim-clad thigh. "I told him I had to ask you."

"You did?" I couldn't help the smile spreading across my lips, and I didn't even try to hide it. "What did he say to that?"

Kyler grinned in return. "He said, and I quote, 'It's about damn time, you asshole,' and then told me to let him know."

I laughed. "Tanner's one smart guy."

"And I'm one lucky asshole." He cupped the back of my neck with one hand and tugged me closer so that when he spoke next, his lips brushed mine. "You're too good for me, baby. One day you're going to realize that and kick my ass to the curb."

"That's not going to happen." I kissed him, and his grip

on my thigh tightened. "Unless you do something stupid, but I don't think that's going to happen. You've hit your lifetime of stupid already."

"Ha. Smart-ass."

I gave him a cheeky grin. "I'd know."

"You would." And then he lifted me out of his lap, placing me on the couch beside him. He reached for the backpack. "Before I forget, I brought over the presents Mom got us."

"Oh." I'd totally forgotten about them. I made grabby fingers at the backpack.

Kyler grinned as he handed over the package with my name on it. Both of them were identical, and I was curious to see what his mom had done. Turning the present over, I slipped my fingers under the tape along the seam in the wrapping paper. I tore the colorful red-and-green paper off as Kyler did the same.

I ended up staring at the black velvet back of a picture frame. I flipped it over and drew in a shaky breath. It was an iron frame with the words "This Is Forever" inscribed along the top. The picture...oh wow, the picture brought a rush of tears to my eyes.

It was a picture of Kyler and me in the third grade. Our school had had what they'd called "Friendship Day" where friends wore matching clothes. Kyler and I had our arms over each other's shoulders, wearing cheesy grins and matching shirts my mom had made for the event that had said, "This Is Forever." Kyler probably would have loved to forget he'd ever worn a shirt like that, and he'd taken a decent amount of teasing from the other boys, but I'd been so happy that day. Even though he'd protested wearing it, he had. I didn't remember our picture being taken, but there it was, a goofy moment captured forever.

Man, I was turning into a crybaby. Seriously. I needed help.

Drawing in a shaky breath, I glanced at Kyler. He was holding an identical picture and frame. He was silent. I nudged him with my elbow. "I bet you forgot about this."

"No," he said. "I hadn't. I've seen the pic a couple of times."

Surprise flickered through me. "You have?"

Kyler nodded. "Mom loves to pull it out whenever family comes over. Funny that she gave us this now, all things considered." He looked at me. "Almost like she knew we'd finally figure this out, huh?"

"Yeah." I smiled, smoothing my fingers along the edges of the frame. "I love it. Seriously. I really do."

"Same here." He slipped the picture into his backpack. "I don't want to forget it."

I couldn't figure out if he really did like the picture or not, but I stopped myself from overanalyzing it. I gathered the wrapping paper and carried it into the kitchen, disposing of it in the trash. When I returned to the living room, he was standing in front of the Christmas tree. The present I'd gotten him a few weeks ago was still nestled underneath.

"You're not getting your present right now," I told him.

He turned to me, a mysterious grin etched across his lips and his dark brown eyes intense. "There's something I want right now, and it's not what's under the tree."

Warmth stole through my veins, and liquid heat pooled low in my belly. "And what would that be?"

"I can give you one hint."

I was already breathless. "Okay."

Kyler prowled up to me, placing his hands on my hips once more. He tugged me against him, fitting his hips against mine. I could feel him through our clothes. "That's your hint."

Shivers coursed through me, and the tips of my breasts tightened under my sweater and bra. "I think I know what you want."

"You do?" His lips brushed across my forehead and over my temple. My body relaxed and tensed all at once. "What do I want?"

I gripped his arms, and his muscles flexed under my touch. "Me?"

"Bingo," he growled, and who knew someone could make *that* word sound sexy? "I want you."

And those last three words were the sexiest words thrown together in the human language. Then Kyler kissed me, and I stopped thinking about words and languages because there was nothing beyond how smooth and firm his lips felt against mine. My senses snapped alive, shooting hot fire through my veins as his tongue expertly slipped past my lips.

Good Lord, Kyler knew how to kiss.

A sexual charge thrummed through me as his hold on my hips tightened. Without breaking the kiss, he lifted me, and I wrapped my legs around his narrow hips.

"Good girl," he murmured against my lips. And then he started walking. When he hit the stairs, I knew where he was heading, and I *so* approved.

My bedroom door was ajar, and Kyler turned sideways, nudging it all the way open. He put me on my feet beside the bed and then closed the door.

"Lock it," I said. No one else was home right now, but why take the chance?

He grinned, flipping the lock, and then turned to me. Our eyes met, and excitement hummed through me. I reached down, wrapping my fingers under the hem of my sweater and pulling it over my head. I let it fall to the floor.

Kyler's eyes flared. "God. Damn."

I flushed as I bit down on my lower lip, flicking the button on my jeans. He took a step forward and gripped the waistband.

"I'm impatient," he grumbled, and he was. In one quick motion, he swept the jeans and socks right off me. Standing before him in my bra and panties was suddenly easier than I had imagined it ever could be. "You're beautiful."

That helped.

His clothes came off rather quickly, and I got caught up staring at the hard dips and planes of his stomach. I touched him, slipping my hand under the band of his boxers. "You're not too bad—"

My words were cut off by the sheer intensity of the way he kissed me. His hands went to unhook my bra, then to my panties. He stripped me bare, and then we were a tangled mess of flesh on my bed.

I moaned against his mouth as his hand slipped between my thighs, his fingers brushing over the wet cleft. His kisses were intoxicating and addictive. Since he timed the thrusts of his tongue with the plunge of his finger, I was quickly on the verge of coming apart, and when his thumb pressed against the bundle of nerves, I tumbled right over the edge.

In the midst of the shattering release, he slid into me, skin against skin. Sensation roared through me, a feeling I'd never get used to as long as I lived. The powerful cords of the muscles along his back bulged under my hands. He rocked into me, a deep invasion that curled my toes and had my back arching.

"I love you," he said, and he kissed me again. Feral. Possessive.

I gasped out, "I love you, too."

And then I was incapable of talking. A sharp swirl of tingles spread over me as his hips moved fiercely, bringing me closer and closer to the edge once more. He moved fast and hard, his face beautifully strained. His mouth pressed to mine as my ankles locked around his back, and then it hit us both at the same time. Our bodies shuddered together, our names on each other's lips. It was a stunning moment that threw me up so high, I wasn't sure I would ever come back down.

Afterward—long, long afterward—we snuggled together under the covers. He was tracing idle circles along the curve of my spine, and I was content listening to his heart. It was quiet and peaceful, making me think of that one Christmas rhyme.

I laughed because that was wholly inappropriate.

"What?" Kyler's hand stilled.

Giggling, I pressed a kiss to his chest. "I was just thinking of the Christmas poem 'Night Before Christmas,' and it made me laugh."

"You're weird."

"I know." I lifted my head so my chin rested on his chest. "But you love me?"

His lips tipped up at the corners. "I love you as much as a kid loves Santa."

I laughed. "That's serious."

"Hard-core," he murmured, tucking my hair back from my face. "Though, I have to say, what we just did was the best Christmas present ever."

I flushed with pleasure. "Well, if you're nice, you'll get another present."

His brows rose. "What if I'm naughty?" My mind went

straight to the gutter, and Kyler must've sensed it because he chuckled deeply, and the sound rumbled through me. "I like where this conversation is going."

"I bet you do."

"I could pretend I was Santa. You can sit on my lap and tell me what you want for Christmas."

I laughed again. "That sounds like it would only benefit you."

"Hence the sitting-on-my-lap part. Naked."

Lifting myself, I kissed his slightly parted lips. That led to more kisses and more touching, which led to me straddling his hips, and before too long, we both were beyond talking. We explored each other like it was our first time, and we took things slower, making the experience more tender and intimate, but the results were just as beautifully breathtaking.

Much later, when it was time for us to leave, he stood to find his clothes, and I admired the nice view I was getting of his backside. My gaze finally moved up his spine, and I rose, trailing a finger over the intricate lettering of the mystery tattoo that had always fascinated me. He looked over his shoulder at me but didn't move away.

"What does this say?"

He didn't answer for a long moment. "You really want to know?"

I settled back on my side. "Yes, I do."

Kyler finished buttoning his jeans and sat beside me. He leaned down and kissed me. "I got the tattoo after high school, right before freshman year of college."

"I know." It wasn't like I'd only recently started checking Kyler out. The day I'd seen the tattoo for the first time was the day I'd committed it to memory.

One side of his lips tipped up. "You're probably either

going to think it's really stupid, or you're going to be really surprised."

"Now I'm really curious. Tell me." I tapped on his bare chest. "Please?"

He watched me for a moment. "It's in Sanskrit. It says, 'This Is Forever.'"

My heart skipped a beat as I stared up at him. "Does it mean what I think it does?"

"Yeah, it means what you think it does."

I pressed my hand to my chest, blinking back tears. "You did this after we graduated high school? That long ago?"

"Yes. It just felt like something I needed to commit to, you know? That our relationship, no matter in what way we were together, was forever."

I couldn't speak for a full minute. "Surprise" didn't cover how I felt. I wanted to cry again, like a baby, because that was the confirmation of all that he'd said. Of how he'd felt about me this entire time, and I'd never known. But deep down, he had known. My chest filled to the point I felt like I'd burst.

He studied me intensely. "What are you thinking?"

"I'm thinking...I'm thinking it's perfect." I sat up, placing my hands on either side of his face. "You're perfect."

Kyler pressed his forehead against mine. "I wouldn't go that far."

"Look at you, being modest for once in your life," I teased, but the lump of emotion was sitting at the top of my throat. "Kyler?"

He pecked me on the lips. "Syd?"

"I love you." I paused, taking a deep breath, and our eyes locked. I saw the world in his gaze. I saw our future. "And *that* is forever."

READ ON FOR A SNEAK PEEK AT THE NEXT BOOK IN THE FRIGID AND SCORCHED DUOLOGY

Chapter 1

ANDREA

This had to be the absolute wildest thing I'd ever seriously considered agreeing to do. That was admitting to something pretty epic because I'd done a lot of stupid stuff in my twenty-two years strutting around on planet Earth. And I mean, a *lot* of stupid.

At the ripe age of six, I'd shoved a fork in my pappy's toaster when my Toaster Strudel got stuck—though I'm pretty sure even back then I knew that wasn't a clever thing to do. That ended in a trip to the emergency room and a near heart attack for the dear old man, who, after that, had refused to babysit me again. Then, when I was ten, I'd allowed my older brother—older by *barely* a year—Broderick to convince me that jumping from the porch roof into the pool below was a totally cool idea and not dangerous at all. That had also ended with a trip to the ER, this time for a broken leg, and a summer-long grounding for Brody.

Not all my stupid actions resulted in hospital visits, but that didn't make them any less ridiculous. When I was fourteen,

I'd been positive that I could take my parents' car around the block without them ever finding out. Unfortunately, in the excitement of doing something naughty, I'd forgotten to lift the garage door and ended up driving *through* it.

In their shiny new Benz.

Then I'd dated Jonah Banks, all-star quarterback, in high school, and while that didn't necessarily sound like a bad thing, he'd been under the impression—and probably still was—that the sun revolved around the Earth. And because everyone else was having sex, I'd given him my V-card and had immediately wished I could grow that damned hymen back because the awkward fumbling in the back of his truck and all that sweating *so* hadn't been worth the pain and weirdness.

I was also beginning to think changing my major at the start of the school year from premed to education hadn't been a smart choice, because *cheese and rice*, I was going to be in school forever, and when I graduated, I'd be so far in debt that Sallie Mae would be the godmother of any children I had. Not to mention my parents were still reeling from my latest string of decisions that they didn't necessarily approve of. Both were doctors, successful ones, and Brody was already in med school, continuing the family tradition like the good child he was.

But becoming a doctor … well, it had been what *they* wanted. Not me. Seeing Kyler, my best friend's boyfriend, change his major last year had given me the courage to do the same. Not that I'd ever tell him that, though. Or really admit that to anyone.

However, one of my latest and greatest foolish decisions to date, and probably the most painful, was allowing myself to be charmed by Tanner Hammond. Because I totally,

totally knew better. From day one, I'd recognized Tanner for what he was—a player's player. After all, I'd grown up with a brother who'd had the attention span of a gnat when it came to girls. Tanner was no better.

Fucker.

But I was about to make another epic bad decision because as I stared into Sydney Bell's bright blue eyes, I couldn't tell my best friend no.

Well, I *could* tell her no. I'd told her no a lot, but I couldn't in this situation because telling her no meant I would be stuck here by myself, and nothing bothered me more than being … well, alone.

"Please," she said, clapping her tiny hands as she hopped, causing her thick black ponytail to bounce.

Everything about Syd was small. Standing next to her, I felt like Bigfoot—a redheaded Bigfoot. "Please. It will be so much fun. I promise you. And it's going to be the last time any of us really have a lot of time to get away. Summer is almost over. Kyler is doing the vet-school stuff. My grad school classes are going to suck up all my time."

And I'd be puttering around, being lame and useless, still taking undergrad classes like the loser I was turning out to be.

Plopping down on the edge of the bed in the apartment she now shared with Kyler, I tried not to think about all the indecent things those two had done on said bed. Nor think about the constant reminder that all my friends were either paired off, entering grad school, or starting their careers, while I was … unchanged.

Stuck.

Even though I kept changing my mind about, well, everything, I was still *stuck*.

"But it's a cabin in the woods of West Virginia," I said, shaking off the troublesome thoughts before they festered into something I couldn't ignore. "That's like the start of every horror movie featuring cannibals."

Syd narrowed her eyes. "You had no problem going to the cabin in Snowshoe."

"That's because that cabin is in a tourist town, and this cabin sounds like it's in the middle of nowhere," I pointed out. "And may I remind you what happened the last time you went to Snowshoe? You got snowed in, and some crazy dude attacked you."

"That was a freak occurrence," she insisted, waving her hand. It had taken her a long time to be so flippant about the event, but I noted that for this trip, she and Kyler had rented a different cabin, rather than go back to the one his family owned. I honestly wasn't sure if Syd would ever go back to that cabin. "And the house Kyler and I rented is actually near Seneca Rocks, so it's not that remote. It isn't like you're going to run into the chupacabra or a pack of aliens."

I snorted like a little piglet. "I'm more worried about serial killers."

She folded her arms across her chest. "Andrea..."

Exhaling, I rolled my eyes. "Okay. I know there aren't serial killers running around." Truthfully, I'd found West Virginia to be very beautiful every time I'd visited.

"The cabin is fully loaded and gorgeous. It's huge. Six bedrooms. Has a hot tub and a pool." Moving over to the dark cherry dresser, she started arranging the bracelets sprinkled across the top, organizing them by color. What a neat freak. "It will be a week in paradise."

I lifted a brow in doubt. To me, paradise was lounging

on an island in the Caribbean with a margarita the size of a toddler in my hand, but hey, what did I know?

"And the house is big enough that you won't even know Tanner is there," she added as she cast a sly grin over her shoulder. "If that's what you want to do. Of course, you don't *have* to ignore him."

"You had to invite him, didn't you?" Needing to move, I popped up from the bed and stalked past her, heading into the bathroom—the ridiculously clutter-free bathroom, with its deep-blue floor mats and matching toilet seat cover. Ugh. Couples.

I leaned against the sink and stared into the mirror. Yikes. My eyeliner was trying to mate with my cheeks. How had Syd failed to mention that?

"*I* didn't invite him." Her voice carried from the bedroom. "Kyler did. And what's the big deal? I thought you two were getting along now."

After swiping my fingers under my eyes, I dropped my hands to the cool rim of the porcelain sink with a sigh. "Just because we're getting along *right now* doesn't mean we'll get along tomorrow or next week or an hour from now. He's ... he's moody like that."

There was no answer from the bedroom.

Rising onto the tips of my toes, I peered closer into the mirror and then cursed under my breath. Was that a zit forming on my chin? A huge one, too. I puckered my nude lips. At what point would my face outgrow the pimple phase? "And why would Kyler even invite him? Tanner is as interesting as getting my eyebrows plucked. Speaking of which..." I pulled back from the mirror, wrinkling my nose. "My eyebrows look like caterpillars, Syd. Hairy and bushy caterpillars."

Syd cleared her throat. "Um, Andrea—"

"Actually, let me rephrase that." Settling flat on my bare feet, I smoothed my hands over my shoulder-length ringlets. My hair was a deep auburn in normal light and much redder out in the sun. Syd thought I looked like the old-school Little Orphan Annie since I also had freckles. "Plucking the hair off my chin would be more interesting than spending a week with Tanner. And why *do* we get hair on our chins? Don't answer that. You'll probably have some kind of logical explanation, and I'm against all things logic right now."

"Andrea—"

"But plucking any piece of body hair would be less painful. *God*." Yep. I was getting riled up, like I always did when I thought about Tanner. "Do you know what that dickhead told me after you and Kyler ditched me at the park the night of the fireworks? And I don't even need to guess what you two were doing behind those trees. Perverts," I went on, anger resurfacing as I remembered what Tanner had said. "He told me I drink too much. And he said this while holding a beer in his hand. What kind of fucked-up double standard is that? Plus, I need to drink so I don't want to punch him in the gonads."

"Nice."

I stiffened, my eyes widening when I recognized a voice way too deep to belong to Syd. Two pink splotches formed on my cheeks as I turned toward the open bathroom door.

That was definitely Kyler's voice, and if he was home, there was a good chance he wasn't alone, which meant…

Oh, for fuck's sake.

With my face burning and most likely matching my hair, I briefly considered hiding behind the shower curtain, but that was weak and would be really weird. I walked out of the bathroom and quickly discovered that I'd just inserted my foot and my entire leg into my mouth.

Kyler Quinn was in the bedroom, with one well-defined arm draped over Syd's slim shoulders. Her cheeks were flushed pink, so I was assuming he'd given her a heck of a greeting with his mouth and hands. He was a multitasking kind of guy. Right then, he was grinning at me like a cat that had devoured an entire box of mice. Kyler was hot. With his messy brown hair and Prince Charming smile, he was a perfect match for Sydney, who sort of reminded me of a living, breathing Snow White.

Sydney and Kyler? Gah, they made me want to puke rainbows of the My Little Pony variety.

Their whole story was a thing of fairy tales, what little girls dreamed of—what I still kind of dreamed of in a really pathetically sad sort of way.

Growing up together, basically best friends for life, they had been secretly in love with each other, and last year, while snowed in together at the cabin in Snowshoe, they'd finally fessed up to their feelings. They'd been together ever since, and even though I was a wee bit envious of their love, I couldn't be any happier for them. Those two deserved their happy ending.

The walking penis leaning against the doorframe? Another story.

My gaze slid to Tanner Hammond. He wasn't hot. Oh no. "Hot" was too weak a word to describe all six feet and four inches of sexiness packed into well-formed arms, tight abs, and a broad chest, complete with narrow hips and an ass one could ogle for days. His bright, crystal-blue eyes were legit bedroom eyes, always half-hooded, sleepy, and sensual. His face was almost perfectly pieced together—high cheekbones and a lower lip slightly fuller than the top lip, his nose faintly crooked from a break he'd suffered long before I knew him.

I usually liked my guys with a bit more hair, but he rocked the buzzed–at–the–sides and cropped–at–the–top look. Once, when I'd been... well, drunk, I'd gotten the great idea to rub my palm across his head. Probably another foolish idea, but I'd about died over how the prickly softness of his hair felt against my palm.

It had felt *go-oo-od*.

The first time I'd seen Tanner had been in my packed English 101 class, and my tongue had practically lolled out of my mouth and smacked the floor. He, of course, hadn't noticed me. Hell, Kyler and Syd thought we'd only met in the past two years or so. Not true. I'd known *of* Tanner since my freshman year. That year alone, he'd been in two of my classes, and I had crushed on him hard—super hard—right up to the end of spring semester.

Tanner lifted a brow. "I stand by my word. You do drink too much."

My hands clenched as I drew in a sharp, stinging breath. "I didn't ask for your opinion, Dr. Phil."

"All I'm saying is that I've seen you puke more times than I would hanging out in an emergency room during flu season," he added dryly.

The vein along my temple started to tick, while Kyler tipped his chin down, not doing a good job at hiding his smile. I said, "Oh. So roughly the same number of times you screwed random chicks this week?"

His lips curled into a half smile—the kind of grin that would've been mind-numbingly sexy if I didn't want to smack it off his face. "Sounds about right—no, wait. There's probably been one more random chick than you puking, if we're keeping count."

"Guys…" Syd murmured.

My shoulders tensed as I readied for a verbal battle, round five million. "So that means you've probably caught chlamydia *and* gonorrhea this past weekend alone then?"

He raised one shoulder as he eyed me lazily. "Probably the same likelihood of you vomiting in your date's lap."

Warmth crept over my cheeks. I'd done that before. Once. Wasn't pretty. "How about this? Why don't you go fu—"

Tanner pushed off the wall, turning to Kyler and Syd. "Is she going to the cabin? If so, I need to pack hazmat gear."

I was going to hit him. Seriously. Plant my fist in his solar plexus, right at the exact moment he inhaled.

Struggling to keep a straight face, Syd looked at me. "I don't know. I was trying to convince her before you two showed up, but now that seems like a giant waste of time." She shot a dark look at Tanner.

He smiled broadly. "Sounds good to me." Clapping his hand on Kyler's shoulder, he started to walk back into the hall. "I was thinking about inviting Brooke."

My jaw hit the floor. Brooke Page? Blond and big boob-a-licious Brooke Page?

"You are *not* inviting Brooke," Syd said, sighing.

Tanner chuckled. "How about Mandie?"

A choking sound came from Kyler.

I rolled my eyes. Now he was just being silly. "You have such classy taste in women."

Casting a long look over his shoulder, he winked. "At least none of them are spoiled little rich girls."

"I am not a spoiled little rich girl!" I shrieked, and Syd

suddenly found something interesting on the ceiling. Okay. Being that both my parents were very successful plastic surgeons, they were well off. The apartment I lived in? Paid for by Mom and Dad. As was most everything inside said apartment and the car—an older Lexus—I drove, but just because I came from money didn't mean I was spoiled. My parents were never afraid to remind me of just how much they paid for and how quickly all that could go away— they were making me pay my tuition now that I'd switched majors, and the loans were already adding up.

"So you say," he replied, walking down the hall.

I prowled after him, ignoring the exasperated noise coming from Syd. "What? Tanner-man, you don't want me to go to the cabin?"

"Do I really need to answer that question, Andy?" He headed for the galley kitchen.

My lip curled. I *hated* that nickname. Made me feel like a dude with big shoulders... and I kind of did have manly shoulders.

Before I could reply, Tanner said, "It's Friday night, shouldn't you be plastered by now?"

"Ha ha." Actually, I *was* usually a bit tipsy by this point on a Friday night, but Syd was staying in tonight with Kyler, and the rest of our friends were gone.

I can't go to the cabin.

The moment that thought finished, a slice of panic twisted my stomach, and my throat dried. If I didn't go, I'd be... stuck here. I'd be alone. And if I were alone, I'd just sleep and be...be lame, and if I didn't sleep, then I'd spend all the time *thinking*.

Sometimes thinking didn't end well. I had to go to the cabin. Stopping in the entry to the kitchen, I looked down the hall, back to where Kyler and Syd lingered. "When are you guys planning to go to the cabin?"

"Next week." Syd appeared, her hair mussed and out of the ponytail. Jesus. Kyler was a man of opportunity *and* a fast worker. "We're going to leave on Monday morning."

"Hmm." I turned to Tanner and smiled sweetly. "Well, since I'm a spoiled little rich girl, it's not like I have to get time off from work. I'm free next week."

Tanner reached into Kyler's fridge and pulled out a beer. Wisps of cold air rolled up from the neck. Screwing the top off the bottle, he raised it to me. "Well, since I don't have a drinking problem, I can have one of these."

"I don't have a drinking problem, asshole."

He took a long and slow drink as he rested his hip against the counter. The half grin was back in full force. "You know, I've always heard the first step to recovery is acceptance that you have a problem."

I drew in another cutting breath and felt the warmth spread across my face. Tanner and I gave each other a hard time, that much was obvious, but for some stupid reason, a knot exploded in the base of my throat and the back of my eyes burned as I watched him take another drink. Embarrassment seeded in my stomach before blossoming into a tree that only bore rotten fruit.

I *didn't* have a drinking problem.

Tanner lowered the bottle, and the moment our gazes collided, the grin faded slowly from his striking face. His brows knitted as his lips parted, and I quickly turned toward Sydney, my voice embarrassingly hoarse when I spoke. "Count me in."

ACKNOWLEDGMENTS

I wasn't planning on writing this book until Patricia Riley asked me to write something for the former Spencer Hill Contemporary line. So a huge thank you to you for asking me, therefore having a lot to do with the creation of Kyler and Syd. Thank you to Kate Kaynak for always supporting me no matter what. Thank you to Stacey Morgan for willingly subjecting herself to my first drafts. No one can truly understand how painful that is until you've seen one of my first drafts.

Thank you to my friends and family for putting up with me. I'm always writing, it seems, which is something I love to do, but leaves little time for them. They are owed major props for allowing me to dedicate my time to fictional characters.

And to all the readers out there—I write because it's what I love to do, but it is because of each and every one of you that I'm able to do this. There are not enough ways I could possibly thank you guys.

ABOUT THE AUTHOR

#1 *New York Times* and #1 international bestselling author Jennifer L. Armentrout lives in Shepherdstown, West Virginia. All the rumors you've heard about her state aren't true. When she's not hard at work writing, she spends her time reading, watching really bad zombie movies, pretending to write, hanging out with her husband, her Border Jack Apollo, Border Collie Artemis, six judgmental alpacas, two rude goats, and five fluffy sheep. In early 2015, Jennifer was diagnosed with retinitis pigmentosa, a group of rare genetic disorders that involve a breakdown and death of cells in the retina, eventually resulting in loss of vision, among other complications. Due to this diagnosis, educating people on the varying degrees of blindness has become a passion of hers, right alongside writing, which she plans to do as long as she can.

Website: jenniferlarmentrout.com
Facebook: JenniferLArmentrout
Instagram: @jennifer_l_armentrout